WHO KILLED ALYS

TONY SPALLONE

WHO KILLED ALYS
Published in the United States of America by Long Walk Publishing
www.TonySpallone.com/Tsonroad@aol.com

This is a work of fiction. All names, characters, businesses, places, roadways, events, law enforcement agencies and incidents are either the products of the author's imagination or used in a fictitious manner. Any resemblance to places, actual persons, living or dead, or actual events is purely coincidental.

ISBN-978-0-9864271-8-3 (paperback)
Cover Design by Langao, 99design

OTHER BOOKS BY TONY SPALLONE

Murder at Breeze Canyon

Murders in the High Desert

Murders on Pigeon Mountain

Revenge is not Justice

Eagle Wind

TO JOHNNY AND TOMMY
BRIGHT LIVES LOST TOO SOON

ACKNOWLEDGMENTS

It took a village. Thank you Patti, Mark, Lynn, Rose, and Sandy for your incisive critiques.

CHAPTER 1

Maura Quenneville drove out of her tree-lined driveway on the way to her Sunday morning beauty appointment at the prestigious Canyon Spa in Santa Fe.

A moment later, a car pulled away from the curb and followed her as she drove onto Breeze Canyon Road. Maura didn't pay any attention to the vehicle until it accelerated to only a few feet behind her Mercedes.

With its multiple blind turns overlooking deep canyon, the road was fraught with danger for anyone who drove recklessly or over the speed limit. Maura, normally an aggressive driver, drove the road with caution. Ahead was a short stretch of road with a passing lane that allowed cars to pass safely. She slowed to allow the tailgater to pass, but the car stayed glued dangerously close to her back bumper.

She tapped her brakes, thinking the tailgater would get the message that he was *too damn close*.

There were no other vehicles in front of or behind Maura and the tailgater on this pleasant New Mexico morning.

Maura was getting more and more irritated by the tailgater. Her temper was always at a hair-trigger level anyway, and this tailgater wasn't helping her mood. She opened her window and reached out to wave the driver on.

The tailgater did not attempt to pass.

Frustrated, Maura threw her hand up. She screamed, "If you don't want to pass, don't pass, but stop tailgating me."

She accelerated to earn some distance between them, but the trailing car caught up quickly. When the driver flashed the car's high-beam lights at her, Maura thought, *Maybe there is something wrong with my car*. She looked at her dashboard for any indication there was a problem, but nothing was blinking. No check-engine warning. Nothing.

The trailing car pulled away from Maura's tail as though to pass but instead pulled alongside the Mercedes. The driver wore a full ski mask.

Maura tapped the brakes to allow the driver to pass, but the driver slowed down equally.

"I'm calling the cops," Maura shouted through the open window.

The tailgater laughed, then drew closer alongside the Mercedes, mere inches away. Maura tapped the brakes and skidded dangerously close to the metal guardrail.

The tailgater reached for a pistol he had placed on the passenger seat and raised it toward her.

Maura panicked. *Good God, he's going to shoot me.* She slowed down, but the tailgater had her boxed in between his car and the guardrail.

The driver leaned across and fired one shot through Maura's driver's side window, striking Maura in her temple.

The Mercedes scraped the guardrail then slid across the road, rammed the barrier on the other side, then flipped end-over-end, catapulting over the metal barrier. It exploded when it landed on the canyon floor.

Cacophonous noise shattered the desert quiet on the remote road.

Several minutes passed before a driver traveling in the opposite direction approached the scene and witnessed the automobile ablaze.

The driver called 911, but by the time the police arrived, and paramedics were able to descend to the desert floor, nothing was left of the smoldering Mercedes except the metal frame and the charred remains of Maura Quenneville.

CHAPTER 2

Police scraped the soot from the barely legible Mercedes license plate and learned that the car was registered to Doctor Ronald Quenneville. However, the person was burned beyond recognition, and the medical examiner was uncertain if it was a male or female.

Two hours later, a police lieutenant drove to the Quenneville estate on Mountainview Place and announced himself through the intercom embedded in the stone wall of the driveway entrance. "I'm with the Santa Fe Police Department. I've come to inquire about a Doctor Ronald Quenneville."

A woman with a slight foreign accent answered and advised the officer, "I will inform Doctor Quenneville that you want to speak to him. Just a moment, please."

A few seconds later, Quenneville answered. "I'm Doctor Quenneville. What can I do for you?"

"I would like to speak with you."

"About what?"

"I'd rather talk to you face to face."

Quenneville opened the gate for the lieutenant and greeted him with a handshake as he exited his police car.

Quenneville was a handsome man with a slender build, refined features, and thick, prematurely white hair. With a smile he said, "Before you start, I want to let you know I've already contributed to the Santa Fe Police Benevolent Association."

The lieutenant was a couple inches taller than average height and was dressed in a brown, ill-fitting suit that stretched over his large belly. He addressed Quenneville with a sorrowful look. "I'm not here for that. I'm sorry to tell you, Doctor, that a Mercedes registered in your name was in an auto accident, and the occupant is deceased."

"You mean my wife?"

"Doctor Quenneville, we don't know that for sure. We tracked the license plate to you. As of now we can't tell if the decedent was a male or a female. Until an autopsy is completed, all we can confirm is that the car was registered in your name. I don't know how else to tell you this, but whoever was in the car was burned beyond recognition. The medical examiner will have to determine who the person is. Who else other than your wife might have been driving your car?"

"No one. Maura went to a spa this morning. She said she would be back by noon. It must be my wife."

"As I said, we won't be sure until an autopsy is done. As far as we know, it appears the driver may have lost control of the car, and it flipped over the roadside barrier on Breeze Canyon Road. As you may know, the roadside barriers are very low on some sections of that road. The car fell to the canyon floor and apparently was engulfed in flames immediately upon impact. Because it was in the canyon, the fire department wasn't able to get to the wreck until after the fire totally consumed the vehicle. Paramedics rappelled to the scene, but they couldn't do anything except stand by."

"We need to find out for sure if it was Maura," Quenneville said. "I'll call the spa. Maybe she's there now. Maybe it wasn't Maura in the car, but someone else who was killed."

The lieutenant said, "It's Sunday, are you sure she was going to a spa? Aren't they closed on Sundays?"

"I don't know. That's all she said to me when she left. I

don't know if she got them to open up for her, or if they're normally open on Sundays. I don't know."

Quenneville used his cell phone to Google the number of the Canyon Spa. A woman answered. Quenneville said, "I want to speak with my wife, Maura Quenneville. She told me this morning she was going to your spa."

The woman did not sound sympathetic. "She's not here. She did not show up for her appointment. We tried calling her cell phone, but we didn't get an answer."

"Are you normally opened on Sundays?"

"No, only for special customers like your wife. I wish she told us she was not going to make her appointment. I have the staff in today specifically for her. Is she okay?"

The doctor hung up without answering. He turned to the lieutenant. "It must have been Maura. She didn't show up for her appointment this morning." Quenneville appeared to lose his balance and leaned against the foyer wall for support.

The lieutenant reached for Quenneville's elbow. "You might want to sit for a second."

"I'll be okay. Just stunned."

The lieutenant expressed his condolences. "I understand. I'm very sorry for your loss. I'll ask the medical examiner to contact you as soon as possible. Is there anything I can do for you in the meantime? Do you want to call someone to be here with you?"

"I'll be okay. I appreciate your concern. When will I get a definitive answer that it was or wasn't Maura?"

"As I mentioned, the ME will contact you. I'm sure it will be soon, but perhaps as late as tomorrow."

Forty-eight hours later, Doctor Aaron Safford, Santa Fe's

medical examiner called Clay. He said he relied on dental records read by a forensic odontologist to confirm that the individual who died was indeed Maura Quenneville. The ME suggested that it was up to the doctor if he wanted to come to the morgue to identify the body, but he suggested that the doctor not do so since the body was not recognizable.

CHAPTER 3

Monday afternoon, Santa Fe's Captain of Detectives, Matthew Ellsworth, called Detective Clay Bryce into his office.

Ellsworth explained, "Yesterday there was an auto accident up on Breeze Canyon Road. The victim's car ran off the road and ended up at the bottom of the canyon where it was consumed by fire."

"Who was the victim?"

"Maura Quenneville, the wife of Doctor Ronald Quenneville, a prominent plastic surgeon in the city. I want you to take on the case."

"If it was an accident, why do you want me to investigate?"

"At first, the accident investigators thought she may have been speeding and lost control of her car. However, the ME notified me that Quenneville's death was not an accident. He discovered a bullet lodged in her cranium. She was murdered. I told the ME that I was assigning you the case."

Clay had distinctive traits that made him the best homicide detective on the Santa Fe police force. Confident, smart, and introspective, he had an impressive record of having solved one hundred percent of the murder cases assigned to him. Square-jawed with broad shoulders, he was a ruggedly handsome forty-two-year-old, well over six feet tall, and packing 240 pounds on a muscular frame. His imposing size alone put the fear of God in crime suspects.

Clay drove to the ME's office at the Institute for Forensic Science, where the bodies of all suspicious deaths were transported for examination.

The ME explained the cause of Maura's death. "She was

shot. I discovered a bullet that entered her temple above her left ear, lodged in her skull. She was probably killed instantly. When I asked our forensic odontologist to review her dental records to confirm who the victim was, he discovered the bullet lodged in her skull. Mrs. Quenneville probably lost control of her car after she was shot, and it ended up crashing into the canyon. The car was consumed by fire and the body burned beyond recognition before first responders could reach the wreck. The cause of her death was homicide." He handed the bullet to Clay in an evidence bag. "Here's the slug I extracted from the victim."

Clay asked, "Is there any indication that the shot could have been fired by a second person, perhaps someone seated in the passenger seat?"

The ME said, "It's possible, but short of having an eyewitness there's no way to know."

Clay added, "In any event, could it have been a case of road rage?"

"Yes, that's possible and probably likely."

Clay left the ME and headed back to police headquarters to talk with Santa Fe's Forensics Chief Examiner, Dan Carton, and his assistant, Dick Cook.

Clay explained, "A woman by the name of Maura Quenneville, the wife of Doctor Ronald Quenneville, was killed Sunday morning. Initially, it was believed she died in an auto accident. However, the ME found a .38 caliber slug embedded in her cranium. She was murdered, perhaps as the result of a road rage incident."

Clay handed Carton the slug that killed Maura. "This is what the ME recovered. See if you can find a match to this in your database. And check out Quenneville's Mercedes to see if you can learn anything else about her murder."

"Where is her car now?"

"It's in impound. I'm heading out to talk to Doctor Quenneville to see if he can shed any light on her murder. I'll check back with you later to find out what you've been able to find."

CHAPTER 4

The day after Maura was killed, Clay drove to Doctor Quenneville's home and asked to speak to him. The doctor opened the entrance gate to his large home and stepped outside to wait for Clay on the front landing.

Clay thought it strange that there was only one car in the driveway, a silver Maserati, and no sign of anyone else. In most cases that he had investigated where someone was killed, it was common for a steady stream of people to flock to the victim's family, offering condolences, bringing food, flowers, and sympathy cards.

Clay climbed the half-dozen steps to the landing and extended his hand to Quenneville, who was dressed impressively in tailored slacks, Italian loafers, and a custom-made dress shirt.

Clay said, "Thank you for seeing me. I'm sure you've got a ton of things to do regarding your wife's death, so I'll try to be brief. First off, let me express my condolences."

"Thank you, Detective. Maura's death comes as a tremendous shock. I've closed my practice for a few days to deal with my loss. I will miss her tremendously."

Clay said with sincerity, "I'm sure you will."

"Let's go inside. May I offer you something to drink?"

"No, thanks."

Before arriving, Clay researched Quenneville's background and learned that he was forty-nine years old and was a highly successful plastic surgeon sought after by wealthy patrons, mostly women and celebrities, some traveling from California and other states to have him tighten sagging jowls, necks, wrinkled brows, and other real or perceived aging and cosmetic conditions.

Pointing to a couch in the living room, he said, "Detective, let's sit. I appreciate your department putting so much effort into Maura's death. Is this the usual procedure when someone dies from an auto accident?"

"No, sir, only those of unusual circumstances. Unfortunately, I'm here to inform you that your wife did not die in that automobile accident."

"What do you mean?"

"We learned today from the medical examiner that your wife was murdered."

"Murdered?" Quenneville stood up abruptly. "What are you talking about? What do you mean, 'murdered'?"

"I mean someone shot her."

"You're not serious?"

"I'm afraid I am. Apparently, when she was shot, she lost control of her car, and it ended up crashing to the canyon floor, where it was engulfed in flames."

"Who did it? Who shot her?"

"We don't know. That's why I'm here, to see if you can help me make sense of what appears to be a senseless murder. Let me begin by suggesting that we are trying to determine if she was killed in a road-rage incident. Unfortunately, as of now, we can't confirm that. No other passing driver has stepped forward as a witness to what may have happened. Apparently, she was shot on an uninhabited stretch of canyon road where there was no security camera footage to view."

"That's downright crazy that someone would shoot Maura. Why? Because of a traffic incident, is that what you're saying?"

"I want to emphasize that we are not certain why she was killed. But we're working on the theory that it was road rage. Let me ask you about your wife's temperament when she drove. Did she drive aggressively?"

"I don't know what you mean by driving aggressively."

"As you no doubt know, when road rage occurs, it usually involves a person who speeds or weaves through traffic, tailgates other cars, gestures, cuts off other drivers, or cuts into traffic."

Quenneville shook his head. "Are you suggesting she was at fault?"

"No, I wouldn't know that. At this point in my investigation, I'm trying to determine if it was a road-rage incident, and if so, how she might have contributed to the incident. However, I'm not implying that her being shot can be justified under any circumstance."

Quenneville's eyes flitted away from Clay. "It's not so funny now, but I used to call her Mario Andretti because she drove so fast and cut people off sometimes. She was impatient when traffic bogged down. But she was probably no different than the rest of us. No one likes to wait in a traffic jam."

"Do you know if she had ever been involved in a traffic accident where tempers grew out of hand?"

"She had a few fender benders over the years, but nothing that became violent. At least none that she told me about. But it wouldn't surprise me to learn there had been angry confrontations. She was very headstrong."

"Thanks for sharing that about her. If her death was not the result of road rage, do you know of any reason why someone would want to harm her? Did someone hold a grudge against her for any reason whatsoever?"

The doctor sat on the couch, his eyes devoid of tears. After a few seconds, he dropped his head, avoiding eye contact with Clay. "This is all too much for me to process."

Clay said, "I'm sorry, I know I'm causing you additional grief by some of my questions."

Quenneville looked up, "I understand that you are looking for answers. I appreciate that you have to do your job, and I admit she had a sharp tongue, but I don't know who would have wanted to murder her."

"What do you mean by 'a sharp tongue'?"

"She never held back—about anything. She would bulldoze ahead to get what she wanted. She never took no for an answer. Sometimes she could be embarrassing about her demands."

Clay asked, "Tell me about your marriage."

Quenneville looked quizzically at Clay. "It was good." He hesitated before adding, "And sometimes bad, like any marriage."

"How long were you married?"

"Twenty-eight years. I was twenty-one when we married. Maura was a couple of years older."

Quenneville suddenly expressed irritation by Clay's line of questions. "Why are you asking me these questions about our marriage? What are you suggesting?"

"Just routine. Nothing to be upset about. I'm trying to establish a picture of your wife's character and personality. Tell me about her. What made her tick? What did she like and dislike? Who were her friends? Or enemies?"

Quenneville answered, "She didn't have any close friends, not anyone she would hang out with or go to a movie with. She was pretty much a loner. We were different in temperament. I guess you can say I am more gregarious than Maura was. She found fault in everyone, whereas I try to find the good—you know, the glass half-filled or half-empty analogy."

"Sounds like you and she were total opposites?"

The doctor added defensively, "Yes, we were different."

Clay nodded and stared at Quenneville for several seconds but did not respond. He was a skilled interrogator who knew how to gain information from a reluctant suspect or witness by exercising a period of silence. Typically, such a silence made suspects uncomfortable and invariably led to the individual divulging more information than he or she otherwise would have offered.

Quenneville finally broke his silence. "Even though she was strong-willed, she was selfless. I mean, she would have gone to war on my behalf. She was so loyal to me. If it wasn't for her, I would not have become a physician. We married when I was in med school. Maura was a nurse at the time. She worked her butt off, working double shifts so she could pay for my education. We had shared dreams of my becoming a surgeon. Because of Maura, I was one of the few students who did not have a huge debt to pay after thirteen years of medical school, residency, and fellowship programs. And that was mostly thanks to her."

"At the time of her death, was she still employed as a nurse?"

"No, she quit several years ago, when we didn't need her salary to make ends meet."

"You're saying she sacrificed her own interests on your behalf?"

"That's a blunt way of saying it, but yes, I'll always be grateful to her."

Clay spread his arms to encompass Quenneville's mansion, and said, "This beautiful house of yours would suggest that you've done very well for yourself. I noticed a silver Maserati in front of your garage. Can I assume it belongs to you?"

"Yes, one of the fruits of my labor."

"You mean one of the fruits of your wife's labor?"

The doctor appeared to be irritated at Clay's comment. "Yes, you could say that. I wouldn't have my toys without her help."

"Was she able to have any toys, too?"

"Yes. She drove that Mercedes, for example. I didn't hold back on anything for her. Whatever she wanted—first-class travel, country clubs, jewelry, or anything she wanted for our house. Whatever she wanted." Quenneville appeared to have become uncomfortable.

Clay decided to ease up on his questions for a moment. "I wonder if I might trouble you for a glass of water."

"Of course." Quenneville walked to the kitchen.

Without being asked, Clay followed. As he walked behind Quenneville, the smell of a perfume that was evident to him when he first walked into the house seemed to get stronger as they entered the kitchen.

The doctor was startled when he realized Clay was immediately behind him. "Oh, you didn't have to come with me. I'll get it for you."

Clay answered, "I don't mind. Great kitchen you have. It seems like it's got everything a gourmet cook would ever want. I'm envious." He laughed. "I'm a bachelor chef."

The kitchen was state of the art, with elegant white

shaker cabinets, Wolf commercial appliances, a Sub-Zero freezer, a separate built-in Sub-Zero refrigerator, and other high-end small appliances.

"Thanks for noticing. Maura basically designed the kitchen herself. This was her sanctum sanctorum. She spent a lot of time here working on new recipes. I always chided her for trying to fatten me up."

Clay said, "It looks like you stay fit. Do you work out?"

"Yes, three or four times a week. Early morning at the gym, usually."

"What about Maura, did she work out?"

"I'm not sure why you're asking, but the answer is no. As she was getting older, she was starting to gain weight. I tried several times to get her to stay with an exercise program, but she would falter after a short while. She always seemed to be fighting a weight issue and would argue she was too old to start exercising."

Clay interrupted Quenneville's train of thought. He lifted his head slightly to one side and then to the other, subtly breathing in the smell of perfume. "Is there someone else in the house right now? I didn't notice another car when I drove up."

The doctor mumbled, "No one else is here. Why do you ask?"

"I smell perfume."

Quenneville immediately corrected himself. "Well, yes, of course. I'm sorry. The perfume is probably from our nanny, Reveca. Maura gave her a bottle of Chanel No. 5 for Christmas. You can always tell when she's been in a room. She wears it often. That's probably what you're smelling. It's very fragrant."

"Does she live-in?"

"Yes, she has her own bedroom off the kitchen, but she's upstairs now tending to our son, Adam. She does a little bit of everything for us, kind of like a Girl Friday."

"How many children do you have?"

"Just one. Maura was unable to have a child of her own, so we adopted Adam when he was a baby about a year ago. Of course, that didn't stop us from trying to have another child, if you know what I mean."

Clay smiled to acknowledge Quenneville's failed attempt at humor.

"I would like to speak to Reveca. You said she was upstairs? Would you ask her to come down?"

"Sure, but why?"

"I want to see if she can help us learn why your wife was killed."

"Yeah, fine." The doctor visibly clenched his jaw and walked to the bottom of the staircase to call for the nanny.

CHAPTER 5

Reveca was halfway down the stairs when she saw Clay. She darted a nervous look at Quenneville, who nodded and beckoned her to come down. Clay thought her to be in her mid to late twenties, a very pretty woman, tall, and slender. She wore her light brown hair up in a sexy, carefree way.

"Reveca, this is Detective Clay Bryce of the Santa Fe Police Department. He wants to ask you some questions."

She offered her hand to him with a soft, tentative handshake. "I am pleased to meet you."

Clay said, "I sense you have an Eastern European accent."

"Yes, I am from Slovakia."

"What is your last name?"

"Gabova. My name is Reveca Gabova." She spelled it for him so he could jot it down on a small notepad he kept in his jacket pocket.

"Reveca, I want to ask you some questions about Mrs. Quenneville."

Quenneville said, "Detective, if I might, I can explain why."

Clay nodded his okay.

Quenneville explained, "Reveca, Detective Bryce told me that Maura was murdered. It wasn't an accident as we were first told. The detective is trying to learn who killed her."

Reveca threw her hands to cover her mouth. "Murdered? Oh, my God, no. I did not know." Again, she looked at Quenneville. "I thought you said she was in an automobile accident."

Clay explained, "That's what we thought at first, but we learned she had been murdered. We're trying to find out why. As of now, we think she may have been shot in a road-rage incident involving a driver of another car."

"That's so awful. You mean another driver shot Mrs. Quenneville?"

Clay said, "That appears to be the case. It could have been that maybe Mrs. Quenneville, or the other driver was driving aggressively. Who knows how road rage begins? It could have been that one or the other was honking their horn, or maybe she attempted to block the other car from changing lanes. It doesn't take much to incite some drivers."

"I cannot understand how someone would shoot another driver because of that."

Clay asked, "Doesn't that happen in Slovakia?"

"Yes, it does. We have so many guns there now. Not like in the United States, but yes we have a lot."

Clay asked, "How long have you been working for the Quennevilles?"

The doctor started to answer for her. "She's been with us for ..."

Clay looked at Quenneville and said pleasantly enough, "With all due respect, please let her answer my questions."

The doctor nodded to Reveca that it was okay to answer Clay's questions.

"I have been with the Quennevilles for almost a year."

Clay asked, "A year? How did you learn to speak English? You speak so well. You must have been fluent before you came to the States."

"I learned when I studied at the University in Slovakia, and ..." she smiled at Quenneville and added, "Doctor Quenneville taught me sometimes."

"He must be a good teacher."

"Yes, he is."

Clay sensed a familiarity about the two.

"Did Mrs. Quenneville teach you too?"

She shook her head. "No. As Doctor Quenneville knows, she was not patient with me."

"You said you've been employed for about a year, so I gather you got to know Mrs. Quenneville fairly well."

"I don't understand your question."

Quenneville asked Clay. "May I?"

"Okay," Clay reluctantly permitted him to explain.

The doctor prompted Reveca. "The detective wants to know about your relationship with Maura. For example, did the two of you get along?"

"She was nice, but sometimes she would be irritated with me when I did not understand what she was asking me to do."

Clay asked, "Did you ever drive with Mrs. Quenneville?"

"Yes, sometimes."

"When you were with her in the car, did you ever see other drivers get angry at her, or did she get angry at other drivers?"

Reveca nodded while looking at Quenneville. "Yes. Both. She scared me because she had such a temper. Honestly, I did not like driving with her. She swore a lot. I mean a lot. And sometimes she would get so mad at another driver that she would drive behind the car very close and very fast, then sometimes she would cut in front of another car and the other drivers would honk their horn at us." She demonstrated with her hands how Maura weaved in and out of traffic. "Forgive me, Doctor Quenneville, but I am telling you the truth. She frightened me."

"Did you ever see someone aim a gun at Mrs. Quenneville?"

"Not a gun, but sometimes they would wave a finger at her. But honestly now that I think about it, and Doctor, you can fire me for saying this, but if she died from a road rage it was because she might have caused the other driver to be mad at her first."

Quenneville nodded to Reveca. "Thank you for your honesty. I understand. Thank you. You have been very truthful."

She said to Quenneville, "I hope I did not say the wrong thing."

"No, you didn't."

Clay said, "You may go back to Adam now."

After Reveca returned upstairs, Clay said, "She was very honest about your wife's driving. Based on her recollection, Maura might have been the one to cause a rage incident, although there's no way to know and no factual basis to believe she did."

Quenneville said, "Detective, I knew Maura had a temper, and sometimes she was abrasive with Reveca, and other people. She had zero patience and was hell on wheels when she drove. I wish now I could have controlled her bad temper."

Clay said, "Sad to say, but it appears her death may have been a case of road rage. However, I'm not sure we'll ever learn who shot your wife. The murderer might have to kill someone else with the same gun used to kill your wife for us to determine who killed Maura. Forensics will inform us if they ever find a match. I'll stay in touch with you and notify you if we come up with anything else. I'm sure you have many things to do, so I'll take my leave. Again, I offer my condolences."

Quenneville extended his hand loosely to Clay. "Thanks."

As Clay walked to the front door, he noticed a shadow on the staircase from the second floor. When he looked up, the shadow disappeared.

He wondered what Reveca's relationship was with Quenneville. Although there was an age difference, they seemed to be close.

CHAPTER 6

After Clay interviewed Dr. Quenneville and Reveca, he realized he was miles away from solving Maura's murder. Forensics did not find a match to the .38-caliber cartridge that killed the wife of the plastic surgeon. There were no witnesses to the accident. No CCTV footage. And the blaze was so intense it liquefied the aluminum wheel rims of the car and left nothing but a carcass of steel.

Three weeks had elapsed after Maura Quenneville's murder when a break of sorts in the case occurred at the Emerson Hotel. The Emerson was a two-hundred-room four-star hotel five miles from the center of Santa Fe in a desert setting. At a little before eleven o'clock a.m., the hotel's security guard was making his rounds in the vast parking lot and noticed a car idling in the farthest area of the lot, where there was limited lighting. The guard had seen the scene play itself out many times. *Most likely a sexual meeting between two adults, maybe a hooker earning her stripes.* He was not happy about it but decided to continue with his rounds.

He returned to the site on his next round two hours later and saw the same car idling. This time he decided to intervene. *Enough is enough.* He approached the car from the driver's side. He saw a woman who seemed to be asleep at the wheel, her chin resting on her chest.

He knocked on the window, but the driver did not respond. He tried to open the door, but it was locked. The guard thought the woman might have had too much to drink and had passed out. He tried to open the back door, but it was locked. He walked around the car and observed the passenger-side window was rolled down. He shined his flashlight into the interior and saw blood trickling down the woman's cheek from a hole in her right temple. He didn't know if the woman was murdered or had committed suicide and hurried back to his vehicle to call the police.

In less than five minutes, a patrol officer arrived in a squad car with flashing lights. The officer donned gloves and opened the front passenger door, then stretched across the passenger seat to feel for the woman's pulse. There was none.

The officer carefully backed out of the car and called his patrol supervisor, Sergeant William Rizzo. Rizzo was responsible for the activities of all the officers and dispatchers under his watch. The patrol officer explained the circumstances and reasoned that the woman may have been murdered.

Sergeant Rizzo informed the cop that he would dispatch a detective to the crime scene immediately and to keep the crime scene clear of intruders.

Detectives in Santa Fe, as in many other cities, worked normal eight-hour shifts keeping up with various offenses, and were also on call on a rotating basis for after-hour emergencies involving serious offenses such as homicides. On this day Clay Bryce was scheduled for on call duty. He had barely gotten two hours of sleep when his phone rang. Captain Ellsworth informed him there had been a murder in the parking lot of the Emerson Hotel and he assigned him to investigate.

Clay splashed water on his face to help shake off the cobwebs from his interrupted sleep. He dressed quickly and raced to the Emerson in his unmarked Ford Explorer.

The security guard introduced himself and explained that he was the one who had discovered the body. He assured Clay he had not entered the car nor disturbed the crime scene, but that his prints might be on the door handles.

Clay put on gloves, reached into the victim's car to unlock the driver-side door, and searched for a gun. If he found a gun, her death may have meant she used the weapon to commit suicide.

However, Clay did not find a weapon and turned to the security guard. "It is evident the woman has been murdered. Do you know her?"

"I think I've seen her in the hotel on the surveillance tapes, but I can't say for sure."

The guard was a thinly built man with narrow shoulders, brown hair parted an inch above his left ear in a combover. He was dressed in a white golf shirt with the Emerson Hotel logo and the word "Security" printed in purple on the top left-front of his shirt.

The guard said, "We had a murder like this back some years ago."

"Just like this one?"

"It was a woman who was shot in her car in the parking lot like this woman was. The police never found the killer. They believed she was a hooker and was shot by one of her johns. And if I recall correctly, I think the murder occurred in almost the identical location as this murder."

"Do you remember the name of the victim? I'll want to look up the file on her. Maybe there are similarities that will help me with this case."

"Yes, she went by the name of Cinnamon Stixx."

"Cinnamon Stixx? I'll check her out."

The guard said, "Let me know if I can help you."

Clay studied the guard for a second. "What's your name?"

"John Paul Kozłowski. Some people call me J.P. but I prefer John Paul."

"John Paul, how long have you been working at the Emerson?"

"Fourteen, almost fifteen years."

"I guess you've seen the good and the bad here, haven't you?"

"Yes, I sure have. And the ugly too. But it's a good place to work. A lot of nice people."

Clay said, "The forensics investigators will be here shortly. I'm going to need your help to find out what happened to this victim."

"No problem. I look forward to helping."

Two additional police units arrived. Clay directed them to tape off a wide circumference around the victim's car as a crime scene and to search the parking area for any evidence: shell cartridges, cigarette butts, chewing gum wrappers, or anything on the ground that the killer might have inadvertently left behind that could be analyzed for trace DNA.

The victim's purse lay on the passenger seat. Clay opened it and discovered her name was Alys Chapman. There were two hundred and ten dollars in cash along with two credit cards in her billfold.

A robber would not have missed taking the currency and credit cards, so Clay quickly concluded the murder was not the result of a robbery gone bad but was a targeted homicide. Clay picked up a small, plain white card that was sitting on the passenger seat alongside Alys' purse. It was like a memorial prayer card, often given to family and friends in Catholic funeral services.

On one side the Act of Contrition was printed in small font: *O my God, I am heartily sorry for having offended Thee. I firmly resolve with the help of Thy grace to confess my sins, do penance and to amend my life. Amen.*

On the reverse side, the word SINNER was printed in bold letters.

It was obvious to Clay that the killer left the prayer card as his calling card. *What message was he trying to impart? Was the murderer apologizing that he murdered Alys? Or was the Act of Contrition supposed to represent Alys' repentance?*

Clay put the card in an evidence bag for further review by forensics to determine if they would be able to collect DNA from the card to compare against DNA in the CODIS database maintained by the FBI. Clay also wanted to know if other prayer cards had been placed at other murder scenes in Santa Fe or at hooker Cinnamon Stixx's murder scene.

The victim's driver's license showed she was thirty years old and lived at an address in Santa Barbara, California. A car rental contract in the glove compartment showed she had rented her car at the Santa Fe airport.

She had two phones in her purse, an iPhone and what appeared to be an inexpensive burner phone. In her iPhone's Wallet app he discovered an American Airline ticket stub that showed she had arrived in Santa Fe three days earlier.

She had been ticketed to return to California on Monday afternoon.

Clay asked John Paul to check with the hotel's reservations staff to confirm that Alys Chapman had been a guest at the Emerson.

The guard called the front desk. "This is John Paul. The police are here investigating the probable murder of a woman that I found dead in her car in the parking lot at the rear of the hotel. I think she was murdered. The detective in charge of the investigation agrees. Her name is Alys Chapman. We would like to know if she was a guest at the hotel and if so, when she was scheduled to check-out."

The desk confirmed she was registered as a guest in room 410 and was scheduled to check out by eleven o'clock that morning.

Clay scrolled through Alys' iPhone contacts and discovered that a Mackenzie Stanton was shown as an emergency contact. It was early in the morning, but he decided to dial Stanton's number. He knew the sooner he pieced together a profile of the victim, the better his chance to learn why she was murdered and who the killer was.

A sleepy voice answered Clay's call. He called Mackenzie by name, but she hung up, irritated by what she believed was a spam call.

Clay called a second time, but this time Mackenzie did not answer. Clay left a voice message. "I am Detective Clay Bryce of the Santa Fe, New Mexico Police Department. If you want to verify who I am, call the Santa Fe Police Headquarters at 505-428-3710 to confirm my identity. Once you are satisfied that I am who I say I am, please call me back." Clay understood, of course, that Mackenzie was unsure who he was. Certainly, a call in the middle of the night could have been a spam call.

When the Santa Fe police administrative officer identified Clay as a Santa Fe detective, Mackenzie called Clay back. Obviously irritated by the call, she said, "Detective, it's the middle of the night. Do you know what time it is? What do you want?"

"Are you sitting down?"

She didn't answer. "Just tell me what's going on with Alys. Did she get caught speeding or something?"

"I'm sorry, but I have no other way to inform you of this bad news. Alys Chapman is dead. She has been murdered, found dead in the parking lot of a hotel in Santa Fe where she was a guest. We don't know who killed her or why. Now please tell me who you are to her?"

"Oh, no," she screamed.

In between sobs, Mackenzie said, "Alys is—was my friend and roommate. We've been friends for years."

"What can you tell me about her? Do you know why she was in Santa Fe?"

"She said she had met someone she really liked there. I asked her who it was, but she wouldn't tell me. I don't know anything about him. She never told me his name. I was always so worried about her. It's like I knew something would happen to her. She was very naive in some ways, gullible, if you know what I mean. She didn't have any street smarts."

"I show Alys' address as 23 Lincoln Boulevard in Santa Barbara. And you said you were her roommate?"

"Yes, we've been roommates for several years. We own a condo together at that address."

Clay informed her he would be traveling to Santa Barbara

in the next twenty-four hours to gather more information about Alys. "I will want to talk with you when I arrive."

"I understand. Just let me know when exactly you'll be here. In the meantime, is there anything I should do?"

"Do you have another place you can stay until I arrive?"

"Why, am I in danger?"

"Maybe. I don't want to take a chance that whoever killed Alys thinks you know more about him than you do, and because of that he might decide to make you a target also."

"I can stay with my parents. They're a half-hour away."

"Okay, good, do that. In the meantime, I want you to stay put until I get an escort for you from your local police department. When we hang up, I will contact the police in Santa Barbara to inform them of Alys' murder. I will ask them to secure your condominium with a lockbox so I can examine Alys' belongings for possible leads when I arrive. In the meantime, do not inform anyone of Alys' murder, not even your folks."

"What do I tell them?"

"Make up a story. Tell them you locked yourself out of your condo. I want you to keep all the details of Alys' murder confidential until I have a chance to explain to everyone what happened."

"What about her employer? They'll want to know where she is."

"Do not tell them anything. If they inquire, tell them she's under the weather. I will explain what occurred when I meet with them."

"And her family?"

"I will contact them and ask them to come to Santa Fe to identify Alys. Please do not speak to them at this time. I will contact them tomorrow morning."

CHAPTER 7

Santa Fe's forensics investigators arrived at the Emerson and quickly set about to illuminate the crime scene with their portable lighting system. With bright lights in place, the two examiners began a meticulous search for trace evidence.

The medical examiner arrived shortly thereafter. As mandated by New Mexican police procedure, the ME, took control of the body. After a cursory examination, Safford offered Clay a time of death and cause of death. "The victim was shot in the head about eleven o'clock."

Clay had worked with the ME often over the years and knew the results of his examination would be detailed in scope and would include the actual cause of death, and blood alcohol measurements to determine if she had drugs in her system. Safford said, "I'll arrange to have the body transported to the morgue for an autopsy and inform you of my findings as soon as possible."

After the ME left the crime scene, Clay entered the Emerson lobby, accompanied by the forensics team and John Paul. Clay introduced himself to the night clerk and explained he would be examining Alys' room for clues.

Before they took an elevator to room 410, Clay stood for a few moments and studied the Southwest-themed lobby. A bar situated at the far end of the lobby caught Clay's attention. It was apparent that the bartender had a bird's eye view of the hotel's comings and goings, and he might be able to provide valuable insight about Alys Chapman's actions and her companions during the several hours before her death.

Clay planned to interview the bartender later that afternoon when the bar reopened for business. The front desk informed Clay that the bartender's hours were five p.m. to midnight.

In Alys' hotel room, the forensics team of Carton and Cook collected her laptop, her clothes, and other personal belongings for further analysis at the forensics lab. They dusted for fingerprints and collected the room's bed linens and towels to examine for DNA from possible sexual activity. After forensics processed the room for evidence, Clay had the room taped as a crime scene and had a lockbox installed. Carton promised they would get back to Clay as quickly as possible with any pertinent evidence they might uncover.

Clay questioned John Paul about the hotel's surveillance cameras. "Where are all the cameras located?"

He provided a litany of locations. "We have cameras outside the hotel focused on the parking lot, two more at the front entrance, two covering the lobby, one at each side and back entrance, one at the service entrance, cameras in each corridor, inside the three passenger elevators, at stairwells, the boiler room, the restaurant, and breakfast area. We have all the interior spaces, and all ingress and egress points to the building covered. We have cameras that cover virtually every square inch of the building and property that is used for public access. Of course, guests' rooms and public rest rooms are not included, for obvious reasons."

"Who monitors the screens?"

"I do. The monitors are in the security room adjacent to the front desk. Whether I'm in the security room or making my rounds, we have state-of-the-art mobile apps that allow me to view our camera feeds and receive instant motion alerts on my smartphone, my tablet, or my computer. And I can play back footage anytime."

Clay nodded. "You're pretty much married to your job, aren't you? Do you ever get tired of watching these camera displays day after day?"

"No, I enjoy the quiet. I'm never bored. I can shut out the outside world. There's a lot of drama here in real life. And I have the pleasure of watching people go about their lives like actors in a movie. Ha, that's what I do. Don't tell my boss, but my job is like watching movies all day. I should be paying my boss for doing what I do. I'm a movie fanatic. My favorite shows are the Spaghetti Western films with Clint Eastwood. I bet I've seen them a hundred times each. I love black-and-white movies. One of these days I'm going to write a movie script about what I do and what I've seen here, and I'm going to have Clint play my part."

Clay said, tongue in cheek, "I hope you write that movie. I'd like to see it, especially with Clint Eastwood as the star."

"You can be my guest on opening night."

"Sounds like a plan. John Paul, to change the subject, how far back in time do the security tapes go?"

"They cover the past thirty days, then the system overwrites the oldest footage. If you want, we can review the tapes now."

John Paul escorted Clay to the security room where multiple panels of CCTV screens captured footage of activity from all the cameras advancing on regular cycles.

Clay said, "From what you told me, you were making your rounds when you discovered Alys' car idling in the far reaches of the parking lot."

"That's right." John Paul showed a furrowed brow. "You know, the more I think about the woman's murder, the more I think I should have pursued the person who shot her."

"Do you mean you saw the suspect when you arrived on scene?"

"It may have been my imagination, but I swear I saw something in the desert when I first saw the victim's car idling. It was only a half a second, a microsecond, and then whatever it was, it disappeared. I probably was seeing things. When I made my rounds again, I didn't see anyone or anything unusual other than the fact that the victim's car was still idling. That's when I pulled up and parked behind her car."

"Are you normally armed?"

"No, not normally, but I have a pistol in my desk just in case. I'm licensed to carry it."

"Okay, let's look at the footage. Maybe we can spot the individual you may have seen. Let's start with the cameras covering the parking lot."

Clay sat next to the guard and watched as John Paul played the footage from various cameras. There was diminished vehicle activity as the night drew longer. However, at ten forty-five p.m., the parking lot camera focused on Alys' car and captured the grainy low-resolution image of an individual wearing what appeared to be a ski mask entering the crime scene from the adjacent desert. The suspect approached Alys' car and leaned down to chat with the victim through the open passenger-side window. Every few seconds he would straighten up and look around, conceivably to see if anyone was watching. Alys was not identifiable on camera nor was the individual with the ski mask. Three minutes later, at ten forty-eight p.m., there was a flash of light.

"Play that again. That was the killer, and the flash of light was probably the muzzle-flash from the gun the murderer used."

Clay observed that the suspect looked around one last time, then hurried into the adjacent desert and disappeared.

Two hours later, the tape showed John Paul parking behind the victim's car, going out to inspect the scene, trying to enter the victim's car, then walking around the car before returning to his car to call the police.

Clay suggested, "It appears the shooter was familiar with the layout of the hotel property. That might indicate the killer is an employee of the Emerson. Let's see if there's footage that shows any employee entering the hotel after the shooting."

The guard played footage from the front and side entrances, but no employee entered the hotel between ten forty-five p.m. and one a.m.

After the parking lot surveillance footage played out, Clay asked to view the CCTV footage from the fourth-floor hallway beginning on the Friday when Alys checked in.

Clay witnessed Alys putting a *Please Do Not Disturb* hanger on her door on the first day of her three-day stay. The sign remained on the door for the entire three days.

About one o'clock on Saturday afternoon, a man dressed in sweats, a baseball cap, and sunglasses knocked on Alys' door. She opened the door and allowed the man to step in. Alys peeked down the corridor then closed the door. About two o'clock that afternoon, the man exited the room and walked down the emergency exit stairwell.

John Paul announced, "That's probably our killer, but I don't know who it is."

John Paul and Clay continued to watch surveillance footage. It showed Alys leaving her room twice a day. In the morning, she took an elevator to the first-floor café for the hotel's complimentary breakfast. Fifteen minutes later, she returned to her room alone. Then about five p.m. each day, she left her room, went to the bar in the lobby, ordered a cocktail, then chatted with the bartender for several minutes. After she finished her drink, she exited the hotel. Then several hours later, a little before eleven, she returned and ordered a nightcap at the bar before going to her room.

About noon each day, room service knocked on her door and delivered a tray of food. Alys accepted the tray at the door, gave a tip to the deliverer, looked up and down the corridor, then closed the door.

The only other time someone entered her room was on the second day of her stay. A man carrying tools and a toilet plunger knocked on her door and waited patiently for Alys to let him in. After a few seconds, he knocked again and put his ear to the door, apparently to hear if anyone was in the room. He knocked a third time and when no one came to the door he used a keycard to open the door. He entered the room, but six seconds later, the surveillance tape showed him leaving abruptly, backtracking so quickly he banged into the corridor wall in his haste, then walked hurriedly to the exit stairs.

Clay asked John Paul, "What was that all about?"

"I don't know. He's the hotel maintenance man. Max Bruder is his name. I'll check with the front desk to see if he was asked to address a maintenance issue in the room."

Later that day, Carton reported to Clay that they had identified prints in room 412 belonging to Alys. There were a number of other random prints from past hotel guests, but none that forensics could match to anyone in their database.

Clay contacted Alys' parents to inform them of their daughter's death. They took the news badly, as one would imagine when parents lose a child. They had no idea why Alys was in Santa Fe or who she was seeing.

Later that afternoon, they arrived to identify Alys, talked to Clay, and arrange to have her body transported to a Santa Barbara funeral home.

* * *

Clay called on the medical examiner at the morgue to find out what he had learned about Alys' death. The ME reported that he had extracted a bullet that was lodged in Alys' temple and gave it to forensics to determine if it was a match to any cartridge in their ballistics database.

The ME offered, "The only other finding of interest is she had breast augmentation surgery relatively recently, probably within the past several weeks. The plastic surgeon who performed the surgery was very skilled. Her scars were visible only after close examination. It's just a guess on my part, but it's possible she was in Santa Fe to follow-up on her surgery."

CHAPTER 8

Clay went to the forensics lab to learn if they were able to find a match to the .38 slug that killed Alys.

Dan Carton, the normally placid chief examiner, was pleased. He explained, "I was just going to call you. We found a match to the cartridge that killed Alys Chapman. It was fired from the same gun that was used to kill Maura Quenneville."

Clay said, "I'll be damned. So, chances are Maura Quenneville was not involved in a road-rage incident. She was targeted, as was Alys Chapman. What else did you come up with?"

Carton explained, "The security guard's fingerprints were found on the car door handles. Apparently, it was when he tried to open the car door to check on Chapman. There were no other fingerprints other than Alys' prints, so it was likely the killer wore gloves."

Clay asked, "What did you come up with in Alys' room?"

"We uncovered dozens of prints. However, as you might expect in a hotel room, many guests would have been registered to the room before Chapman checked in. There are too many prints to pinpoint a suspect. However, we did check the prints that were most evident and learned they were from the maid who cleaned the room."

"Anything else?"

"Here's all we came up with." Carton handed Clay a file, which included multiple photos of the interior and exterior of the car, close-ups of Alys dead in her car, and at the morgue before autopsy, and finally a detailed listing of what forensics found in her hotel room.

"What about the prayer card that I found on the passenger seat?"

"It did not tell us anything. There were no fingerprints. And no DNA. It was printed on a standard computer printer, such as an HP. The paper was cut using scissors. In other words, it was not professionally printed. The paper was sixty-pound glossy text. Fairly common. Staples and other outlets carry it. I'm afraid it doesn't lead us anywhere. However, we learned from our archived files that some years ago a similar prayer card was found at another murder. The murder was about fifteen years ago, and ..."

"And it occurred at the Emerson, right?"

"Yes. Exactly."

"The Emerson security guard told me the circumstances were similar, except the victim was a hooker."

Carton added, "We checked with every priest in every Catholic Church in Santa Fe and surrounding towns to see if anyone could identify prayer cards like this one, especially one that had the Act of Contrition on one side. No one could identify a similar card."

Clay asked, "What about Alys Chapman's cell phones?"

"As you know, she had two phones. Her iPhone has well over 100 contacts, primarily business contacts, and only two numbers with a New Mexico area code—one was the phone number for the Emerson Hotel, and the other was the High Desert Plastic Surgery Center."

Clay asked, "Any voice messages to or from Santa Fe?"

"No, that's probably why she had been using a burner phone. Her incoming and outgoing calls were deleted or 'burned' and were not traceable. Not sure why she would have used a burner phone."

Clay said, "Maybe to hide an illicit affair or even drug transactions, although there was no indication that she was involved with drugs or that drugs played a part in her murder. My guess is that in her case she was protecting someone's identity, maybe someone in the public eye, or possibly a married man."

"Here's another list. This one details the entirety of what was in her purse." The list contained 210 dollars in cash, two credit cards, some loose change, lipstick, a small bottle of Advil, fourteen remaining birth control pills in a blister pack, three condoms, pepper spray, and a pack of matches from the Saddleback Saloon in Santa Fe.

CHAPTER 9

The Saddleback Saloon was a popular bar and grill situated a short block from the iconic Plaza at the center of Santa Fe. The restaurant served the self-proclaimed best hamburgers in the Southwest and was a meeting place for both tourists and Santa Fe citizens alike.

Clay parked his Explorer in the rear parking lot then entered and surveyed the noisy restaurant. Diners sat at picnic-style tables while a few tourists danced the country two-step on the 1,300-square foot dance floor. Bartenders and servers were dressed in period outfits that added to the Wild West atmosphere.

On one side of the dance floor, a mechanical bucking bronco stood waiting for the next fearless tourist to try their luck on the wild, bucking ride. Laughter and shouts of encouragement added to the din as another tourist mounted the bronco.

It was past one o'clock, and the restaurant was in the middle of a typically hectic lunch rush. Clay sat at a suddenly unoccupied barstool and flashed his badge to get the attention of one of the two bartenders behind the long mahogany bar.

"I need to talk with you."

The bartenders were rushed. "Man, you couldn't have picked a worse time. We're really jammed. Can you give me half an hour? This rush will be over by then."

"Yeah, sure, no problem." Clay motioned toward an emptying two-top table. "I'll grab a seat over there. It'll give me a chance to get a bite to eat." He ordered a cheeseburger with all the fixings.

As the lunch crowd subsided to a manageable number, the bartender walked around the bar and sat at Clay's table. He asked, "What can I do for you?"

Clay identified himself, then showed the bartender a photo of Alys. "Last night, about midnight, this woman was murdered at the Emerson Hotel. When we searched for clues, we found a pack of matches from your restaurant in her purse. We believe she was here sometime during the past three days. Do you recognize her?"

The bartender studied the photo for a few seconds then nodded as he looked at Clay. "Yep, I recognize her. She was here last night. I couldn't take my eyes off her. She was drop-dead gorgeous. You said she was murdered? Sorry to hear about that."

"What time was she here?"

"I don't know exactly, around five-thirty or six, about then. It was just starting to be a madhouse here."

"Was she with someone?"

"Not at first. But after a while a guy tapped her on her shoulder and sat next to her. She must have known the guy because she gave him an air-kiss on both cheeks."

"Can you describe the guy?"

"Handsome dude. Dressed in a suit. Swept-back white hair."

Clay immediately recognized that the bartender was describing Doctor Quenneville.

"Would you be able to identify him?"

"Yeah, I think so. He's been here a few times. He drew my attention because there aren't many people who come in dressed in a suit and tie." The bartender gestured at the crowd and said, "As you can see, it is pretty casual here."

"Did the guy leave with the woman?"

"I don't know. He sat alongside her for a while, then at one point when I turned around, they both were gone. He left a nice tip, but I didn't see them leave. The guy must be a hotshot. Always with a pretty woman. I remember he was here a couple of other times with another woman, also a beauty."

"Can you describe her?"

"Yes, she was a tall girl, brown hair, and much younger than he was, and oh yeah, she had a foreign accent."

"I know I'm really testing your memory, but do you know what name the foreign girl went by?"

"Yep, I overheard him introduce her to someone. It was a different kind of name."

"Reveca?"

"Yeah, that was it."

CHAPTER 10

Clay drove to Quenneville's office to interview the doctor about his whereabouts when Alys was killed the prior night. The doctor greeted Clay with a handshake and a disingenuous smile. Clay sensed the faint smell of Chanel No. 5 on him.

"Bryce, come on in. Have a seat. Are you here with news about my wife's murder?"

"No, not specifically, however someone killed a woman last night, and ballistics tests showed the killer used the same gun that was used to kill your wife."

Quenneville asked, "Who was the murder victim this time?"

"A woman by the name of Alys Chapman. She was staying downtown at the Emerson Hotel and was shot in her car in the hotel parking lot around midnight."

Quenneville did not act surprised or upset. "Sounds like you have a serial killer on the loose. Who do you think the killer is?"

"Unfortunately, we don't know that yet. All we know is, the gun was used to kill your wife as well as the woman last night. I was hoping you could help me tie the two murders together. Is it possible you knew the victim?"

"What was her name again?"

"Alys Chapman." Clay paused for a second. He was surprised by the doctor's uncertainty. "Our medical examiner discovered that she had breast augmentation surgery, most likely within the past six months, and you might have done the surgery."

"Detective, there are many other plastic surgeons in

Santa Fe, and they all do breast augmentation surgery, among other procedures. Why would you think she was my patient?

"Your office name was on her cell phone contact list."

The doctor shook his head slightly. "I have many patients."

Clay removed a photo of Alys from his inside coat pocket and showed it to him. "Do you know her? This photo was taken immediately before her autopsy."

Quenneville bit his lower lip and looked away for a few seconds, seemingly crestfallen. Finally, he composed himself and nodded. "Alys Chapman, of course. You're right. She was a patient of mine. Pardon me for not remembering her name. I have dozens of patients. I can't remember all of them."

"Sure, I understand. When did you see her last?"

"I must be losing it. I totally forgot she had a follow-up visit yesterday. You don't think I had anything to do with her murder, do you?"

Clay said, "A follow-up visit this late after surgery, is that normal?"

"Yes, I have several follow-up visits after surgery for each patient. That's my normal procedure. Between you and me, the follow-up visits serve two purposes—one to check on the surgery itself, and secondly to help promote interest in doing other types of surgeries. Oftentimes, if a surgery proves successful in the eyes of a patient, she will opt for additional procedures."

"By the way, is it possible that Alys might have known your wife?"

"I can't imagine how they would have known each other."

Clay nodded and said, "Tell me what you know about Alys."

The doctor said, "There's not much I can tell you. I believe she was from California. A pretty woman. Unfortunately, she admittedly did not have confidence in herself because she had extremely small breasts. There are several reasons why that condition occurs in a woman, but the primary reason why some women have breast augmentation is they suffer from a lack of confidence. Whether it's someone's nose, or breasts, or facial wrinkles, it's all pretty much the same. After a patient's initial visit, I find that virtually everyone is uncertain if they should proceed with surgery. I tell them if they are unsure what impact surgery will have on their lives, they should have psychological counseling before they commit to surgery. I usually end up referring them to a local psychologist if they don't already have someone they're seeing."

"Doctor Quenneville, I have an eyewitness who informed me that you were with Chapman last night at the Saddleback Saloon."

The doctor took a deep breath, exasperated by Clay's doggedness. "I wasn't with her. I happened to see her there. I didn't even remember her name. I said hello and we chatted for a few minutes before I left."

"Did you leave the saloon with her?"

"No, I left by myself."

"Where did you go afterward?"

"Home."

"Who can confirm that?"

"Reveca, my nanny."

"Is Reveca at your home now?"

"Yes, of course. She's taking care of Adam. He had a bit of a fever this morning."

"I'd like to talk to her."

"Why? This is starting to irritate me, Detective. I'm a very busy man and I can't afford to go back and forth to my home to answer your questions about Alys Chapman. I understand you're doing your due diligence, but I've already told you where I was last night. I don't get why you need to talk to Reveca."

Clay glared at Quenneville. "Relax, Doctor. I'm not accusing you of anything."

Quenneville calmed down. "Fine, I'll take your word on that. Let's get going. I've got a full schedule today. Besides, it's a good opportunity for me to check on Adam. I'll meet you there."

Clay did not want Quenneville to race back to his house and prompt Reveca about where he was last night. "No, I'll drive us. We'll be there and back here to your office before you know it."

CHAPTER 11

When Clay and Quenneville arrived at Quenneville's home, the doctor called out to Reveca. "It's me. I'm home for a minute. Please come down to the living room."

Reveca answered from upstairs, "I did not expect you home this early. I'll be right down." She entered the living room, casually dressed in tight-fitting jeans and a sexy tube top. With her lean and long physique, Clay felt she could have been a model.

Reveca was surprised to see Clay. "Oh, Doctor, I did not know the detective was here. Did I do something wrong?"

Quenneville answered. "No, Reveca. He simply wants to talk to you."

Clay greeted her pleasantly. "Hello, Reveca. Good to see you again. I understand Doctor Quenneville's son is not feeling well."

Clay observed that she tilted her head toward the doctor, seemingly seeking assurance from him that she could answer. "Yes, but he is better now."

Clay said, "I won't keep you very long. Let me explain why I'm here. Last night, a young lady was murdered in the parking lot of the Emerson Hotel. Her name was Alys Chapman. We're interviewing everyone who may have known her or may have seen her."

Reveca shook her head. "I do not know anyone named Alys Chapman. And I did not murder her."

Quenneville stifled a laugh. "The detective's not accusing you of her murder. Tell her, Detective."

Clay said, "Doctor Quenneville, if you don't mind, I'd like to talk with Reveca in private. Please give us a few minutes."

The doctor was annoyed by Clay's insistence to talk with Reveca without him guiding her responses. "Not sure what you're trying to get at, but I insist that you do not intimidate her, and further, I expect you to explain her rights. I hold Reveca in high regard, and I don't want you to walk rough-shod over her because she's naïve about our country's customs, especially as they deal with our law enforcement process."

Clay remained calm, although he did not appreciate Quenneville's insinuation that he would treat Reveca cruelly. "You are overreacting, Doctor. I simply want to talk with her for a few minutes to see if she can provide me with any information concerning Alys Chapman's whereabouts last night leading up to the time she was killed."

"How could she know about Alys when she was here tending to Adam all night?"

"I am sure you have an alternate babysitter if Reveca cannot be available. Let me explain where I'm coming from. First off, the bartender at the Saloon can identify Reveca. He said he has seen her there several times with you. Is it possible Reveca may have met Ms. Chapman during one of her times there?"

Quenneville said, "Why didn't you say so to begin with?"

Clay suggested, "Perhaps you can check on your son's condition while I talk with Reveca in the interim."

Quenneville walked up the steps to tend to Adam, but when Clay's back was turned, the doctor looked down at Reveca and furtively shook his head at her.

Clay handed the photo of Alys to Reveca. "Please take a good look at this photo of the girl in the picture. That's Alys. Do you know her?"

She studied the photo. "Maybe, but I am not sure."

"The doctor has indicated the woman was a patient of his."

"I do not know the doctor's patients."

"You obviously are familiar with a restaurant called the Saddleback Saloon? I understand from the bartender that you've been there a few times."

"Yes, I am familiar with the restaurant. I've gone there several times, either with the doctor or by myself so I could meet people my age."

"That was nice of him to take you there. I understand he was at the restaurant last night before he came home. He was seen with Ms. Chapman."

Reveca was taken aback by that news.

Clay said, "That news seemed to surprise you. Was it that he was with another woman so soon after his wife's death?"

Reveca said, "No, I am not surprised. It is not my business what Doctor Quenneville does or who he sees."

"Of course not. I understand that you are an employee of the doctor and really have no say in what he does?"

She looked away.

Clay said, "Did you know if he left the restaurant with Ms. Chapman?"

"Why would I know that?"

"True. You were here tending to Adam, right? But afterward, did she visit with him here at the house?"

"No, she did not."

"What time did he come home?"

"Nine o'clock."

"That's late. Is that normally when he comes home?"

She answered Clay sharply. "You should ask Doctor Quenneville those questions. I take care of Adam, not Doctor Quenneville."

"Did the doctor leave the house last night?

"No, he did not."

"Are you sure?"

"I was ..." she started to explain but stopped.

"What were you going to say?"

"Detective, I do not want to answer any more of your questions. I am frightened what I say will be used against me to deport me back to Slovakia. You should ask the doctor what he did last night, not me."

Clay stared at her, surprised at her sudden strong and defensive attitude. She closed her mind to further discussion and was no longer going to answer his questions. Clay believed it would be best if he continued his questioning another time.

"Thank you, Reveca. No more questions. Would you allow me to take a photo of you?"

"Why?"

"For my records."

She hesitated but agreed. "It's not to deport me, correct?"

He smiled, "No, not to deport you."

"Okay then."

Clay used his cell phone to take a photograph. Afterward, at the foot of the stairs he shouted for Quenneville that he was going to be leaving. "I'll wait for you in the car."

Quenneville came downstairs and peered through the front-door's side window to ensure Clay was not within sight, then he approached Reveca. He kissed her on the cheek. "Thank you," he said.

CHAPTER 12

Clay dropped Quenneville off at his office, then drove back to the Emerson. He parked his Explorer at the entrance under the hotel canopy and notified the valet that he would be a while. He entered the hotel and strode to the lobby bar, where the bartender was setting up the bar for its five o'clock opening. The bartender was a good-looking man in his early forties with a stubble beard, a short ponytail, a small tattoo of an eagle on his right wrist, and another tattoo of an otter on his left forearm.

"He addressed Clay tersely. "Hey pal, we're not open yet. Give me fifteen minutes."

Clay showed his badge. "I'm detective Clay Bryce of the Santa Fe Police Department. I'm not here for a drink. I'm investigating the murder of Alys Chapman." Clay took out the photo of Alys from his pocket. "This is the woman who was killed. She was murdered last night in the parking lot at the rear of the hotel."

"I'm sorry to hear that. No one told me. I know who she is. She came to the bar from time to time. Who killed her?"

Clay said, "I don't know."

"How can I help?"

"First off, what is your name?"

He answered without looking at Clay. "Jeremy Voit. V-o-i-t."

"I've viewed the hotel's surveillance tapes and saw that on Friday and Saturday evening she was at your bar when you opened and then again when you closed, but not on Sunday. Do you remember serving her?"

Voit nodded that he recognized Alys. "Yes. A very pretty

woman. She was my first customer both Friday and Saturday nights. She always ordered a vodka martini, straight up, with two olives."

"What time was that?"

"Five o'clock. We would chat for a while until I got busy with other guests and then she would thank me, sign her check to her room, and leave."

"Did you ever notice if she was with anyone, or if anyone was waiting for her in the lobby or outside?"

"Not that I remember. She always seemed to be by herself."

"What about when she returned to the hotel? The surveillance tapes show she would be back at your bar about eleven o'clock."

"Yeah, that's when she'd order a sherry and afterward, she'd take the elevator. I assume she went to her room. But come to think of it, I didn't see her Sunday evening. I understand now why."

Clay asked, "What did you talk about with her?"

"Nothing in particular, just stuff."

"Like what stuff?"

"Where she was from and what she liked to do in Santa Fe. Her favorite restaurants—touristy, casual stuff. She said she lived in Santa Barbara, California, and worked for the Hilton there."

"Did she say why she was in Santa Fe?"

"She said she was here for a follow-up on a medical procedure. I asked her what kind. She said it was a woman thing, so I didn't push it."

"You said you didn't see her last night, but you said she was here when you opened yesterday. When I viewed the lobby surveillance videos of Saturday night, I saw a crowd at the bar, half of them were men in suits and ties. Alys, the woman who was murdered, was seated at the bar in the middle of everyone. What was that all about?"

Voit continued to set up his bar but paused to answer Clay's question. "They were from a wedding rehearsal party. A noisy group. They were getting out of hand, so John Paul had to ask them to tone it down."

Clay said, "The men seemed to be all over Chapman. Do you know if she left with anyone from that group?"

"Not that I saw. When she first arrived the bar was empty, but five minutes later, men and women from that wedding party arrived. Some of the men took turns hitting on her, but from what I saw she didn't give anyone the time of day. Most of the time she looked straight ahead and disregarded them. Then I remember she got a phone call on her cell and left the bar. She stayed in the lobby for a while with her phone to her ear."

"What time did you close down the bar?"

"Usual time, midnight."

"Then what did you do?"

"I headed home."

"Can anyone vouch for you?"

"I live alone, so no, no one can vouch for me. Why are you asking?"

"We believe she was seeing someone, but we don't know who. Was it you, by any chance?"

"No."

"Did she give you any idea who that person may have been?"

"No. She wasn't a hooker, was she?"

"No. I don't believe so. From your vantage point behind the bar, overlooking the lobby, did you ever see her with anyone?"

"Nope. Like I said, she was a beauty, a magnet for men, but no one was going to get to first base with her."

Clay asked Voit point-blank. "Did you have sex with her anytime during the last three days?"

Voit recoiled from the question and nervously shifted from leg to leg. "I don't like where this is heading. I'm not going to answer that."

Clay replied angrily. "You can answer now or with your lawyer present. Up to you."

Voit's breathing quickened. "I do not have a lawyer. And the answer is no, I did not have sex with that woman. I didn't have anything to do with her murder. You can't blame me for trying to hook up with her, but I didn't stalk her or anything. She wasn't interested. You must understand that on a one-to-ten basis, she was an eleven. I tried, but I swear nothing happened. I am not lying. Yes, I tried to get together with her, but I struck out. That's all there was to it."

"Did you know a woman by the name of Maura Quenneville?"

He shook his head for several seconds as he ran the name through his memory bank. "No, not that I can think of. Who is she?"

"Another murder victim."

After Clay spoke with Voit, he went to the front desk to talk with Rose, the attractive, smartly dressed employee who had checked Alys into the hotel the past Friday. He was suspicious about Voit's relationship with Alys and asked Rose, "Anything you can tell me about Alys Chapman and Voit? Did they seem to be in a relationship after hours?"

"No, she didn't seem to be Jeremy's type. She was a loner. I don't think he got to first base with her."

"Tell me about Voit. What kind of reputation does he have?"

"Jeremy's a good-looking man and he knows it. Women find him exciting."

Clay asked, "Do you find him exciting?"

"There's something about him. He has a bad-boy image, and some women like that in a man, but he likes himself too much for my taste."

"What about a woman by the name of Maura Quenneville? Is that name familiar to you?"

"No."

"Might she have been a guest here at the hotel?"

"I can check quickly."

She looked the name up on her computer and shook her head. "No, she's not in our database under that name."

Clay removed a photo of Maura from his jacket pocket. "Does she look familiar?"

Rose studied the photo for a moment. "Yes, she does. I've seen her before. She was here a few times to pick up Max Bruder, our maintenance guy, so he could do some handyman work for her at her house."

"That's interesting. I'll have to talk to Max about her. In the meantime, what can you tell me about Alys Chapman?"

"She was a guest at the hotel a number of times."

"Any idea why she was here so often?"

"It's not unusual for businesspeople to stay here multiple times, so it wasn't odd that she was back here often. Interestingly, though, she always requested the same room on the fourth floor, and she always booked the connecting room, 412, for a night or two during each visit. She used her own name when she registered for both rooms and didn't explain why she wanted the second room—and I never asked."

Clay asked Rose, "I didn't think there was anything special about the two rooms. Am I missing something?"

"Not that I know of. As you may know, the two rooms are adjoining rooms accessible through a connecting door. They overlook the parking lot and don't have the best views, but that's the room she always asked for. I'm sure you're aware that the parking lot where Alys was killed is visible from 410."

"I'll want to visit the room again after we finish talking."

"No problem. I'll get you a key card."

"When were the other times Alys checked into room 410?"

"I'll run a printout." She punched in Alys' name on her computer. "Each stay was for three nights, starting on a Friday, with checkout on the following Monday. She charged her bar drinks, room service lunches, and parking fees to her room but did not incur any other hotel expense."

"Is there any relevance to the dates when Alys stayed here, any activity that would draw her to book a room when she did?"

The receptionist studied the printout, and said, "I don't know of any event going on in the city during those dates. I guess it could have involved her business, but I don't know what she did for a living."

"Did she always check in by herself or was she accompanied by someone?"

"I can't remember for certain, but I believe she was always by herself."

Clay laid out his plan to learn more about Alys. "I want to access her room first, then I'd like to talk with any other employee who might have had contact with Alys. Can you tell me who those employees are?"

"Jeremy, our bartender, for one. I'll put together a list of others who might have dealt with her. After you come back from inspecting room 410, I'll have the list ready for you."

CHAPTER 13

Clay took an elevator to the fourth floor, then unlocked and entered Alys' room. He looked around and said out loud, as though Alys was in the room with him, "Okay, what is so special about this room that you insisted on staying here?"

He went to the window, pulled the drapes, and looked out at the parking lot and the desert beyond it. The sun was setting. Cactuses were in bloom, watered by recent desert rains. But other than access to a connecting room, Clay could not understand why this room had been so special to Alys. *Was she meeting with someone in the next room? Was it their rendezvous place?*

As he continued to study the desert scene, he saw a reflection of something bright in the desert just off the parking lot where Alys had been shot. Clay immediately suspected it was the killer who returned to the scene of the shooting through the desert to ensure he did not leave any evidence behind.

Clay hurried down the exit stairs and through the side entrance of the hotel, then ran into the desert for a short distance. But he was too late. If it had been the killer, he was gone now.

Clay phoned the forensics team and instructed them to examine the desert environ adjacent to the crime scene for footprints or any other possible evidence.

❋ ❋ ❋

Clay returned to the lobby to question the employees whose names Rose had scribbled down for him. The list included:

the bellhop, the hotel's concierge, the valet, the maintenance worker, and the maid who cleaned 410 and 412. "The housekeeper is off duty now, so you'll have to wait until tomorrow to talk with her, or if you want to meet with her today, she's only a couple of blocks away at the Albertsons grocery store on South St. Francis Street. She works the afternoon shift there beginning at three o'clock, after she signs out here."

"What's her name?"

"Emily Embers."

"I'll drive over to Albertsons when I'm finished here."

The first person on the list that Clay questioned was Max Bruder, the maintenance worker.

Rose gave Clay directions to Bruder's basement workshop across from the boiler room and phoned to tell him that Clay was on his way to see him.

Max was a hulk of a man, with a square jaw and black hair that could have used a trimming. He carried his tools on a belt around his waist. At first glance, he reminded Clay of John Steinbeck's Lennie Small, the character in *Of Mice and Men*, a giant of a man with shoulders wide enough to wrestle a steer.

Clay said, "I assume you are aware of the death of a hotel guest by the name of Alys Chapman."

"Yes."

"Why did you go to her room the day after she checked in?"

"My boss told me to go to her room to unclog the shower drain."

Clay said, "The surveillance tape on the fourth floor showed you entered her room, but you left abruptly. You couldn't have been in her room for more than ten seconds.

Why was that? You could not have spent enough time in her room to resolve the shower drain problem."

"I knocked on her door a couple of times, and I didn't get any answer, so I assumed no one was in. I used my master key card to get in. At first, I didn't realize she was there, but then I heard voices coming from the room next door. As it turned out, the connecting door to 412 was wide open. I took a couple of steps into the room and said, 'Hello, maintenance here.' The next thing I know, the woman shrieks and slams the connecting door shut. She was naked as a jaybird."

"What did you do then?"

"I backed out of the room as fast as I could."

Clay said, "Do you understand she was the woman who was murdered last night?"

"Yes, but it was not me who killed her. I didn't have any reason to do that."

"Do you have any idea who might have killed her?"

"No. I saw some guy in there with her. He was wearing a towel around his waist. Maybe it was him."

"Can you describe him?"

"Doubt it. He was quick to turn away from me."

"What happened next? Did you ever fix her drain?"

"No, I was supposed to work on it after she checked out, but you've got crime-scene tape on the door and a lockbox on it, so I haven't worked on it yet. You might need to know that the naked lady, the one you said was murdered, reported me to my boss, and claimed I went into her room without warning. She claimed I was a peeping tom. That is not true. I knocked on her door a couple of times and, even after I opened the door, I said out loud that I was from maintenance."

"What did your boss say about all that?"

"He was not pleased with me. He said the woman threatened to sue the hotel and me, too, because I walked into her room when she was naked. My boss was going to fire me because I did not get permission to enter her room. Can you believe that? She wants to sue me. She can try, but I don't have two nickels to rub together, so good luck trying to get any money from me."

Clay said, "Well, she isn't going to sue anybody now. She's dead, remember?"

Max smiled. "Oh, yeah. But like I said, it wasn't me that killed her."

"One last question. I understand you knew a woman by the name of Maura Quenneville."

Max fidgeted in his chair before he answered. "Yes, I knew her. She had me do some work at her house several times. But then she died in an automobile accident a few weeks back."

"What was she like?"

"Nice enough. All business. She'd pick me up after five o'clock here, tell me what she wanted me to do, and that was it. She paid me in cash."

"Did you ever meet her husband?"

"No. He was always working late."

"What about Reveca, the nanny, did you meet her?"

"Yes. Pretty girl. I didn't see much of her. She was always taking care of the son, Adam I think his name was."

Clay said. "Max, thanks for talking with me. I'll have more questions for you, but I'll check back with you later."

Except for the maid who cleaned Alys' room, Clay spoke with each of the Emerson employees on Rose's list who might have had any contact with Alys. The valet saw Alys most often, but he said she did not engage in small talk. Alys would give him the valet ticket, then give him a couple of bucks as a tip after he retrieved her car. He said Alys was not with anyone when he parked or retrieved her vehicle, and she seemed to know her way around the city. She asked for directions one time only.

"And where was that?"

"How to get to the Saddleback Saloon."

CHAPTER 14

Clay drove to the Albertsons grocery store and introduced himself to the store manager, Alonzo Garcia, a middle-aged Hispanic man who wore his thick black hair piled high on his head and buzzed it short on the sides in a modern-day Mohawk.

Clay explained, "I'm investigating the murder of two women. One was named Maura Quenneville and another by the name of Alys Chapman. I need to talk with Emily Embers to see if she could shed some light on the murders. Without going into a lot of details, the two women are linked, but I'm not sure how. Chapman was a guest at the Emerson Hotel, but we don't have much background information about Maura Quenneville other than she was married to a prominent plastic surgeon here in Santa Fe."

"Are you saying Emily was involved in their murders?"

"No. I'm hoping she can provide me with some pertinent information about the victims. What can you tell me about Embers?"

"Not a whole lot. She's an hourly employee, a checkout clerk. She's very dependable. Always on time, and seldom misses a day's work. She's an absolute whiz, ultrafast, and chats up customers like they're long-lost friends. Actually, she's one of our better employees. I wish I had a dozen more employees like her," the manager said.

"Can you get someone to cover for her so I can ask her some questions?"

"Sure, you can use the conference room next room down to talk to her."

"Emily, thanks for meeting with me. I understand that besides working here, you're employed at the Emerson."

"Yes, I'm a maid at the hotel."

Emily was around Clay's age, early forties. She was about fifteen pounds overweight, with red hair flecked with gray. She plopped down in the chair across from Clay and folded her arms across her significant chest. She gave Clay a fake grimace. "Detective, what did I do?"

Clay smiled. "Nothing that I know of. I need to ask you some questions about a woman who was killed at the Emerson. Do you know about the homicide that occurred Sunday night?"

"Yes. When I first got to work this morning, I saw cop cars all over the place, and everyone was jabbering about a hotel guest being murdered. But that's not the first time someone has been killed there. I don't remember exactly when it happened, but quite a few years ago, another woman was killed in the hotel parking lot. She was shot to death too. Apparently, the police believed she was a high-class hooker, and management didn't want that kind of news to leak out about a hooker doing business at the hotel, so it was kept pretty hush-hush. Do you think the woman killed there yesterday also was a hooker?"

"We don't think so."

"Wow, this is exciting stuff. I love reading murder mysteries, and here we have a murder right in our backyard. Do you think I should be worried about myself? I mean, does the guy who shot her prey on women?"

"I don't think you have anything to worry about. As always, just be aware of your environment."

"Do you have a suspect?"

"Not yet. That's the reason why I wanted to talk to you. The woman who was killed, Alys Chapman was her name, stayed in room 410 at the Emerson. I understand that's one of the rooms you're responsible for cleaning."

"Yes, but she never wanted her room cleaned the entire time she stayed there. And she stayed at the hotel often over the past year, always in the same room. Funny, that she never wanted her room cleaned. I guess she didn't want to be bothered."

Clay continued his questioning. "Did she ever talk to you or say why she was in Santa Fe?"

"No. The only time she talked to me was when she had a problem Friday with the drain in her shower. She approached me in the corridor when I was cleaning another room, and she said the drain was clogged and she had to stand in dirty water when she showered. She asked if I could arrange to have it unclogged as soon as possible. I told her I was sure she could be moved to another room if she was uncomfortable in that room, but she said she preferred to stay where she was. She liked the view of the desert. I told her I would tell maintenance about the clogged drain and get it unclogged right away. She said to make sure maintenance notified her in advance when someone was going to work in the room."

Emily said, "Yesterday, she told me that the shower was still clogged. I apologized and told her I would call maintenance again right away, but she was very nice about it and said she would live with it."

"Is there anything else you can tell me about her?"

"Other than she was a very pretty woman, I can't add anything. She had this regal appearance, like Kate Middleton. I didn't see her again after we talked about her shower problem. I knocked on her door one time to give her fresh towels that she asked for. She said, 'Thanks, please leave them at the door.' I didn't know what she was doing in the room and it wasn't any of my business. I'm sure she had her reasons. Frankly, I think she was doing it with the guy in 412, and that's probably the reason why she didn't want maintenance back in to unclog her shower. She could use the shower in the connecting room."

"Can you describe the guy in 412?"

"No. He checked out yesterday. When I went into the room to clean, I saw that the connecting door to that woman's room, 410, was partially open. You know in some rooms, there's a door between two adjoining rooms so if guests are traveling with children they might want to keep the door open to keep an eye on the kids. Anyway, that woman didn't have any kids, so I think she and the guy in 412 were doing a little shagging, if you know what I mean. Not that there's anything wrong with that." She gave Clay a wicked smile.

"Was she still in the room?"

"I don't know. She was either in the bathroom or down for breakfast. I closed the door quietly and went about my business."

"So you didn't see the person in 412?"

"Not a good look, no. He had a *Do Not Disturb* sign on his door the entire time too. I only saw him once. It was late Saturday afternoon. He passed by the room I was cleaning and was headed down the stairs. He didn't have a suitcase or anything. It was like he was sneaking out."

"Do you think you would recognize him if you saw him again?"

"I doubt it. I only caught a glimpse of him as he walked

by. He was wearing a baseball cap low on his head. I see that same look all the time with men at the hotel who don't want to be identified on the security cameras."

Clay asked, "Anything you can tell me about the room after the guy left yesterday?"

"There were glasses and an empty bottle of wine, and there was a room-service tray with leftover food that sat on a table in the room. The bed sheets were off the bed, towels were on a chair and on the bathroom floor. All the same stuff I see every day."

When Clay initially viewed the surveillance tapes with John Paul, he did not pay any attention to anyone entering or exiting 412. He had focused solely on 410. Now he decided to view the fourth-floor surveillance tapes again but with the emphasis on room 412.

The tapes showed that about noon on Saturday morning a man dressed in sweats, a baseball cap and sunglasses knocked on 412. Alys opened the door and allowed the man to step in. She peeked down the corridor to ensure the coast was clear then closed the door.

About two o'clock that afternoon, the man exited the room and entered the emergency exit stairwell. His back was intentionally always to the surveillance camera.

❋ ❋ ❋

Later that day, forensics reported to Clay that they had identified prints in Room 412 belonging to Alys and Emily

Embers. There were other random prints from past hotel guests but none that forensics could match to anyone in their database. In addition, Carton said they had searched the desert adjacent to the parking lot per Clay's instructions and did not discover any evidence useful to the investigation.

CHAPTER 15

The day after Alys was murdered, Clay flew to California to interview Alys' roommate, Mackenzie Stanton. A detective from the Santa Barbara Police Department met him at Alys' condominium to help Clay search for clues into Alys' murder. The detective unlocked the police lockbox and extracted a key to open the door. Once inside, Clay called Mackenzie and asked her to meet him at her condo.

Mackenzie was a beautiful blonde about thirty years of age, tall, at nearly six feet, with a flawless complexion, a lean, athletically toned figure, with eyes the bluest Clay had ever seen. He was attracted to her instantly. He thought, *she has to be one of the prettiest women in all of Santa Barbara.*

"I'm sorry for your loss," he said as he extended his huge hand that enveloped hers. He held onto her hand a few seconds longer than she expected.

She asked through welling tears, "Detective Bryce, are you sure it was Alys who was murdered? Could it have been someone else, maybe someone who was using her identity?"

"Her parents identified her, so no, I'm sorry, but we've confirmed that it was Alys."

Mackenzie could not hold back her tears any longer. "I was always frightened for her. Who would have done such a thing?"

Clay said, "That's what we're going to find out. Mackenzie, tell me about Alys. Start off by telling me how you knew each other."

"We knew each other in high school, then we renewed our relationship five or six years afterward and we've been best friends and roommates ever since. We had a lot of interests in common. We've never had a harsh word between us."

"What did she do for a living?"

"She worked as an events coordinator at the Hilton Hotel Beach Resort only a few miles from here."

"Do you know why she was in Santa Fe this past weekend?"

"She went to Santa Fe a number of times. When I asked why, she told me it was to follow-up on the plastic surgery procedure she had done there. And after I bugged her enough times about going so often, she finally admitted she was seeing someone there. At one point, she mentioned he was married and planned to divorce his wife so they could get married. I said to her, 'Please do not be gullible.' I questioned that he was really going to divorce his wife, but she said she was certain of it."

"Did she tell you his name?"

"No, she wouldn't tell me, but I think I know."

"Who?"

"The guy who operated on her—Dr. Ronald Quenneville."

Clay said, "I don't know anything about plastic surgery, but I assume breast augmentation is a major procedure that requires a lot of pre-surgery prep and post-surgery recovery. But you're saying that wasn't the real reason for her frequent trips to Santa Fe?"

"Yeah, my guess is her trips were primarily to see her lover."

"Quenneville?"

"Yes."

Clay found a letter on Alys' bedside table from someone who signed his name as G.H. The envelope did not have a return address, but the postmark showed it was from New York City, New York. The letter read, in part: "I love you very much and am quitting my job here and returning to California to try to make a go of it again with you. I'm very sorry if I hurt you. I was wrong, and I promise I won't hurt you again. Let me put it this way. I love you a lot more than I like my job; I don't care how much money I can make here. I hope you'll give me another chance. I am working hard to control my temper. Love, G.H."

Clay asked Mackenzie, "Who is G. H.?"

"Gardner Hicks. He is Alys' ex-boyfriend. They were together for several years, but she broke up with him about a year ago."

Clay held the letter in his right hand. "The impression I get reading this is that he was abusive to her. Was he?"

"Yes, that's why they broke up. He had anger issues. He would rage at the drop of a hat."

"Could it be he's the one Alys had been seeing in Santa Fe?"

"It's possible although their breakup was pretty intense. Alys told me after she first broke it off with him that he had taken a job in New York, working for a startup IT company, and he was making a huge salary."

Clay asked, "Do you know if Alys gave him another chance like he asked for in this letter?"

"I don't know. But I do know she told him she was seeing someone else. I didn't think that was the smartest thing to tell him because he was extremely jealous."

"I'd like to talk to Gardner. Do you have his address or phone number?"

"Sorry I don't."

"What about the name of the company he worked for?"

"I don't know that, either. As I said it was a startup, and I don't know its name."

Clay pointed to a photo on the bureau that showed Alys posing cheek-to-cheek with a male on a beach and with the ocean as a backdrop. The photo showed a heavily tattooed and fit Gardner Hicks in a bathing suit with six-pack abs and Alys in a white micro-bikini.

"Is this the guy who Alys is seeing in Santa Fe?"

"No, that's Gardner."

Clay remarked, "So she must have had some feelings for him even after they broke up. Otherwise, she wouldn't have kept a photo of the two of them in her bedroom."

Mackenzie shrugged. "I guess so. You have to understand, they had been going together for several years. It took a while for Alys to adjust without him. I think she still loved him, even with his abusive behavior."

"It's never easy to regain your equilibrium when a breakup happens, regardless of the reason," Clay said.

Mackenzie said, "Sounds like you're a man with experience."

He nodded and acknowledged that he was. "Yes, I recently broke up with someone who I was very fond of. In time we decided to go our separate ways. We stay in touch and wish each other the best."

Mackenzie said, "I hope you don't mind me being forward, but if I were your ex, I never would have let you go."

Her flirtatious comment seemed to embarrass Clay. He didn't know how to respond, and said simply, "Thanks."

Clay removed the photo from the picture frame to take

with him back to Santa Fe. He wanted to see if anyone at the Emerson might recognize Alys' former boyfriend.

After studying the photo again, Clay said, "Obviously, Alys had breast augmentation surgery sometime after this photo was taken."

"Yes, that's true."

"Do you ever hear from Gardner?"

"Not anymore. He used to text me or try to reach me by phone. I never answered, but a few days ago I accidentally answered the phone. I thought it was someone else, but it turned out to be him. He asked where Alys was and said he needed to talk to her. I told him she was away on business in Santa Fe. He wanted to know where. I lied and told him I didn't know. He said he wanted to say hello and to tell her he was moving back to California. He asked if she was still working at the Hilton and if she was seeing anyone. I said yes, she was going with someone in Santa Fe—and that she was head-over-heels in love with the guy. I wasn't trying to bait him. All I was trying to do was to get him to understand that Alys had no interest in starting up a relationship with him again."

"How did he respond?"

"He wanted to know who the guy was that she was seeing."

"Did you tell him?"

"No, but I did tell him I thought the guy was a doctor she knew there."

"What did he say about that?"

"He went off the wall as usual. He said, 'You mean the plastic surgery doctor who operated on her boobs?' That's when I realized I had told him too much. I told him I thought he should just drop it and let Alys live her life."

"What did he say to that?"

"He cursed a blue streak. First at Alys, and then he cursed me for protecting her. He swore to get even with Alys, and me too. He was cursing at me so badly that I hung up on him. He called me back three or four times, but I didn't answer. I blocked his calls from that point on. I haven't heard from him since."

CHAPTER 16

Clay wrapped up his search for evidence at Alys' condominium and thanked the Santa Barbara detective for assisting him. He said he would be in touch with him as the case continued to develop. After the detective left, Clay questioned Mackenzie. "Tell me more about Gardner Hicks."

Mackenzie explained, "A very smart guy. A techie. He could tell you anything you wanted to know about computers or anything for that matter. He always thought he was the smartest person in the room, always certain and never wrong."

"What about his temperament?"

"Abusive."

"In what way?"

"In every way. It was mind-boggling to me that Alys put up with him for as long as she did. I never could understand that. How is it that some women continue to stay in abusive relationships? I'm sure you've seen victims of abuse in your time with the police force."

Clay agreed. "It happens more than you can imagine. There are many reasons unique to each woman. Maybe the woman is afraid of being physically harmed if she tries to leave, or she doesn't want to be alone, or she might have a feeling of worthlessness, or lack self-esteem."

Mackenzie cleared her tears and said, "It was upsetting to me that Alys would take such abuse and go back to Gardner time and time again and, worse yet, forgive him for his behavior. She always blamed herself, never him. He had jealousy issues and accused her of cheating on him, only one of the million things that made him lose his temper.

He'd pick a fight at the drop of a hat in a bar, or anyplace for that matter. I'd see him with bruises on his face or a black eye sometimes, and he would admit he had been in a fight."

"What about bruises on Alys?"

"She'd have bruises on her arms and wrists. She would explain them away by saying she bumped into a wall or she tripped or whatever, but I knew she was trying to cover up for him." She paused and looked Clay in the eye. "Detective, you may think what I'm going to tell you is crazy, but a lot of times, what I think is going to happen in the future—happens. Like I have ESP. I've been worried about Alys for a long time. I thought something terrible was going to happen to her. Obviously, now it turns out I was right."

"Did you tell her about your conversation with Gardner?"

"Yes, in so many words, but she wouldn't listen. She laughed it off and called it my 'ESP gibberish.'"

"If you truly have ESP, then you should know who killed her." He smiled at her, and at the same time tried hard to keep the smile from turning into a mocking look. He wasn't successful.

"Now I sense you're making fun of me. I'm sorry to say I don't know yet who killed Alys. But I will know, and when I do, I'll let you know who it is. Sometimes my extrasensory perception, my psychic gift, takes a while to sort itself out."

Clay realized Mackenzie was serious about her supposed powers. He thought Alys was right, it is gibberish. *She's a kook? But, oh, yes, she is a beautiful kook.*

"Anything else you can tell me about Gardner?"

"Yes. Alys tried to talk him into going to therapy, but he wouldn't go. As much as she tried to hide her bruises, it was obvious to me that they were caused by him. I pleaded with her to leave him, but she would argue that he was really a nice guy, and she was trying to help him change his anger traits. But I thought he was mentally ill, really, and I knew things were only going to get worse. He was always picking a fight with her and his temper was getting worse by the day, not only verbally but physically as well. The last straw in their relationship happened right here in our condo. I was in my bedroom when I heard him yelling at her."

"What happened?"

"After a little while Alys screamed. 'Mackenzie help! Help me!'"

"I raced out to see what was happening and I found Alys on her back, pinned to the floor, crying her eyes out, screaming, and Gardner sitting on top of her. When he looked at me, he had a wicked look on his face. It was an evil look. Like he was crazed. You know what I mean? He said, 'You can tell her I'm not going to get off her until she apologizes to me.'"

"I said, 'You're crazy. You're the one who's on top of her. You're the one who's hurting her.' I had my phone in my hand and told him to get off her before I called the cops. The whole time Alys was trying to free her arms. She was hysterical. 'Get off of me. Get off!' She finally freed one of her arms and reached up and raked his face with her fingernails. When she did that, he slapped her. Hard!

"I told him, 'I'm calling the cops. You have five seconds to get off her and leave or I'll make sure you will be charged with assault.'"

"What did he do?"

"He got off her slowly and ordered me to put the phone down or he would hurt me. Then he accused me of being the one who was trying to change her."

Clay asked, "What did he mean about you trying to change her?"

"Apparently their argument was about her wanting to have plastic surgery to enlarge her breasts. You can see from that picture of the two of them on the beach that she was totally flat-chested and was always self-conscious about her breasts. But he was vehement against her having the surgery and blamed me for her wanting to have it done."

"Were you in fact the reason she decided to have her surgery?"

"No, why would I care one way or the other? But I told her that whatever she decided to do I would support her. My guess is that Gardner thought her having her breasts enlarged was a sign that she was cheating on him. Yet ironically, she wanted to have the surgery because she thought he would like her better with larger breasts. Go figure. When Gardner stormed out of the condominium he swore, 'You'll both pay for this.'"

"What happened then?"

"She was scared. That wasn't surprising after what she had been through. The poor girl cried her eyes out. She was bruised and obviously hurt. But then, unbelievably, she said she was the one at fault and she should have just apologized to him like he wanted her to. I said, 'You're crazy to think that. You do have to get away from him. He's a bad guy. He's mentally ill, and he's going to hurt you very bad some time. You have to get him out of your life."

"Did she agree with you?"

"About a month after that incident, he left Santa Barbara for a job in New York City. I was tickled that he wouldn't be around to hurt Alys anymore, and I personally wouldn't have to look over my shoulder, afraid that maybe he was going to try to hurt me."

Clay said, "The bottom line was Gardner did not want Alys to have her breasts enlarged, and he falsely blamed you for supposedly talking her into having that surgery."

She said, "Correct. I was so happy that she finally decided to leave him."

Clay explained, "Good for her if she was true to her word about leaving him, but you probably know this, oftentimes a woman who has been abused will gravitate to the same kind of person she just left. It's possible that it was Gardner who returned from New York, tracked her to Santa Fe, and killed her as he said he would."

Clay added, "Let me share something with you. Doctor Quenneville's wife, Maura Quenneville, was murdered a few weeks before Alys was killed. Quenneville is the guy you thought Alys was going with. Evidence indicates the same person killed both Quenneville's wife and Alys. If we find a link between Maura Quenneville and Hicks, we may have found Alys' killer."

Clay thanked Mackenzie for her help. He said, "I'm going to visit with the folks at the Hilton to see if they can share any information on Doctor Quenneville."

❊ ❊ ❊

Clay was taken by Mackenzie Stanton's beauty even if he didn't agree with her claim of having extrasensory perception. He left with an offer to her. "Let me know if you're ever in Santa Fe. I'd be happy to show you around." He gave her his card.

Mackenzie showed Clay a beautiful smile and the two locked eyes. She said, "Actually, I was going to offer you a tour of Southern California if you're ever back in town. But I'll keep Santa Fe in mind as well."

CHAPTER 17

Clay drove to the 360-room Hilton Hotel Beach Resort and asked to speak to the hotel's general manager.

Kelvin Green, a short, balding, affable man, introduced himself to Clay. "What can I do for you?" he asked in a surprisingly deep voice.

"Are you Alys Chapman's manager?"

"Yes, I am."

"I'm Detective Clay Bryce of the Santa Fe, New Mexico Police Department." He told Alys' manager about her death. "I'm sorry to have to tell you that Ms. Chapman was killed last night in Santa Fe. I'm here to investigate her murder."

"Oh my God. What do you mean, her murder?" Green was stunned by the news. "Who killed her?"

"We don't know. That's the reason I'm in Santa Barbara, to see if we can identify a suspect or at least identify persons of interest."

"I'm shocked and saddened. Terrible, awful news! Terrible! Whatever I can do to help you, please let me know."

"I've met with her roommate, a woman by the name of Mackenzie Stanton, to try to learn why Alys was in Santa Fe. Unfortunately, she doesn't know why. Perhaps you can explain why to me. You can start by telling me what Alys' job was."

"She was one of our event coordinators. She was responsible for promoting the Hilton to companies or organizations that planned to have an event, such as an educational or sales meeting, a trade show, or a product launch. She spent a lot of time hobnobbing with organization coordinators. Once she got a commitment to have the event take place in our facility, she would help the organization's coordinator finalize all the details. She was perfect for the job: very detail-oriented and she could turn on the charm. She dazzled anyone with her beauty alone. She was such a dynamic employee who brought in such a significant amount of business that the folks in Hilton's corporate headquarters in Virginia talked about making her Hilton's national events coordinator."

"How many events coordinators do you have in Santa Barbara?"

"Two total—Alys was one, and a woman by the name of Nicole Anderson is the other. In addition, each coordinator has a staff of employees who handle all the nitty-gritty details to ensure events run smoothly. Nicole worked very well with Alys. They made a good team. If you wish, you can talk to her about Alys."

"Before I talk to Nicole can you tell me why Alys had traveled to Santa Fe this past weekend. Was she there to drum up event business?"

"That's possible, but she didn't confide in me if that was her intent." Green said, "I didn't have her on a tight leash. I trusted her to bring in the business, and if it meant she had to travel to convince a company to have their event here, so be it. I approved virtually all of her business expenses. She was as honest as the day was long and never filled out an expense report that included personal expenses."

"I'd like to talk to Nicole to see if she can tell me anything more about Alys."

"Of course. She's down the hall. I'll introduce you to her. She can provide you with any information you need about our events and which ones Alys had been involved with. Nicole has access to all the files."

Green walked Clay to Nicole's office and introduced him to the pleasant, middle-aged woman.

Clay said, "I'm with the Santa Fe, New Mexico Police Department. I explained to Mr. Green about the tragic occurrence involving your colleague, Alys Chapman."

She braced for bad news. "What do you mean?"

"Someone murdered her in Santa Fe Sunday night."

"What?" Nicole recoiled and tented her hands over her mouth as though in prayer.

"I'm sorry to inform you of her death in this manner, but I need your help to review Alys' business activities. I'm the detective in charge of investigating her murder."

After a few seconds, Nicole lowered her hands and shook her head. She reached for tissues to dab at her tears. "Who killed her?"

"We don't know. I'm hoping you can help me learn who it was."

You can start by providing me with a list of all the events the Hilton hosted in the past two years.

"It will take me less than a minute to generate a report for you."

"Does the surname, Quenneville, ring a bell?" Clay spelled the name.

Nicole chewed on her lower lip in thought before she answered. "The name sounds familiar, but I can't place it right now."

Clay explained. "A woman by the name of Maura Quenneville was murdered a few weeks ago in Santa Fe. We know from ballistics testing that the person who killed Mrs. Quenneville also killed Alys. but we don't know how the two women were connected."

Nicole suddenly remembered. "Wait a second. It just came to me. I do know that name. There was a Doctor Ronald Quenneville who presided over an event here about a year ago for the American Society of Plastic Surgeons. If it's the same guy from Santa Fe, he was a charmer and a very good-looking man."

"Was Alys involved in bringing that meeting to the Hilton?"

"Yes, and she handled all of the details."

"Did she meet with Quenneville in Santa Fe or in Santa Barbara only?"

Green answered, "Some of the times in Santa Fe, and other times she met with him here."

Nicole agreed. "About fifty-fifty."

"What about this past weekend, did she inform either of you that she would be traveling to Santa Fe?"

Both Green and Nicole answered, "No, she did not."

Clay asked, "Over the past year, did Alys ever intimate that perhaps she was in a relationship with Quenneville?"

Green said no, but Nicole said, "I remember having suspicions about the two of them. I asked her about him a few times, but she would shrug and smile, and then give me a vague response, like *He's a nice guy*. It was obvious she was taken by him."

"Nicole, were you friends with her outside of work?"

"We were friendly, but mostly she was all-business and rarely talked about her personal life. Occasionally I would ask her how she spent her weekend or what she did on a holiday, but she never went into any detail. After a while, I stopped asking."

"Did Alys ever mention an ex-boyfriend of hers—a guy by the name of Gardner Hicks?"

"Yes, it was one of those rare times when she opened up about her personal life. She told me that he had abused her physically and emotionally. She asked me if I thought she should get a restraining order against him. She was scared he would try to hurt her. I told her I thought that would be a good idea to get a restraining order. She received the order, but when her boyfriend moved out of town, she said she wasn't as fearful that he would harm her. However, I remember she told me she carried a pepper spray in her purse to protect herself from him in case he returned to Santa Barbara."

Clay thanked the staff at the Hilton and flew back to Santa Fe with scant evidence, but now with two persons of interest: Gardner Hicks and Dr. Ronald Quenneville. Even though there was nothing discernible that linked Hicks to Maura Quenneville, Clay would try to determine if there was a circumstantial connection between the two.

But that meant he first had to find out where Gardner was and bring him in for questioning.

CHAPTER 18

Clay arrived from Santa Barbara and drove directly from the airport to the Emerson Hotel. He was eager to begin his search for Gardner Hicks and wanted to see if anyone from the hotel could identify Hicks from the beach photo of Alys and him.

The Emerson front-office employees and staff recognized Alys, but no one recognized Gardner.

Clay drove to police headquarters. When he got to his desk, he read a telephone message left for him from Alonzo Garcia, the Albertsons store manager. "I have some information for you about Maura Quenneville's death. Please call me back." It was signed, "A. Garcia."

He called the store manager, who explained, "Detective, I've come across something regarding the murder of Maura Quenneville. It probably doesn't have any bearing on your investigation, but I thought I should mention it to you just in case. I was reviewing customer service reports written by employees involved in incidents with customers, and I came across a report from Emily Embers involving Maura Quenneville. You might want to look at the report."

When Clay got to the grocery store the manager handed him a one-page form entitled *Albertsons Customer Service Report.* The manager told Clay, "We are obligated by union rules to document any incident that occurs between a customer and any of our employees. We value our employees and attempt to safeguard them against any issue created by a customer. You had mentioned that you were investigating the death of a woman by the name of Maura Quenneville. Well, it so happens that Emily Embers had an incident with her a few weeks ago. Please read the report, and you'll see what I'm talking about."

Memo from: Emily Embers
To: Alonzo Garcia

A customer by the name of Steve was in my "ten-and-under" checkout line when a lady barreled into him with her cart, and then cut ahead of him in line. She had a lot of groceries in her cart, so I told her that my line was a "ten-and-under" line only. She said she didn't care and told me she was in a hurry and to "just do my job." Steve, the customer she banged into, repeated that my line was for people who only had a few items to check out. The lady told him to mind his own business, and that started a loud argument between the two of them. She insulted Steve and me. Steve tried to defend me, but the female customer continued to berate Steve. Finally, I decided to check her out because I didn't want the incident to escalate more than it already had. The customer's name was Maura Quenneville.

Clay informed the manager he wanted to talk with Emily for a few minutes.

"Hello Emily, good to see you again. I just read a report you filed about the difficulty you had dealing with Maura Quenneville. For your information, she was killed on Breeze Canyon Road several days after your incident with her. I'm hoping you can shed some light about her behavior while in the store."

Emily immediately became defensive. "Well, I didn't kill her. I hope you're not suggesting that I did."

Clay did not dismiss her concern. He said, "I'm not suggesting that. But tell me exactly what happened. From what your customer service report shows, she caused a stink when she was checking out at your line."

"Yeah, she did. Occasionally, I must deal with a rude customer. She was one of the worst I've had to deal with—ever. As you read in my report, it all started when a customer by the name of Steve was in my checkout line. There were a couple of people in front of him with a few items each. Suddenly, BAM, that lady barreled into Steve with her cart that was jam-packed with groceries. I told her that my line was for people with ten items or less, and since she had way more than was allowed, she would have to go to another line. She said she didn't care about Albertsons' quote-unquote, 'asinine' rules and told me to 'just do my job' and check her out.

"The customer who she banged into repeated to her that my checkout line was for people who only had a few items to check out. The lady told him to mind his own business, and the argument went downhill from there."

"What did you do?"

"Nothing I could do. You know. 'The customer's always right,' so the saying goes. The argument was starting to draw a lot of gawkers. I just wanted to end the confrontation. I mean, I wasn't going to call the police on her, so I elected to check her out. The sooner the better. I didn't want the incident to escalate any more than it already had."

"And Steve, what did he do?"

"He asked the lady to apologize for banging into him, but she didn't. What a bitch. He was fuming, but it didn't matter to her. When she was ready to pay for her groceries, she pulled out her credit card from her purse and it slipped out of her hands and onto the floor right at Steve's feet. Steve picked it up and politely handed it to her. She snatched it out of his hand without a thank-you. That's how Steve happened to catch her name on the card and that's how I knew her name."

Clay said, "Unfortunately, now she's dead."

"Too bad," she said with a smirk. "You reap what you sow. That's karma, isn't it? That's what I attribute it to. What comes around goes around."

"Back to that incident, did Steve continue to have words with her after the two of them left the store?"

"You'll have to ask Steve, but yes, I think so."

"What can you tell me about Steve?"

"He's a nice man, a real gentleman. He shops every week on Wednesday, buys a few things, then checks out in my line. He's always very polite and sometimes lets people get through ahead of him if they seem to be in a hurry."

"Do you know Steve's last name?"

"No, I only knew him by his first name, but I know he works at the post office."

CHAPTER 19

Clay drove to the post office on South Federal and identified himself to the postmaster. Clay told him he wanted to speak to one of the mail carriers, an employee named Steve. "I don't know his last name. Do you have any employee named Steve?"

"There's a Steve Aldrich. He's the only person named Steve. What's the problem? Is he in trouble?"

"No. I'm investigating two homicides and Steve might be able to help me."

"That's a relief. We're shorthanded as it is. He's one of our best. Losing him would set us back big time. He should be returning in a few minutes from his route. If you want to wait, you can come round back to the employees' break room."

Steve parked his white, red, and blue USPS vehicle alongside the others in the rear of the building and strode in carrying a tray of mail he collected from several mailboxes on his route. Clay guessed him to be in his mid-forties, not good-looking, but not bad looking either. An everyman. Average height. No distinguishing features. He wore his longish brown hair parted down the center and allowed the sides to hover partially over his ears.

Steve walked in, gave a jaunty hello to everyone, then dropped off the mail he had picked up and nodded to the stranger in the mailroom.

Clay flashed his badge and identified himself. "Steve Aldrich, I need to talk with you for a few minutes."

"Sure. What can I do for you?"

Clay explained, "I learned you were involved in an incident with a woman by the name of Maura Quenneville at the Albertsons grocery store a few weeks ago."

"Yes." Steve showed some nervousness, not unusual when a detective is questioning someone, especially someone as big as Clay. "Why are you asking? Did she file a complaint against me? Is that why you're here? She said she was going to do that. I was the one who should have filed a complaint."

Clay said, "Relax. It was Emily Embers, one of Albertsons' cashiers who explained what happened when Mrs. Quenneville was checking out. From all indications, it appears Mrs. Quenneville was the one who caused the ruckus, not you. And no, she did not file a complaint against you. In fact, Mrs. Quenneville is dead."

"Dead? Oh, I am so sorry to hear that," he said with a large dose of sarcasm evident in his tone.

"For your information, she was murdered on Breeze Canyon Road."

"You're kidding me. Murdered, who murdered her?"

"We don't know yet. Did you kill her?"

"No, I did not kill her," he said emphatically.

Clay said, "I'm surprised you didn't know she was killed. It happened a few weeks ago and it was all over the news. She was the wife of a prominent plastic surgeon in Santa Fe."

Steve shrugged his shoulders. "I don't get the newspaper and I don't remember seeing anything about her on TV, but if you want to know my opinion, she probably made someone mad enough to want to kill her, because she was such a bitch—a prima donna bitch."

"Whoa, don't hold back." Clay chuckled. "Where were you Sunday morning, three weeks ago?"

Steve did not hesitate to answer. "Home. Sunday is my day off. I usually stick around home doing chores. If I leave the house, it's to run errands like go to the hardware store or to get a cup of coffee. Why are you asking me these questions?"

Clay said, "I'm developing a profile of the murder victim. The more information I have about her, the better the chance I can learn who killed her. Tell me, how did your argument with her start?"

"This is very funny. I mean who would have thought that I would end up in a murder investigation because of that bitch? One thing for sure, I didn't kill her. I'm just an ordinary guy. I don't go around killing people."

Clay observed that Steve grew increasingly nervous. "I understand from the check-out woman at Albertsons that you're always there on Wednesdays to do your shopping. Is that right?"

"Yes, that's right. I'm not married, so after work on Wednesdays, I go directly to Albertsons to shop for my weekly groceries. When I check out, I always make a point of going through the same line to pay. I call it Emily's line. She's the cashier you just mentioned. She mans the ten-item-or-less checkout line. That Wednesday was no different than any other Wednesday, except I was standing in line when that obnoxious lady barged into my cart and smacked my shin in the process. There were two or three people ahead of me and no one behind me in line."

"Might she have bumped into you accidentally?"

"No, she did it on purpose so she could cut in line. I

never heard an apology from her. She looked away from me like I wasn't even there. I said, 'Excuse me, ma'am, the line starts behind me.' That's when she said loud enough for everyone to hear, 'You're standing there staring at that checkout lady's tits and holding up the line and I'm in a hurry.'"

Clay asked, "Steve, were you holding up the line?"

"I was not! I was waiting my turn. Detective, I would have relinquished my spot in line if she had asked nice. But she never asked."

"What happened then?"

"She embarrassed me by her stupid comment about staring at Emily's boobs. And how do you think it made Emily feel? That's when I looked at the lady's cart and realized she had at least three dozen things in it, a lot more than was allowed in that checkout lane. I said, 'Excuse me' and pointed to the sign that said the lane was only for ten items or less.

"The lady looked at the sign, looked at her cart, then looked back at me and asked in a loud voice, 'Who are you, the checkout nazi?'"

"Some people snickered, but I didn't think it was funny. People were lining up, but all she wanted to do was to make fun of me in front of them. That really made me mad. I don't like to be embarrassed, and that lady embarrassed the heck out of me—and Emily, too."

"What did Emily do?"

"The line was beginning to get long. Emily said, very nicely, 'Ma'am, he's right. This line is for customers with ten or fewer items. The line is getting busy. It's better if you go to another line.'

"The lady said, 'The other checkout lines are jammed

with people, too. I'm in a hurry and what difference does it make to you? Why don't you just do your job and stop trying to boss me around?'"

Steve said, "That's when I told her there was no reason to talk to Emily that way. I told her I would have let her go ahead of me."

"How did she respond to you?"

"She laughed out loud and shook her head and said something like, 'Oh, you poor soul,' and rubbed her knuckles in her eyes pretending she was crying. That made me madder. My blood pressure must have jumped a hundred points."

Clay said, "Other than the fact that she was rude, what else can you tell me about that lady?"

"She was in her forties, maybe early fifties, short gray hair. She looked like she had a facelift, because she had tight skin around her eyes and lips. She was too old to have skin that smooth."

"Anything else you remember about her? Was she with anyone else?"

"No, she was alone. She was obviously wealthy by the looks of her diamond wedding ring that was the size of a donut hole."

"Did your beef with her continue after she left the store?"

"Yes. After she pushed her cart through the store exit, she turned around and blew me a kiss."

"Go on."

"Well, that pissed me off even more, but I didn't try to continue with our argument, so I walked to my car. Unfortunately, as luck would have it, I found she was parked in the space next to me. It was pure coincidence. She didn't know my car was next to hers. When I walked to my car, she must have thought I was going to do something to her because she opened her purse and got mace or something out and pointed it at me."

"Did she actually use it on you?"

"No, I was too far away from her. She said if I took another step toward her she was going to use it on me, and I quote, 'I'll mace you to kingdom come!' I didn't get any closer to her. I told her my car was next to hers. Then I said to her, 'First you bang into my cart, smack me in my shin, embarrass me and the cashier, and now you're threatening to mace me. You need some anger management therapy. What exactly is your problem, are you demented?'

"She said, 'You are my problem. Do I have to file a complaint against you because you're harassing and stalking me?'

"I laughed at her. 'Go ahead and have me cited. I will look forward to telling my side of the story to a judge. In fact, I think I will call the police on you for threatening me.'"

"What did she do when you threatened to call the police?"

"Nothing. She put the last of her bags into the back of her Mercedes and allowed her empty cart to roll into my car. That only added to how I felt about her. I said, 'You are supposed to return your cart to the space that's designated for carts so your cart doesn't roll off and bang into someone's car like your cart just did to my car.' And she said, 'Oh, I get it, first you're the checkout nazi and now you're the grocery-cart cop.'"

"Did anyone try to intervene?"

"No, a couple of shoppers stood and watched the two of us arguing, but no one stepped in."

"What did she do then?"

"She opened her car door overly wide and allowed it to bang into my passenger door, hard enough to make a small dent. She looked at the ding, looked back at me, and smirked, with no apologies. Not that it mattered what damage she did to my car. My Civic's a 1990, with over a hundred-twenty thousand miles on it and a ton of dents. But it was the principle of the thing that got me mad. I said, 'You banged into my car.'

"She didn't care. She said, 'What's it got, like a million miles on it? It should be in a junkyard. So sue me.' She got into her car and drove off."

Clay asked, "Did you threaten her in any way? Did you follow her out of the parking lot?"

He hesitated for a few seconds before he answered. "Yes, I'll be honest with you. I tailgated her for a while. I wasn't going to do anything, but I wanted to scare her. I probably shouldn't have done that, but I did."

"Go on. What then?"

"I trailed her to the outskirts of Santa Fe. I drove probably no more than three feet from her bumper the entire time. At first it looked like she was trying to lose me, but eventually she pulled into the driveway of her humongous house and opened her entrance gate remotely. While she waited for the gate to swing open, I saw her give me the finger. She set her finger against the rear-view mirror for me to see and kept it there until the gate fully opened. Then when the gate closed, she rolled down her driver's side window, stuck her left arm out, and gave me the finger again. Nice, genteel lady, huh?"

"Did you have any contact with her after that?"

"No, apparently someone beat me to it," he said with a grin.

Clay wanted to see Steve's reaction when he fabricated a story. "For your information, we had an anonymous caller say they saw an old Civic tailgate a Mercedes on Breeze Canyon Road the same day Maura Quenneville was killed. Was that your car?"

"No way. It couldn't have been me. Your witness is full of crap if he said it was me. I was nowhere near Breeze Canyon."

Clay let his lie about an anonymous witness to Maura's death drop without pushing it further.

CHAPTER 20

The company that lured Gardner to work for them offered equity in the company. After nearly a year, the company went public, and stock that was held privately became available to new investors. Gardner profited immensely.

Shortly after the initial public offering, Gardner sold all his stock and flew back to Santa Barbara with the intention of rekindling his relationship with Alys.

He wrote a sorrowful letter to her asking for another chance to recapture their lost love. The letter was the one that Clay discovered in Mackenzie and Alys' condominium.

Alys had no intention of getting back together with Gardner and messaged him that she had found someone else, and they were going to marry. She told Gardner she did not want him to contact her again and reminded him that she still had a restraining order against him that was issued a year earlier.

In earlier phone conversations with Mackenzie, Gardner had pieced together information about Alys: that she stayed in an unknown hotel in Santa Fe and was head over heels in love with a doctor there.

Hicks decided to search for Alys and win her back.

Gardner drove thirteen hours straight from Santa Barbara to get to New Mexico. Tired from his drive, he booked a room at the Days Inn in Española, a small working-class town about a half-hour from Santa Fe. He leafed through a phone directory, looking for hotels in Santa Fe, and called each one with the inquiry, "May I speak with a Ms. Alys Chapman?" She was not a guest at any of the hotels that Gardner called until he called the Emerson Hotel. The operator there seemed reluctant to tell Gardner yes or no that she was or had been a guest there. Finally, the operator suggested that Gardner contact the Santa Fe police for information about Alys.

Gardner asked why, but the operator said, "I'm afraid I can't help you. If you wish I can give you the phone number for the Santa Fe police."

"No thank you," he said and hung up.

Because of the way the operator answered his question, Gardner was convinced Alys was staying at the Emerson. *But why the police? Could it be because of the restraining order?*

Nevertheless, he was pleased with himself for having located Alys and planned to drive to Santa Fe the next day to connect with her face-to-face. He was certain she would take him back.

It was getting late, and he was hungry. He drove from the motel to the first restaurant he came to on the side of the main road into town. He sat at the bar and ordered a hamburger and a beer. Ten minutes later, a trio of ranch hands still in their jeans, cowboy hats, and sweaty shirts walked in. The cowboys were in town for the weekend to blow off steam after a hard week's work at the ranch. Laughing boisterously, they sat on the stools alongside Gardner. He nodded to them and returned to his beer.

The men were loud. When one of the men edged off his stool on his way to the bathroom, he accidentally bumped Gardner's shoulder. Gardner turned to him and dropped his eyes in a scolding gesture.

The man, who was obviously inebriated, saw that Gardner was irritated. "Sorry man," he said.

Gardner didn't say anything.

The man repeated himself, "I said, sorry."

Gardner stared at his food and did not look at him. "I heard you," he muttered.

"What do you want me to do, kiss your ass? I said I was sorry."

"What's your problem, pal? I said I heard you. I'm sure you won't give a damn, but I've just driven thirteen hours straight from California. I'm tired, hungry, and thirsty. I heard you say you were sorry, and I accept your apology. Now let me go ahead and finish my meal, and I'll be on my way."

The man leaned in and bumped Gardner's shoulder intentionally, harder this time than the last bump.

Gardner was jerked forward. Beer spilled from his mug onto his lap.

"Oops, I'm sorry again," the man cackled.

Gardner looked straight ahead. "I get the impression you aren't sorry even a little bit."

The other cowboys snickered. One of them said, "Better not make the man mad. You know how those manly men are from California. He might slap you."

Gardner smiled at the comment. "Come on, fellas. Let me finish eating."

"Fellas? That's what he called us. Fellas."

The bartender knew the three men. They were in the restaurant most weekends. "Hey, Sal, come on man, let the guy finish. He's got to pay me yet."

"Oh, he'll pay you okay, or I'll whup his ass."

"I don't know what you want from me, Sal. Why not let me finish my meal, so I can leave?"

Sal jammed his finger into Gardner's hamburger.

"Gardner got off his stool and turned to face Sal. "Sal's your name? Is it short for Sally?"

The diners in the restaurant stiffened.

Sal's two friends guffawed. "You gonna let him get away with calling you Sally?"

"Ya think?" Sal said, "Well, watch this." He leaned back and tried to strike Gardner's forehead with a headbutt, but because he was drunk he lost his balance, and instead of butting Gardner's head, he ended up with his chin on Gardner's neck in what looked like a hug.

The restaurant crowd roared.

"What's so funny?" the ranch hand slobbered.

His two buddies laughed uproariously. "What are you gonna do next, Sal, kiss him?"

Gardner pushed Sal away. He fell to the floor, but he got up again with a snarl on his face and his fists drawn at his hips, ready to fight.

Gardner did not hesitate. He had enough and nailed the rancher with a right-cross to his jaw.

Sal fell to the floor like a sack of potatoes.

The bartender shouted at Gardner. "Why did you punch him? He couldn't defend himself. Can't you see he's drunk as a skunk? He was just funning you. What the hell's wrong with you?"

Gardner shot back. "Apparently he wasn't too drunk to try to headbutt me."

The bartender did not want a full-scale brawl with Sal's

buddies and ordered Hicks out of the bar. "Alright, get your ass out of here."

"I will when I finish eating. Fix me another hamburger that hasn't been contaminated by Sal's dirty hand." He climbed back onto his stool. "How much do I owe you?"

"Nothing. I want you out of here."

"I insist on paying you."

The bartender picked up the house phone at the end of the bar and called the Española cops. "We have a disturbance here. A stranger assaulted one of my customers and now I can't get him to leave."

In less than three minutes, two burly Hispanic cops entered the restaurant wearing bulletproof vests under their uniforms. They looked around and asked the bartender, "What happened, Joe?"

He lied, "I didn't see what started it, but I saw this guy punch Sal. It was uncalled for. Sal was drunk and couldn't defend himself. The boys were having fun with him, that's all."

Sal was still on the floor bleeding from an open cut to his jaw. The other two ranch hands were trying to lift Sal back up to his stool, but he was out cold and kept collapsing to the floor as dead weight.

The cops asked the restaurant crowd if anyone saw what happened. The diners were Española locals and most knew the three ranch hands. No one came to Hick's defense.

"I guess I know what that means." Gardner got up with his hands raised and said to the police, "I swear to you that I acted in self-defense." Gardner put his arms behind him and turned around, knowing he was going to be handcuffed and arrested for assault. He had been in those circumstances before.

He posted bond and was released from custody, but when he did not show up for his arraignment scheduled for the next day, the judge issued an arrest warrant for failure to appear.

The same day that an arrest warrant was issued for Hicks, Clay issued a BOLO, a "Be on the lookout" advisory, to police departments throughout New Mexico, asking to be notified if anyone knew where Gardner was located.

The police department in Española shortly thereafter contacted Clay with the news that a day earlier, Hicks had been arrested for assault because of a bar fight, and when he did not appear for his arraignment, a warrant had been issued for his arrest by the presiding judge.

The Española police sent Hick's case file to Clay. It included mugshots, basic identifying data, copies of his fingerprints, and details of his bar fight arrest.

Gardner listed his current address as the Emerson Hotel.

CHAPTER 21

Clay was curious why Gardner told the Española police that the Emerson was his address. Was he the mysterious man in 412? Had Alys relented and arranged to meet Gardner at the hotel? Clay contacted forensics and asked them to check the fingerprints they collected in 410 against Gardner's prints from Española.

They did not find matching fingerprints.

Clay reasoned that if Gardner Hicks killed Alys, he most likely killed Maura Quenneville, too, since the same gun was used to kill both women. However, there was no indication that Hicks was acquainted with Maura, and even if he did know her, what motive would he have had to kill her?

Until Hicks was located and brought in for questioning, he would remain a person of interest. But for now, Clay would turn his attention to Doctor Quenneville as the most likely suspect.

Mackenzie Stanton told Clay when they first met in Santa Barbara that she believed Alys was having an affair with Dr. Quenneville. If so, had Maura learned about her husband's affair and confronted him? Clay could imagine her howling at her husband: *"How could you do that after all I have done for you?"*

If Quenneville's affair with Alys had been known, suspicion would point to him as the person who killed his jealous wife, and that would involve sensational media coverage.

* * *

Two weeks after his trip to Santa Barbara, Clay received a text from Mackenzie Stanton stating she was virtually certain she knew who murdered Alys. She wrote she would be in Santa Fe that weekend. Would Clay care to meet with her over a drink to discuss her theory about Alys' murder?

Clay replied to her text. "I look forward to seeing you again. Text me when you will be arriving and include your flight number. I'll pick you up at the airport."

Friday afternoon, Clay watched as Mackenzie was the last to deplane from the American Eagle jet that landed at the small regional airport in Santa Fe. At nearly six feet tall, she had to duck as she exited through the front door of the low-ceiling plane. Clay was surprised she wore the uniform of a flight attendant. Her occupation had never been brought up to Clay in Santa Barbara.

As she climbed down the steps, a sudden burst of wind blew wisps of her shoulder-length blonde hair across her face as though she was in a photo shoot. *Whew, she's beautiful, even prettier than I remembered.*

When she entered the small one-story terminal building, she spotted Clay, who towered over everyone else. She waved and surprised him by giving him a hug, her body folded against his.

She said, "Detective, I've been looking forward to seeing you again."

Clay answered with a smile, "Me, too, but please call me Clay. I'm off duty now and for the weekend, so I can escort you around our historic town."

"Wow, that sounds like the beginning of a TV promotional spot."

"It does, doesn't it, but you'll see. I'm prejudiced, but Santa Fe is everything it's cracked up to be. I was born and raised here."

As they got into Clay's car, he said, "I can drive you to your hotel so you can check in, or we can get you something to eat. It's after twelve-noon. You must be hungry. Whatever you wish."

"I think I would like to check into my hotel first if they allow an early check-in. I'll only be a few minutes, then I'm open to getting something to eat."

"What hotel are you staying in?"

"The Emerson."

"Really, the Emerson? I'm surprised. I didn't think you would want to be reminded that Alys was murdered there."

"But I do. Alys has not been far from my mind since you first told me of her murder. I feel a duty as her friend to learn who killed her. I thought if I stayed at the same hotel, I might be able to get a stronger sense, a confirmation of who I think the killer is. As I mentioned to you in Santa Barbara, I believe in the concept of psychic senses. I think everyone has extrasensory perception—some more than others. I hope to be able to help you identify who the killer is by utilizing my ESP."

Clay said, "I thought from your text that you said you knew who killed Alys."

"To be precise, I said I am virtually certain I knew who it was."

Clay thought, *Why quibble*? "Of course. You're right. That's what you said."

She resumed her discussion of extrasensory perception. "I've studied the concept that our sixth sense can offer us powerful insights, like sensing the truth in certain matters, or recognizing significant events that are about to happen."

Clay looked at his beautiful passenger. "Okay, so tell me what are the winning lottery ticket numbers in tonight's drawing?"

Mackenzie turned toward him. "You're making fun of me, aren't you? I hope I haven't made a mistake asking to meet with you. If you don't accept the fact that ESP is possible with some people some of the time, then you might as well drop me off at my hotel. I can find my way around."

Clay realized she was serious about her intentions to be a psychic sleuth. He decided to respect her beliefs for what he hoped would be a weekend of promise. Having her mad at him at the very beginning of her visit is not how he wanted the weekend to start.

"You're right, I was making light of your ESP. I was wrong to do that. I apologize. I don't know much about ESP, but maybe you can educate me about it. One thing I know is that in certain instances, police departments employ psychics to help them provide clues that are prophetic in their investigations of certain criminal cases, so there's some validity in what you're saying."

"I accept your apology. I hope you will accept my offer to help." She was serious.

Surprisingly, he acquiesced. "Yes, I will." Clay wasn't going to jeopardize the weekend with this beauty. He said to himself, *My mama didn't raise no dummy.*

Mackenzie said, "Like I told you in Santa Barbara, I always

felt something bad was going to happen to Alys. I cautioned her many times to be careful and to share what she knew about the guy she was seeing here. I had a premonition that she was in danger You may think that's ridiculous, but now it seems I was correct."

"You said she never talked about the guy she was in love with?"

"That's true. She did not want to talk about him. She always told me not to worry, and that I would meet him in time."

Clay pulled up to the Emerson. The valet recognized him as he exited the car and opened the door for Mackenzie to exit. "How are you, Detective? Any luck finding out who killed that woman?"

"Not yet. Still working on it. I'm only going to be here for a few minutes while my friend checks in. Okay to leave the car at the curb?"

"Sure, no problem."

Once inside the hotel Clay was greeted by Rose, who welcomed him with a smile at the front desk.

"Hi Rose, any chance my friend here can check in a bit early?"

"For you, absolutely."

Clay noticed Jeremy Voit, the bartender, was not at the bar. "Rose, I see the bar is still closed. Where's Voit?"

"He starts at five o'clock. He'll be here. He lives some distance away and is late from time to time because of traffic, especially on Friday nights when businesses let out. When he comes in, I'll tell him you were looking for him."

"Thanks. I also need to talk to Max Bruder again. But I'll catch up with both of them tomorrow."

Rose said, "Max doesn't work here anymore. He quit a couple of days ago and no one has been able to reach him since."

"Did he give any explanation why he quit?"

"No. He didn't come to work one day. He didn't resign, he just out-and-out quit."

CHAPTER 22

While Clay waited in the lobby for Mackenzie to get situated in her room, he took the opportunity to ask Rose about Max Bruder's departure. Clay said, "When I spoke to Max, he didn't give me any indication that he was about to quit. I thought he was happy in his job. What do you suppose happened to have changed his mind?"

Rose shook her head. "I don't know. As I said, he didn't resign. He just didn't show up for work one day. I tried reaching him, and so did his boss, but we didn't have any luck."

"Maybe he's out of town."

"Doubt it. He never went anywhere."

Clay suggested, "You might want to ask for a wellness check to make sure he's okay. Or I can check on him tomorrow. Let me have his home address and phone number. I'll try to find out what he's up to."

Rose scribbled the information on Emerson stationery and handed it to Clay. "Thanks for doing that. Tell him I miss seeing him. Max and I go back a long time, five, six years at least."

"What is he like?"

"Looks are deceiving. If he hasn't shaved for a few days, or trimmed his crazy hair, he resembles a wild man. His dark eyes seem to look right through you. But he's really a sweet guy, and I find he's handsome too when he's groomed. A strong, silent man. I've never been to his house, but Jeremy Voit said he was there once. He said he lives by himself with what Jeremy calls a 'mean junkyard dog' for company, but otherwise he's a loner."

While waiting for Mackenzie to return from her room, Clay stepped behind the empty bar. His suspicion was aroused when he found a couple of disposable gloves turned inside-out. Earlier in the investigation, forensics had examined Alys' car and could not find any fingerprints other than prints belonging to Alys and the security guard. The crime scene team determined it was likely that the killer wore gloves. *Could these be the killer's gloves?*

Clay confiscated the gloves and put them in an evidence bag that he kept in his pocket for just such circumstances. He would arrange to have forensics determine if Alys' DNA was found on the gloves. If so, it would implicate Voit in Alys' murder.

As Clay sat waiting for Mackenzie, Clay was surprised to spot Emily Embers and Steve Aldrich close-talking together in front of the service elevator. The two did not notice Clay at first.

Clay studied their interaction for a moment until Emily spotted him talking to Rose. She pretended not to see him, casually turned away, peeked over Steve's shoulder, and whispered something. After a few seconds, the two separated. Emily pushed the up elevator button and nonchalantly studied the floor numbers on the elevator as it descended to the lobby.

Before Emily could get on the elevator Clay walked up to the two and greeted them in a cordial manner. "Hi folks, what's up?"

Clay noticed they appeared to be uncomfortable with him.

Steve answered. "I had an express delivery package to deliver to the hotel and I bumped into Emily. Just saying hello."

Clay said, "I wasn't aware the two of you knew each other."

Emily answered as she looked away from Steve. "We're acquainted through Albertsons. Sorry Detective Bryce, nice seeing you again, but excuse me, if you don't mind, I've got to get back to work before my manager fires me. Steve, see you at Albertsons."

Emily entered the elevator, leaving Steve behind to answer questions posed by Clay.

Steve said, "I better get going also. Nice seeing you, Detective." He turned abruptly toward the front entrance where his truck was parked.

It was obvious that Steve and Emily did not want Clay to engage them in conversation.

Clay said, "Hang on a second, Steve. I want to ask you a couple of questions. I'm curious about something. Is the Emerson on your mail delivery route?"

"Yes, it's normally my last stop before I head back to the post office. Detective, sorry, but I really have to get going."

Clay asked, "Yeah, a second more. Do you normally see Emily here?"

"From time to time, I do. Why do you ask?"

"I'm curious."

"I don't want to bother her when she's working, so I wave to her when I see her."

"Have you known Emily for a while?" Clay was wondering if he had caught them in a lie.

Steve took a deep breath and looked at his wristwatch. "Yes and no. Occasionally, I bump into her here, but most of the time, I see her at Albertsons—almost every Wednesday, like I told you. That's my grocery shopping day. Today she happened to be using the service elevator here when I spotted her from the front desk as I dropped off the hotel mail."

"Do you two socialize? I mean do you date? Are you boyfriend and girlfriend?"

"Not really. The truth is I've had a crush on her for quite a while. But I could never drum up the courage to ask her out for a date. I was going to ask her out the day that Quenneville woman ran into me with her cart. But unfortunately, I never got the chance because that bitch caused such a stink in front of Emily."

"What time do you normally finish your route?"

"I'm back at the post office by 5:00 most days."

Clay looked at his watch. "Then the Emerson normally is your last stop? I'm a little confused. It's nearly two thirty now. Why are you here so early today?"

"Like I said, I had to deliver express mail. That takes priority. I'll continue my route after I leave."

Something rubbed Clay wrong about Steve's excuse.

"Steve, are you aware that a hotel guest was murdered here at the Emerson three weeks ago? She was discovered shot to death in her car in the parking lot behind the hotel. We don't know why she was parked there. We think she may have been waiting for someone."

"I heard about her murder. What does that have to do with me?"

"I was hoping you might have seen her when you were delivering mail at five o'clock. That's roughly the same time she was leaving the hotel. Let me show you a photo of her. It might ring a bell for you."

Steve studied the beach photo of Alys with Gardner Hicks. "She's very pretty, but I have to say she's too skinny for my taste. Emily is more my type. I prefer women with more, ah, more curves."

Clay grinned. "Of course, everyone has a different opinion about beauty. But do you remember seeing her before?"

He nodded. "I think I saw her once when she was leaving the building the same time that I was leaving. She thanked me for holding the door open for her. I remember she had such a sweet smile."

Clay asked, "As you drove off, did you happen to see if someone spoke to her or got in the car with her?"

Steve said, "Let me see that beach photo again. That guy in the photo looks familiar. I think I remember seeing him that same day that woman and I were leaving."

Clay handed him the photo again. "Take your time. It's important."

After a few seconds, Steve tapped the photo with his forefinger. "Yeah, that's the guy. When the woman got her car from the valet she started to drive away down the driveway, and that guy stepped in front of her car and waved her down. She almost hit him. The guy went around to the driver's side window and said something to her. I couldn't see if she responded to him. But then he walked around to the passenger side of the car and tried to get in the car but she floored it and left."

"What did the guy do when she sped off?"

"He stood in the middle of the driveway for a second watching her before he walked away."

"Did he go into the hotel?"

"I have no idea where he went."

"Are you sure it was the same guy you saw in that beach photo?"

"Not one hundred percent, but yeah, pretty sure it was the same guy and also the same woman in that photograph."

Mackenzie returned to the lobby from her room wearing a fresh coat of very red lipstick and carrying a light jacket for what the meteorologists were forecasting to be a cool New Mexico evening. She said, "Sorry to keep you waiting."

"No problem. It gave me a chance to follow up on what happened to Max, the maintenance guy," Clay said.

"What did you learn?"

"He quit two days ago, without notice."

Mackenzie said, "Do you think his quitting had something to do with Alys' murder?"

Clay nodded, "It's crossed my mind. I'll be checking in on him as soon as I can."

"Why don't you go now? I'll go with you."

He was irritated at Mackenzie's pushy overreach. "I said, I'll check on him, but not now. Tomorrow is early enough."

She said, "For your information, I sense something has happened to him."

Clay glanced at Mackenzie and simply shook his head at her purported clairvoyance. "Okay, I'll play along with you: explain why you sense that."

"I don't know why. I just know something has happened to him."

Although Clay was suspicious of Max's quitting, he didn't want to concede to Mackenzie's supposed ESP. "I'm sure he's fine. He's been working at Emerson for five or six years, doing the same thing. He may have gotten tired of it, and it was a coincidence that he quit now."

"I hate to keep insisting that something's wrong, but I really think you ought to check on him."

Exasperated by her persistence, he said, "I'll check on him tomorrow. Let's end the discussion, okay?"

"You don't have to get mad about it."

"I'm not mad. I just do not want to argue about it."

"Okay, let's start over."

"That's a deal. I only want to enjoy your company and hope you will enjoy your tour of Santa Fe."

"I will and I'll butt out. I promise." Her voice tapered off. "Unless you ask my opinion."

CHAPTER 23

Clay was skeptical about Mackenzie's claim of clairvoyance. He did not believe in ESP. He felt detective work involved the use of deductive reasoning, a reliance on forensic skills, and advanced technological discoveries, such as DNA profiling, to arrive at rational conclusions. In his view, ESP was nothing more than reliance on Ouija board assumptions and was not based on objective analysis. He had already apologized for making fun of Mackenzie's supposed gift, and his views on ESP were not going to stop him from enjoying his time with the beautiful Mackenzie. However, he didn't want her interfering in his investigation.

He planned to show her some of the many interesting sites in Santa Fe, from the vantage point of the Plaza, the center of the walkable city. Alys' murder was not brought up again until they were dining at the celebrated Compound Restaurant on Canyon Road, the road replete with art galleries and excellent restaurants.

Clay studied Mackenzie without staring at her. He found her to be intelligent, strong-willed, opinionated, stubborn, and likely the most beautiful woman on the long list of beautiful women he had known.

She said, "From what you've shown me of Santa Fe, I can understand why people fall in love with the city. It's beautiful and historic. I knew I would like it. I particularly like the Loretto Chapel and the story behind the stairs that was supposedly constructed by Joseph the carpenter, the father of Jesus."

"You mean you knew you would like it because you have the gift of ESP?" he said and instantly regretted bringing up the subject of extrasensory perception again.

"Yeah, I hope you're not kidding me again, but I can tell you honestly that I do have the ability to foresee some things, not everything, but some things."

"That's great," he said in a matter-of-fact way, clearly not impressed with her supposed ability.

"You've heard of the term déjà vu, right?"

"I'm sure you have felt you've met someone before or have been to a certain place before. That's déjà vu. I know you don't want to get too deep into this subject, but really what that means is we've lived another life before, maybe more than one, and in those lives we've met certain people or have been to various places that are familiar to us in our current life. I'm sure you're thinking I'm a wacko. But honestly, I have been tested and found to have a greater-than-average degree of extrasensory perception. Did you know that two-thirds of all Americans believe in some form of ESP? Apparently, you make up part of the one-third who do not."

He didn't want to question her further, so he wisely tried to change the subject.

But she continued. "For example, I knew from the first time I met you in California that I would be seeing you one-on-one on a social level and that our relationship would get off to a good start."

"Are you saying you think we've been together before in another life?"

"No question about it."

"And what else can you tell me about us?"

She smiled. "I'm not going to tell you. You'll have to wait and see what our future holds. One thing you'll learn is that I'm not shy about offering my opinion on most subjects."

"Opinionated? No, not you," he said.

"Ha, very funny."

"Go on. Besides the fact that you say you're opinionated, what else can you tell me about you?"

"My biggest fault is that I'm attracted to cops."

Clay laughed. "Now I know you're making that up."

"No, that's the truth."

"Seriously? Does it have anything to do with the image of me in handcuffs?"

"Oh, my God, are you ever serious?"

"I will be from now on. No more wisecracks. I promise. Tell me more."

"I was married for a couple of years to a cop. He was a nice guy, but it didn't work out for us."

"What happened?"

"It was my fault. We got married right out of college, but I wasn't ready for marriage. I wanted to do things and see the world. I realized I needed to live unencumbered by marriage or kids. It was a eureka realization. I had been living in a cocoon all my life. I needed to step outside of the routine, and if that meant backpacking across Europe and sailing the seven seas, that's what I was going to do."

"How did your husband handle the new you?"

"He was wonderful. He tried to talk me out of a divorce, but he finally let go of me. I got a job as an airline attendant, and ever since I've been on the road. Working for the airline is ideal for me. I can travel almost anywhere on their nickel. There's so much I want to see and do … and I'm doing it."

She paused for a second and looked straight into Clay's eyes. "Does any of that make sense?"

"Yes, it does."

She turned quiet for a moment as she tried to control her emotions. "Now, enough about me, tell me about yourself."

"Nothing extraordinary. I received a scholarship to play football at New Mexico State. I graduated with a degree in criminal justice and got a job as a cop after I graduated, something I always wanted to be. Even as a kid, I talked about being a cop. After a couple of years as a street cop, I was promoted to detective, and that's my life now. I love my job. I like taking bad guys off the street."

"Ever married?"

"Yes, strangely similar to your life. After I graduated from college, I married my college sweetheart, but we divorced after a couple of years. She thought I loved my job more than I loved her, and she was probably right."

Clay and Mackenzie dined and talked for over two hours, and finally they were diplomatically asked to give up their table for other diners. Clay apologized for holding up other patrons and left a sizeable tip for the server's loss.

It was getting late. Mackenzie said, "I'm exhausted. I was up early. I hope you don't mind, but I'm ready for a good night's sleep."

Clay drove her back to the Emerson and walked her into the hotel.

She asked, "Will I see you tomorrow?"

He said, "You're kidding me now. Your ESP should have

told you I will absolutely see you tomorrow. Call me when you wake up. I know a nice little breakfast place."

"Wish I wasn't so tired. I would have liked to sip a sherry and talked some more."

"You and Alys and your sherry. The bartender told me Alys always drank a sherry before she went to bed."

"You're kidding me. Really? She never drank it at home. And I don't drink it. I don't even like it. I have no idea why I mentioned it. Honest. You see what I mean about my ESP? Oh, never mind."

She gave Clay a kiss on his cheek. "Thank you for today. Now remember, you promised to check in on Max Bruder tomorrow. I'm telling you, something is seriously wrong with him."

"I told you I will," Clay said. He left the hotel and drove home. *How did she know about the sherry? And was she right that something had happened to Max Bruder? I will find out in the morning.*

❋ ❋ ❋

Moments after Clay left Mackenzie, she exited the hotel and explained to the valet that she was going to get a breath of fresh air. The valet cautioned her to be careful. "Miss, it's not a good idea to be out here alone. You should know that a woman was killed in the parking lot a few weeks ago, and they haven't found the killer yet. The parking lot is not well-lit in certain places."

Mackenzie responded, "Thanks for your concern, but I'll be okay."

She walked through the parking lot and stopped in the

exact location where Alys had been killed. Although the yellow tape that designated the crime scene had been removed, somehow she sensed where Alys had been murdered. She closed her eyes, took several deep breaths, opened her eyes again then stared into the desert that was adjacent to the space where Alys had parked her car. *Why would Alys have parked this far away from the hotel entrance, and barely in the security camera range? If she wanted to be with someone why not rendezvous in her room? Was it because Alys' lover feared he would be recognized in the hotel?*

Her voice barely in a whisper, she said, "Goodnight, Alys. I'm going to find out who did this to you."

The evening breeze picked up and swept a gentle kiss against Mackenzie's cheek.

She responded, "I miss you too, Alys."

CHAPTER 24

The next morning Mackenzie called Clay to tell him she was going to have to pass on their breakfast date. Clay wondered if his attitude toward her ESP had soured her. "Are we okay?"

She half-lied. Clay's disparagement of her purported *gift* was unsettling to her. She had expected he would be more understanding and appreciative of her offer to assist him. "Yes, I'm fine. Really, I am. I didn't sleep very well last night. Alys was heavy on my mind. I will miss you this morning, but I'll make it up to you. How about we have dinner instead?"

"Okay, I'll pick you up at six o'clock and we can stroll the Plaza before dinner."

She asked, "What did you learn about that maintenance guy who quit his job?"

"Nothing yet."

Clay took a deep breath. He was not happy with her continued intrusion in his investigation.

Mackenzie called for an Uber to give her a lift to the office of Doctor Quenneville at Parson Boulevard a few blocks from downtown Santa Fe. She took a chance that he would be in his office this Saturday. The office was closed but there was a Maserati parked outside the building at the front entrance. She reasoned that it had to be Quenneville's.

She knocked loudly at the front door, but the doctor did not respond. After a few moments she phoned Quenneville's office phone number, but again he continued to ignore her.

She was getting frustrated and took off one of her shoes to use as a knocker against the glass door. After another sequence of loud pounding, the obviously irritated doctor finally appeared in the empty lobby.

"We're closed," he said. "Stop knocking on the door."

"Are you Doctor Quenneville?"

"Yes, I am, and we're closed today. What do you want?"

"My name is Mackenzie Stanton. I called your office before I left California and asked them to schedule an appointment with you this weekend. They notified me you do not see patients on the weekend, but they were kind enough to say they would squeeze me in for a Monday appointment. My problem is I won't be able to see you then. I'm scheduled to fly back to Santa Barbara on Monday, and I thought I'd take a chance that you would see me today."

The doctor said, "Sorry, Ms. Stanton, come back Monday." He turned his back to her and started to walk away.

She shouted out, "I'm a friend of Alys Chapman!"

Quenneville stopped on a dime, returned to the entrance door, and opened it to let Mackenzie in.

Quenneville said, "You're the friend Alys talked about. You and she were best friends, right?"

Mackenzie said, "Yes, she was my best friend. We owned a condo together. I'd like to talk to you about her."

Quenneville said, "You know she was murdered recently, don't you?"

"Yes, that's why I'm in Santa Fe. I wanted to see if the police had made any progress finding the killer. A detective by the name of Clay Bryce is the lead investigator on the case. I met with him yesterday and learned he's not anywhere close to solving the murder."

"I've met Detective Bryce several times myself. He's investigating the murder of my wife, too."

"Oh, I'm sorry to hear your wife was murdered."

Quenneville said, "Detective Bryce thinks the same person who killed Alys also killed my wife."

"I know you knew Alys. I'm searching for the truth about who killed her. I have so many questions."

"You are better off talking with Detective Bryce."

"You had a sexual relationship with Alys, didn't you?"

"What?"

"I don't mean to throw you for a loop, but didn't you have a sexual relationship with Alys?"

"I did not. I'm prohibited from having a relationship with any of my patients."

"Prohibited or not, I know you did."

"What are you talking about?"

"Alys told me about your affair, so I've known all along about the two of you," Mackenzie lied. "After she was killed, I found a diary that she kept in her bedroom. It was loaded with stuff about the two of you, very descriptive things. Frankly, after reading parts of it, I was very jealous of Alys."

Quenneville said, "I'm very upset about what you are implying. Alys would not have written a diary because there was nothing going on between the two of us. Where is this diary you're talking about? Are you trying to blackmail me?"

"No, I'm not blackmailing you. I'm telling you the truth, and I don't think Alys was making things up. Besides, you might want to know that she painted a very flattering picture of you."

"If you have such a diary, let me see it."

"No, I can't do that. Take my word for it or not. I plan to hold onto it."

"Where is it?"

"It's in a safe at my hotel."

"Where are you staying?"

"The Emerson. For your information, I brought the diary from home to show Detective Bryce."

Quenneville asked, "Have you already shown it to him?"

"No, not yet. I wanted to give you the chance to tell me about you and Alys and to convince me you had nothing to do with her murder. And, by the way, you should know that if something happens to me, like for example, if I fall from the fourth floor of my hotel, my lawyer is instructed to send the diary to Detective Bryce."

Quenneville laughed high-pitch and nervously "Why are you doing this? Why the cloak-and-dagger about Alys and me? I'm not Russia's Putin, ready to find a reason to assassinate you."

Mackenzie answered, "I believe you're not telling me the truth. Did you or did you not have an affair with Alys? That's all I want to know."

"I did not. Let me explain why I did not. I told you since Alys was a patient of mine, I would have been prohibited from having a sexual relationship with her no matter if it was consensual or not. If I had an affair, and it was disclosed to the New Mexico State Medical Board, my license would be revoked, and I would be suspended and unable to practice medicine ever again. No roll in the hay is worth losing everything I've worked so hard to attain."

"Are you saying you couldn't take the chance that Alys would keep quiet about your affair?"

Quenneville took a deep breath before he exhaled and responded angrily. "This is the last time I'm saying it. I did not have an affair with Alys. You know how the media likes to play up sensational news about so-called love triangles. If you suggest that I had an affair with Alys, the newspapers would imply that I killed my wife because of an affair with a younger woman. I'm sure you are smart enough to realize I do not want my name dragged through the muck of sensationalism. Please, for Alys' and my sake, and Maura's sake too, please drop this insinuation of yours that I had an affair with Alys."

Mackenzie lowered her eyes and offered a weak apology. "I'll leave now. I'm sorry I've gotten you so upset. I realize now it's unfair to bring up Alys' diary. I may very well destroy the journal so that it doesn't come back to hurt your reputation. Certainly, Alys would not appreciate me using her diary as leverage against you. She would not have wanted me to jeopardize your career. She really did love you, whether you believe it or not, or admit to having an affair or not."

Quenneville said, "I appreciate you looking at this in a different light."

Mackenzie said, "And I appreciate that you are forgiving me for my brash innuendos. Do you have any idea who might have killed Alys? Any thought at all?"

"I don't have a clue. I'm guessing it was a random killing, but I don't know."

Mackenzie shook her head. "It's so sad, isn't it? A beautiful life ended the way it did."

Quenneville said, "Yes, it is sad." He gave her a close look. "Ms. Stanton, what would you say about you and me getting together to get to know each other better? I can show you around town."

"I would like that. As I mentioned, I've been jealous of Alys and her relationship with you. And I promise: no more questions about her. I'm leaving Santa Fe on Monday, although I'll delay my departure for a day or two if you can arrange your workload to see me."

"I would not mind that. Perhaps we can get together for a drink, or maybe dinner. But one last time, are you telling me the truth about a diary?" She smiled and did not answer. Rather, she extended her hand to him. "I hope to see you soon. You can get hold of me at the Emerson Hotel."

CHAPTER 25

Clay had not considered Max Bruder a suspect in Alys' murder, but news that he had suddenly quit his job at the Emerson without notice stirred suspicion. He decided to question Max to find out if he knew anything about Alys' murder.

Clay drove to Max's house at the end of an unpaved, remote desert road. He parked in the dirt driveway behind Max's two-door Jeep Wrangler.

He stepped out of his car and strode to the front door to announce himself when a pitbull chained to a doghouse at the front of Max's house charged at him.

Clay quickly retreated to the safety of his car.

The dog's angry run ended with a brutal jolt of its neck a few yards short of Clay's car.

Safely in his car, Clay retrieved his taser gun from his glove compartment and sized up the route he would have to take to the front door to avoid the wrath of the pitbull.

The dog continued to snarl at him as he approached the front door of the house, but Clay had his taser ready if the dog somehow was able to free himself from his collar.

With one eye on the dog, he rang the doorbell. When Max did not answer, Clay looked through the entrance's side window and saw that lights were on in the house, but there was no discernable activity inside.

Clay shouted Max's name, but there was no response.

The dog continued to bark and strain against the chain when Clay walked around the side of the house to a concrete patio at the back. There were two lawn chairs around a picnic table, a large cooler on the table with unopened

Miller Lite beer cans immersed in water, and a half dozen crushed beer cans floating on top.

Clay knocked loudly on the sliding-glass door that opened into what appeared to be a great room. Newspapers and an empty fast-food container sat on a table, and a bike leaned against a wall. When Clay did not get a response from Max, he cracked open the unlocked door a few inches and shouted Max's name into the house.

Again, there was no reply.

Clay called Bruder's cell phone number and heard the phone ringing from somewhere inside the house. He cupped his right hand over his eyes to obscure the sun's reflection on the glass door, slid the door open, then shouted Bruder's name and walked in. "Max, this is Detective Clay Bryce. I want to talk to you. Are you in here?" He immediately was struck by the scent of a combined fragrant and earthy smell that he compared to an unventilated odor of an old peoples' home.

A small-screen television in the center of an entertainment center across from a recliner was showing a black-and-white vintage episode of *Gunsmoke*. The fact that Bruder was not responding to his shouts was concerning to Clay. He sensed something was wrong. He withdrew his service revolver and advanced cautiously through the house.

He walked warily from room to room. The earthy smell became more intense the farther he walked through the house. Finally, he found himself in the kitchen with food-encrusted dirty dishes in the sink, and several unwashed pots and pans on the counter.

He made his way to a door that opened into a totally dark, unventilated, and cluttered garage, too cluttered to fit even a single car. An intense odor struck him and drove him to cover his nose and mouth with his handkerchief.

Clay found the light switch on the garage wall, flicked it on, but the bulb was burned out. He used the light on his phone to help him navigate through the clutter that was strewn throughout. He stepped over a ladder on the floor, lost his balance and fell heavily to the concrete floor, his face inches from the face of what appeared in the dark to be a mannequin.

He cursed his clumsiness, stepped over the mannequin, and lifted the heavy garage door to bring light into the garage.

When Clay turned to look at the scene, he saw the harrowing image of what he thought was a mannequin but was Max on his stomach on the garage floor in a pool of dried blood. He was clenching a pistol.

Clay stepped outside to phone the medical examiner and the forensics team.

As Clay waited for them, he walked back through the garage and into the house, looking for any indication that would show if Max committed suicide or had been murdered.

CHAPTER 26

Clay directed the forensics team of Carton and Cook to the garage. "He's in there. You'll need masks. And be careful to avoid the dog. He's a mean SOB. I contacted animal control to have him transported to the SPCA shelter."

Two patrol officers arrived immediately thereafter. Clay had the cops string yellow tape to isolate and preserve the integrity of the crime scene.

Forensics entered the garage and began the investigative process by taking multiple photos of the body and the surrounding clutter in the garage, dusting for fingerprints, and examining the exterior of the house for footprints.

When the medical examiner arrived, he paid particular attention to the way Max held the pistol. Forensics then carefully extracted the pistol from Max's grasp for further analysis back in their lab.

After his initial examination, the ME arranged to have Max transported to the forensic science building for an autopsy. He told Clay he would inform him of the cause of death as soon as practical. Initially, his death appeared to have been caused by a gunshot to the side of his head. "Quite likely a suicide." However, he cautioned that there might be a different conclusion after autopsy and after the analysis by forensics.

* * *

Clay and the forensics team worked their way through the clutter in the house, and in the spare bedroom they discovered a prayer card sitting on the bedside table. The religious card was like the one left in Alys Chapman's car when she was murdered, but this one was worded differently.

I killed m. q and a. c. They do not deserve my grief. I am not sorry. Forgive me my sins and through the mercy of God may their souls rest in peace! ! !

Clay asked Carton, "What do you think: was Max Bruder confessing he killed Alys Chambers and Maura Quenneville and then committed suicide, or was he murdered?"

Carton shook his head uncertainly. "It's almost as though the pistol was placed in Max's hand after the fact. We've seen this staged setup before at other homicides. Our conclusion is his death was a homicide and his murder was staged to look like he shot himself. His prints were on the gun, but the fingerprints were positioned in such a manner that we believe his hand was forced onto the pistol, probably after he had been killed. We don't believe Bruder committed suicide."

Clay asked, "Any likelihood that the pistol was used to kill the two women as well as Bruder?"

Carton said, "When we get back to the lab we'll run a ballistics test to check out that probability.

After further investigation, forensics discovered a trove of jewelry in a toolbox in the garage. They would examine them for fingerprints and try to learn what heist the jewelry was from.

Later that day, Carton called Clay. "Our ballistics tests prove your hunch was right. The same pistol was used to kill Chapman, Maura Quenneville, and now Max Bruder. However, we still don't know if Max killed himself or if he was murdered."

"It would help if we knew who the pistol is registered to," Clay said.

Carton said, "Thus far we have not been able to identify the owner. We'll need more time. The weapon's serial number was obliterated. It looks like the offender filed it off, then used a ball-peen hammer to peen the surface and to make it that much harder for us to discern the serial number. However, the shooter is not as smart as he thinks he is, because we might be able to find out what the obliterated serial number is."

"How so?"

"It's a new approach. Underneath the gun's original serial number there are indentations of the serial numbers caused by the structural abnormalities of the metal from the original stamping. We're working with a technique called Magnaflux Method that uses a magnetizing process to recover the serial numbers. We should uncover the number and the original owner's name soon. We'll let you know as soon as we get it."

Clay asked, "Were you able to check the jewelry to learn if it had been stolen in previous burglaries here in the city?"

"Yes, we were able to match the jewelry to the cache of jewelry stolen from Doctor and Mrs. Quenneville's home."

"And what about prints on the jewelry?"

"There were none. They were wiped clean. We don't know if Max stole the jewelry from the Quennevilles or if the murderer planted the jewelry at Max's house."

"What did you find out from the disposable gloves that belonged to the Emerson bartender. Was Alys' DNA on the gloves?"

"No. Only the bartender's."

Clay ordered that all information about Max's murder remain sealed until further notice. "All the details about his death must remain confidential. We want the killer to think we believe he committed suicide. If he's convinced of that he might screw up and incriminate himself in some manner."

CHAPTER 27

Clay called Mackenzie to tell her he would be at the Emerson to pick her up at six o'clock for dinner. Afterward, if she was up to it, they could stroll the Plaza and catch some of the nightlife in the city.

She was waiting for him outside the hotel entrance and greeted him with a wide smile as the valet opened the car door for her.

She said, "I hope you're not mad at me for breaking our breakfast date?"

Clay said, "No, I'm not mad. I'm sure you had your reasons."

Mackenzie asked, "I did have something I had to do. What about you? What did you end up doing all day? I hope you relaxed and enjoyed a day off."

"Not exactly. Remember you thought it was a good idea for me to check on Max Bruder, the hotel maintenance guy? We both felt it was suspicious that he quit so soon after Alys was murdered."

"Yes, I remember."

"I did check on him this morning."

"He's dead, isn't he?"

Clay shook his head in disbelief. *How in hell did she know Max was dead?*

He turned to her and saw her gaze was frozen, staring at the road ahead. Clay thought she was trying to cement a thought. He asked, "Why would you think he was dead?"

She answered without looking back at him. "He is dead, isn't he? Yesterday when I first entered the hotel lobby, I sensed something dreadful had occurred to someone at the hotel. First, I thought it was because Alys had been murdered. Then I thought it was about you, that something bad was going to happen to you." She started to be emotional. "Thankfully, that wasn't the case. Now I realize it was about the maintenance worker."

She looked at Clay and said, "I'm fairly certain he was murdered, shot in his own home?"

Clay said, "You're right that he was shot to death. Now understand, it is extremely important that you keep any information about Max to yourself. We have sealed the details about his death. We're hoping the killer gets overconfident and does something stupid that will lead us to the truth about his murder. The murderer wanted us to believe Max committed suicide."

Mackenzie pretended to zip her lips closed. "I promise not to breathe a word to anyone."

Clay asked, "So how did you guess what happened to him?"

"It wasn't a guess. The only thing that made any sense to me was that he had been murdered."

She paused then continued after several seconds of more stares. "I'm certain that Max somehow is linked to both Alys and Maura Quenneville, although he was not the one who killed them."

"I'm impressed. Who do you think killed the two women?"

"I'm getting close to knowing who, but I don't know right now. That's the strange thing about my gift. Sometimes I can tell you straight off what's going to happen or what has happened, or where a body can be found, or who killed whom. And then sometimes my mind is a blank and I can't even tell you if the sun will rise in the east. Sometimes I wish I never had the gift, and sometimes, like last night, I'm happy I have it."

"Why last night?"

"After you dropped me off last night, I took a walk to find where Alys had been shot."

"Please don't laugh, but I wanted to say goodbye to her."

"How did you learn where the murder occurred?"

"I was able to walk right to it without anyone telling me where she was killed."

Clay teased her. "And did you say goodbye to her?"

"You're laughing, but, yes, I did."

"And did she respond to you?"

Mackenzie bit her lower lip. "Yes, she did."

"Seriously?"

"I thought you said you weren't going to make fun of me."

"I'm not making fun. I would like to know how you communicated with your friend. Your ESP gift is piquing my interest."

"It's not like I'm communing with the dead or using a crystal ball. I can't really explain it. If someone is clairvoyant, they can visualize people and events at another point in time. In my case, sometimes I can see future events. It's called precognition, but it's not something I have all the time."

"What's it called when you can see the past?"

"Retrocognition."

"And you have both abilities?"

"Not always, but yes."

With a fake smile he said, "Okay, now you're scaring me. I won't be able to think the thoughts I usually have without the fear that you will know exactly what I'm thinking."

"It's too late. I like what you've been thinking." She stroked his hand and laughed. "And I thought I was the naughty one."

Surprisingly, Clay was embarrassed, and his face turned red.

She said, "I'm going to have to tell you why I didn't have breakfast with you. And I don't have to be a psychic to know you're going to be mad at me."

"Good grief. I only left you late last night. How much trouble could you have gotten into?"

"I think more than you're going to like."

"Tell me."

"I had an Uber take me to Quenneville's office on Parson Boulevard. I thought Saturday would be a good time to talk to the doctor. He doesn't have office hours on Saturday, and I sensed he would be alone."

"Go on. What were you hoping to accomplish?"

"I wanted him to admit he had an affair with Alys so we could establish a motive for her death."

"And how did that go?"

"Not too well. The more I pushed him to admit that he had an affair with her, the more he denied it. I couldn't get him off dead-center, so I lied to him and told him I found Alys' diary in her bedroom in Santa Barbara and Alys wrote about the two of them."

"You made up a story about a fake diary? It is a fake story, right?"

"And now he thinks you know all about Alys and him from what she said in a diary, a diary that doesn't exist. How did he handle that news?"

"He got upset and wanted to see it, but I said it was in

safekeeping in my room at the hotel. I said I wasn't going to show him. I told him that I brought it from Santa Barbara to show you."

"Good God, you really told him all that?"

"Yes. He thought I was trying to blackmail him. I denied that, of course."

"What did he say?"

"He was mad. Afterward I tried to make nice with him and I apologized for getting him angry. I said that it was obvious from what Alys wrote in the diary that she was deeply in love with him."

Clay managed to keep his temper in check. "Let me get this straight. You just told a suspect in the death of two women that you had an incriminating diary in your possession, and then you told him where it was located."

"I actually felt sorry for the guy. I think he really was in love with Alys."

"What happened next, did he threaten you in any way?"

"No, not at all. I apologized for badgering him about his affair. He said he understood. Then he asked me if we could go out for a drink sometime."

"I said that would be nice, that I had been jealous of Alys, and now that she was gone maybe the two of us could get to know each other."

"Good God, you didn't, did you really? Don't you see that if you meet with him now, it puts you in mortal danger?"

"Nah, you don't really think so, do you? You're just trying to make me feel guilty for what I did, aren't you?"

"Trust me. I think you are in danger now. The best that can happen is he's not the murderer."

"And the worst?"

"The worst is that he is the murderer."

"If you're really that frightened for me, what do you think I should do about it?"

Clay realized this beautiful woman was terribly naïve. "You've got to get out of the Emerson and stay someplace else. Do you know anyone in Santa Fe you can stay with?"

"No. Maybe I should just go home. I can stay with my folks. I stayed with them after you first told me about Alys' death."

"Quenneville's no dummy. He'll find out where your folks live. And you won't have any security there. The police in Santa Barbara can check on you occasionally, but they don't have the manpower to have a cop stand guard at your house or your parents' house for any length of time."

She asked, "Then can I stay at your house?"

Clay was taken aback by her brazenness. He didn't answer for several seconds. It appeared to be an innocent request on her part. "I guess so. It's too late to work out security arrangements for you to stay at a safe house, so I guess it will be okay to stay at my house for tonight."

CHAPTER 28

Clay drove Mackenzie to the hotel to retrieve her belongings. Afterward, he planned to get her situated at his house. Having her stay at his house and then deem it a safe house did not fall under proper police protocol, but he was genuinely concerned about her safety. The more he thought about her request to stay with him, the more he liked the idea. In addition to the safety aspect, this was one way for him to get to know her better. Clay was uncertain where their relationship was headed. After all, it had been only a few days since she entered his life. She was stunningly beautiful, but impulsive and eccentric, one of those firebrands who creates problems then walks away before she gets the blame.

His focus was to keep her safe while at the same time preventing her from intruding any further in his homicide investigation. He genuinely believed she may have put herself in jeopardy by lying to Quenneville about Alys' diary. It was up to him to see that she would be okay.

His modest two-bedroom home would be her safe house until Monday, when she was to leave Santa Fe and return to work as an airline attendant. Thereafter he would be unable to protect her from harm but if she truly had the ability to see into the future, she would have to rely on her supposed gift to forewarn her of danger.

Entering the Emerson, Mackenzie told Clay she was going to go to her room to collect her belongings before she checked out.

"Let me know if you need any help," Clay said.

"I'll be fine. You can wait for me in the lobby. I'll be right down."

After twenty minutes, Clay was getting impatient as he waited for her to return from her room with her belongings. He shook his head. *What is taking her so long? What trouble is she getting into now?*

The door to the passenger elevator slid open and an elderly couple got off. Clay asked, "Did you happen to see a tall blonde woman waiting to take the elevator?"

"Sorry, no. We didn't see anyone."

Clay thanked them and watched as they took the back exit to the parking lot. Mackenzie still was not back, and Clay observed that none of the other elevators were descending from the fourth floor.

He punched the *up* button and rode the elevator to the fourth floor to see what her delay was. He knocked, but there was no answer. He went to room 412 and knocked again. A man opened the door.

Clay flashed his detective's badge and explained himself. "I'm looking for a woman who is a guest in the connecting room."

"Sorry, Detective, there's no one here, and I don't know who the person is in the connecting room."

A woman showed herself behind the man and spoke. "I'm his wife. Is there a problem? You're welcome to come in and see for yourself that no one else is in here."

Clay entered the empty room. He went to the connecting

door to see if he could get through to Mackenzie's room, but the door from 410 was locked.

Clay apologized for inconveniencing them and went back to 410. He knocked again. Still no answer. He used his cell phone to dial Mackenzie, but she did not answer.

He thought, *I must have missed her when she was going down on one of the elevators and I was going up in another one. She's got to be in the lobby.*

CHAPTER 29

Clay took an elevator to the lobby and looked around, but Mackenzie was nowhere to be found. He was concerned and asked Rose about her. "Mackenzie Stanton was checking out today. I went to her room and didn't find her there. Have you seen her?"

"She settled her bill about half an hour ago. I haven't seen her since."

"Let me have a key to 410 please, so I can check if she's okay."

Clay entered Mackenzie's room. Her clothes, cosmetics, and toiletries were neatly packed in her open suitcase and overnight bag, but she was not there.

He walked out into the empty corridor. There was no sign of her. He spotted Emily Embers cleaning room 417. She was wearing earbuds, so Clay had to nudge her elbow to get her attention. "Emily, have you seen the woman who was in room 410?"

Emily nodded. "Yes, a while ago. I saw her go into her room, but I haven't seen her since."

He went back to Mackenzie's room and dialed the front desk. "Rose, I'm calling from Mackenzie Stanton's room. I'm still looking for her. She's not in her room. All her belongings are in her room but she's nowhere in sight. I'm afraid for her safety. Is John Paul in? I need to talk to him."

"Yes. He's in the security room."

Clay hurried down the emergency exit stairwell to the security room and explained to John Paul that Mackenzie was missing. "I need to see the CCTV footage for the fourth floor. She is a guest staying in room 410 and checked out half an hour ago, but her belongings are still in her room. I'm trying to find out what's happened to her."

"Why do you think anything happened? Who is she, anyway?"

Clay answered calmly. "She was Alys Chapman's best friend. I'm concerned she's been targeted by the same person who killed Chapman. I promised her a safe haven at a different location and had her check out first, but I haven't seen her since she went back to her room. I need you to pull up footage for the fourth floor to see if we can find out where she is."

The security guard ran the video for Clay and pointed out a woman getting on one of the elevators. "Is that her getting on the elevator from the lobby half an hour ago?"

"Yes, that's her. There she is again, getting off the elevator on the fourth floor. Room 410 is around the corner. She appears to be heading there. She's entering her room. Nothing suspicious there, either."

Clay said, "Stop. Roll it back, John Paul. There. Stop. There's someone looking out from the ice machine alcove. Roll it forward slowly."

They witnessed a man exit the ice machine alcove and walk slowly down the corridor. He hesitated at each room that he passed on both sides of the hallway until he stopped at Mackenzie's room. Mackenzie had kept the door ajar by placing the security latch across the door jamb. The video showed the man nonchalantly walking into her room. He was dressed in sunglasses, a floppy hat pulled down to his eyes, dark warmups with silver or white stripes down both legs, and New Balance sneakers with a large logo "N" printed on both sides of each shoe.

Mackenzie and the man were in her room, hidden from the hallway camera. There was no other activity on the tape for a moment. After a minute, the man peeked out of the room, keeping his back to the security camera. He made sure the coast was clear, then stepped into the corridor, holding Mackenzie with her one arm bent painfully high behind her back. He closed the door behind Mackenzie and pushed her toward the emergency exit.

Clay observed that Emily Embers surprisingly walked in and out of the room she was cleaning a few doors down the corridor. But on camera she didn't seem to notice what was happening.

Clay said, "The guy is forcing Mackenzie to go to the emergency exit, but I don't know if they're going up or down the stairs."

John Paul clicked on the footage that covered the emergency exit. It showed the man walking down the steps, holding onto Mackenzie's elbow. Once they reached the basement corridor he peeked to see if the coast was clear and pushed Mackenzie into the hallway. Several steps farther down the corridor, he and Mackenzie entered the door leading to the hotel boiler room.

The surveillance footage in the boiler room suddenly went dark. Clay asked, "What happened?"

The security guard said, "The camera is not picking up any activity. We have only one camera in the boiler room, and it looks like he may have spray painted the camera lens.

"He must know we're tracking him. John Paul, stay here.

Dial 911 and ask for backup for me. I'm heading down to the boiler room. Track where they go from there. Phone me on my cell when you find out."

John Paul said, "Be careful." He used the hotel phone to dial for Santa Fe police backup assistance.

Clay raced through the lobby and down the steps of the emergency exit leading to the basement. When he got there, he tried to open the door to the corridor but discovered it was blocked. The kidnapper had jammed a simple but effective rubber doorstop under the door to keep anyone from entering the corridor from the stairs. Clay put his shoulder to the metal door several times but was unable to ram it open. He rushed back up the stairs to the lobby, then out the rear exit.

❊ ❊ ❊

Still in the boiler room, the kidnapper threatened Mackenzie and continued to bend her elbow painfully. "If you don't do exactly what I say, I will shoot you right here and now. Do you understand? I have nothing to lose."

"Are you Gardner Hicks? You're hurting me."

The man was disguising his voice. "I am not Gardner Hicks. Now shut up. We're going to go through a door to the parking lot, and if you shout for help, you're dead. I will shoot you and anyone else who gets in my way. It's getting dark, so no one will pay any attention to us unless you shout out. If you do ..." he didn't finish.

The kidnapper proceeded to shove her through the room and around boilers, pipes, and heat exchangers to get to the outside door.

As he stepped outside, the kidnapper looked both ways to see if the coast was clear.

He saw the elderly man and woman who Clay had observed earlier standing alongside their car in a handicap parking space. They had called AAA and were waiting for someone to arrive to change their flat right front tire. The kidnapper disregarded the couple as a threat and pushed Mackenzie into the parking lot in front of him toward the desert.

Mackenzie heard the older couple talking. She screamed, "Help me! Help me!"

The elderly woman shouted. "Mister, what are you doing to that woman?"

The kidnapper waved his pistol at the couple. "Shut up."

The elderly man shouted to his wife, "Get down. The guy has a gun. Stay down." The man reached inside his open car window and honked the car horn nonstop.

The kidnapper fired his gun at the man, with the bullet ricocheting off the top of his car.

John Paul phoned Clay. "The cops are on the way. My surveillance footage shows the subject exited the boiler room and is in the parking lot with the woman. He has a gun."

When the kidnapper was diverted by the sound of the car horn beeping non-stop, Mackenzie spun away from the kidnapper. The man tried to latch onto Mackenzie's arm, but she tore loose from his grasp. She was surprisingly nimble and darted between cars like she was playing a game of hide-and-go-seek.

"Help! Help!" she screamed as she continued to elude the kidnapper. The elderly man continued to honk his horn, window shades were opened, and multiple hotel guests stared down at the commotion. The parking lot cameras picked up the entire chaotic scene.

As Clay raced through the side exit, he heard Mackenzie scream and saw the gunman about fifty yards away. Clay fired once in the air to draw the kidnapper's attention away from Mackenzie.

The kidnapper turned and fired wildly at Clay but missed. Clay dropped into a crouch behind a car.

Responding to John Paul's 911 call, two cop cars arrived with sirens blaring.

John Paul met the cops at the front entrance. He told them that Clay was confronting the assailant in the rear of the hotel and that shots had been fired.

The cops drew their revolvers and rushed around to the back of the hotel.

Clay saw them and gestured for them to flank the kidnapper. But as Clay and the cops closed in on the assailant, he ran off into the desert and disappeared into the darkness.

Clay hurried to Mackenzie. She was with the elderly couple, and amidst tears, she thanked them for putting themselves at risk to help her escape. "Thank you so very much. If you hadn't diverted his attention, I don't know what would have happened."

Clay led everyone back to the hotel lobby. He asked one of the cops to take a statement from the elderly couple while he comforted Mackenzie.

"I'm not letting go of you," she cried.

Clay tried to calm her down. "You're okay now. The bad guy's gone."

Clay asked her to start at the beginning and recount exactly what had happened.

She explained to Clay, "It happened so quickly. I was in my room, packing my bags, when that guy walked into my room and grabbed me. Stupidly, I had kept the door ajar for easy in and out. He twisted my arm behind my back and said we were going for a walk, and if I shouted, he would kill me."

Clay said, "We saw from the surveillance tape that he had been hiding in the room where the icemaker is located."

"When he walked into my room, he scared me nearly to death. He stuck his gun against my side and dragged me down the stairs of the emergency exit. He took me through the boiler room, then he pushed me out the basement door and into the parking lot." She pointed to the elderly couple. "Luckily that nice couple over there saw I was being abducted, and they beeped their horn to divert his attention. That's when I was able to tear loose from his hold. When he saw you and the other cops circling around back, he stopped chasing me and ran into the desert." She said, "At first I thought it was Gardner Hicks, but I'm not sure who it was."

Clay said, "Okay, listen to me. You're okay now. Let's go back to your room and get your stuff so I can take you away from here." She continued to hold his hand as he escorted her through the lobby and into the elevator.

He asked, "Could it have been Quenneville?"

"Yes, maybe. Gardner and Doctor Quenneville are built somewhat the same. It could have been either one. Whoever it was obviously disguised his voice the whole time so I can't say for sure who it was. I'm so sorry."

Clay said, "It was my fault. I should never have let you go back to your room alone, especially after you met with Quenneville this morning."

Mackenzie calmed down. "It's not your fault. I'm so upset at myself. My stupid self. I thought I could help you find the killer, but I've ended up nearly getting myself killed. What's ironic about all this is I've been telling you about my extrasensory perception and now when it could have helped me avoid being abducted, it failed me. I should have known that the guy was hiding in the ice room, waiting for me. I should have sensed that I was in danger."

Clay said, "Someone obviously is after you. It could be Gardner or even Quenneville, or maybe someone altogether different. I understand you might have a special extrasensory gift, but you can't rely on it. If someone wants to hurt you, today's event proves they can do it despite your ESP."

CHAPTER 30

Mackenzie collected her belongings from her room and rolled her suitcase to the elevator. Clay was with her step-by-step and on high alert. When the elevator opened to the first floor, Clay checked the lobby to ensure no one was lurking. Several guests were checking in and other guests were milling about the concierge desk asking questions about what touristy things they could enjoy doing.

Jeremy Voit was setting up the lobby bar, one hour later than normal. It was after six o'clock.

Clay asked Voit, "You just get in?"

"Yeah, traffic on 25 was a bitch again, as usual. This time a fender-bender bollixed up traffic for about five miles. There wasn't anything major, just a lot of gawkers who slowed traffic to a crawl. It was like a parking lot out there. They need to do something about the traffic. It's really getting bad, especially with so many people moving into the area. It's ridiculous."

Mackenzie stood alongside Clay. Both she and Clay had a full view of the lobby to ensure they would not be surprised if the kidnapper returned.

Clay leaned over the bar to glance at Voit's shoes to see if they were New Balance sneakers which the kidnapper wore. They were not.

He asked Voit, "Are you aware of what happened here this afternoon?"

"Yeah, Rose told me that someone apparently tried to abduct a hotel guest? I missed all the excitement." Voit used a bar rag from behind the bar to wipe his hands then used the rag to dab sweat from his forehead.

Clay put his hand softly on Mackenzie's back and introduced her. "It was this woman who the guy tried to abduct. Jeremy Voit, this is Mackenzie Stanton. Mackenzie was Alys Chapman's best friend and roommate and is in Santa Fe looking for closure regarding her friend's death."

Voit glanced at Mackenzie for the first time, nodded, extended his hand and said, "I'm sorry for your loss."

Mackenzie said, "Thank you. Did you know Alys?"

Several hotel guests approached the bar and stood waiting impatiently to order drinks as Voit spoke with Clay and Mackenzie. Voit briefly turned his attention to them and said, "Sorry, folks, I just got in and am running a little bit behind. What's your pleasure? It's on the house."

After Jeremy filled the orders for the hotel patrons, he turned back to Mackenzie and Clay. "About your friend, no, I didn't know her, except that we would chat at the bar when she ordered a drink. I don't know if you know this, but she stayed at the Emerson a few times before, so I recognized her. I remember she always ordered the same drinks and followed the same routine. She would be at the bar about five o'clock, give or take, and order a vodka martini, straight up, with two olives. Then about eleven o'clock each night, after she had her car parked for her, she would return to the bar for a nightcap and order a sherry on the rocks. Hard not to be aware of someone as pretty as she was. California girls are beautiful."

"Are you flirting with my date?" Clay asked and followed with a burst of laughter when it appeared he had embarrassed Jeremy. "Only kidding."

Voit turned away for a second then smiled at Mackenzie and said, "Like I told Detective Bryce when he asked me about your friend, she and I would talk touristy stuff. That was it, pretty much. A beautiful woman for sure. A real tragedy that she was killed with her whole life ahead of her."

"Yes, you're right." Mackenzie pulled a tissue from her purse to wipe away a tear that was beginning to roll down her cheek.

Voit said, "I'm sorry if I upset you."

"No, I'm okay. Not your fault. Thank you though."

Clay wanted to change the subject. "Did Rose also tell you about Max Bruder?"

"No, what about him?"

"He's dead. Shot himself."

Clay studied Voit's reaction to the news of Max's death and observed how Voit visibly recoiled at the news. But he couldn't tell if he was sincerely surprised at the news, or if he pretended to be.

"I guess it should not surprise me. He's been battling a lot of demons."

"Why do you say that?"

"He served two one-year tours in Iraq and Afghanistan; he was wounded twice and was suffering from PTSD. He was in all-around terrible health."

Mackenzie asked, "Did he try to get help for himself?"

Voit looked away. "No. One time I tried to get him to go to the VA in Albuquerque and get therapy, especially for his PTSD, but he didn't want any help. He said he was fine and didn't want to talk about it. No question, it was the war that made him suffer the post traumatic stress. He was a rough-looking sonofabitch, pardon my French, but some women were attracted to him. For the most part he didn't care how he looked or what people thought of him. His boss tried to keep him away from any contact with hotel guests because of his appearance and his gruffness. On the other hand, he was unbelievably handy. He could fix just about anything that needed fixing."

"Ever hang out with him?"

"No, not really. Although he invited me to watch a football game with him at his house one Sunday some months back. I was shocked by the condition of his house. Here's a guy who could fix anything, but his own house was a freaking nightmare. Electrical cords hanging down from the ceiling. One room had a dirt floor, and the house had a half-inch of dust on everything. It was like the house had been hit by a major dust storm."

"You said you were there only the one time?"

"Yeah, that's all I could stomach. It was pretty gross inside." He chuckled. "I suggested that we sit outside on the patio to enjoy the nice weather we were having. Subtle, right? I didn't stay long. We had a beer and talked about politics mostly. It was obvious we didn't have a lot in common, so I made up an excuse why I had to leave. Never watched the football game. I'm a little OCD, so I couldn't wait to get home so I could take a shower after being in that house."

Clay changed the subject. "Did you know a woman by the name of Maura Quenneville?"

She was the woman who was killed out on Breeze Canyon a few weeks ago. Her death was in the local papers and on TV. She was the wife of a wealthy plastic surgeon here in town."

"The name sounds familiar. If I remember correctly, Max might have done handyman work for her."

"Did he ever tell you that he had a sexual relationship with her?"

"I have no clue. He never bragged about it if he did."

Voit appeared to be getting irritated by Clay's line of questions. "Excuse me, Detective Bryce, but why are you asking all these questions about Max? If that woman was married to a wealthy plastic surgeon, I can't imagine that Max would have been involved with her sexually. It sounds like she was high society, and Max sure was not."

Clay answered, "Since he was your buddy, I thought maybe he spoke to you about her"

He said, "Max was not my buddy. I told you, I only hung out with him the one time."

"You said he could fix anything that needed fixing. A handyman like that is in demand in today's world. It would have made sense if he worked for Mrs. Quenneville."

"Yes, he seemed to like her. She paid him very well for what he did at her house."

Hotel patrons were starting to flock to the bar. Voit was rushed, filling drink orders. He told Clay and Mackenzie, "We'll have to take a break for now and talk later." Voit walked to the other end of the bar to take drink orders from several customers.

When he returned, he asked, "Is that it with the questions about Max?"

"One last question. Did he ever tell you where he got the gun that he shot himself with—it was a .38 special?"

"I don't know anything about guns. I have no idea what caliber it was, and he did not tell me where he had gotten it."

Clay was uncertain about Voit. He planned to look into

his background when he got back to headquarters. "Thanks for chatting with us, Jeremy. We've got to get going now. I know where to reach you if I have any more questions."

Clay walked Mackenzie out the front entrance.

She whispered to him, "He's staring at my ass."

Darkness enveloped the city. Apart from some retail shops, most building lights were off. Clay looked often at his rear-view mirror but didn't see anyone following them. He finally stopped looking when Mackenzie reached over to hold his hand rubbing it softly. Clay did not say anything. He looked at her and smiled. She smiled back at him. There was an obvious sexual tension between the two of them.

On the way to his house, they spoke about Jeremy Voit.

"What do you think of Voit?" he asked.

"If I tell you what I think, are you going to be nice to me or are you going to make fun of me again?"

Clay pretended to be hurt by her comment. "What do you mean by that? I've been nice to you all along."

She whispered plaintively. "Hardly. You've made fun of me from the time I stepped off the plane."

He nodded. "You're right. I'm sorry," he said. "I really am. Please go ahead and give me your thoughts about Voit. I really would like to know."

Mackenzie reluctantly gave Clay her observations. "Let me see. When he finally looked at me, he stared at my chest the entire time at the bar, and he stared at my behind the entire long walk out of the hotel."

"Whew, okay, other than asking you how you knew he

was studying your behind from behind, I get it, he thought you were hot. But, of course, you are." He looked down at her hand locked in his. "Do you think he might have been the kidnapper?"

"I don't think so, but did you notice how much he was sweating? And don't you think it was strange that he looked at me in a sexual way? Was it because he didn't want me to tag him as the guy who tried to abduct me? I do think it was interesting and very coincidental that Voit said he was stuck in traffic while someone was assaulting me. It makes for a good alibi, doesn't it?"

Clay said, "Good observation. Was he really bogged down in traffic?"

Mackenzie asked, "Is there any way to prove he was tied up in traffic that long?"

"All I can do is check with the Department of Transportation to see if there had been a major delay on 25. But that wouldn't tell me if he personally was in traffic."

"When you first introduced him to me I wondered if he was the guy who tried to kidnap me. But then I asked myself, what would his motive have been? Maybe Gardner Hicks or even Quenneville had motives, but not Voit, at least no logical motive that I can come up with. I think you can rule him out as my kidnapper suspect."

CHAPTER 31

Clay pulled into the driveway of his two-bedroom adobe-styled home. Mackenzie cooed her approval. "What a handsome house."

"Thanks. I didn't expect company today, so close your eyes when you walk in. It probably is a mess."

To the contrary, Clay kept a neat house, atypical for a bachelor. She mentioned the home had a warm lived-in feel, with a place for everything and everything in its place. There was an empty bottle of beer and a short stack of newspapers sitting on the living room coffee table, a novel on the end table, a bag of pistachio nuts, and a small bowl of pistachio shells. "I'm very impressed, Clay. It's not what I expected. It's very neat and clean."

"I know your ESP probably pictured me as a slob, right?"

"Well, not quite a slob, but not a neatnik either."

"I have a lady come in every two weeks to clean for me. Otherwise, a slob is the right description."

Clay walked Mackenzie to the spare bedroom. "This is yours. The bathroom has towels under the vanity. Let me know if you need anything else."

She said, "Very nice. This is everything I need. I'd like to unpack and take a shower."

"Of course. There's a bathrobe hanging near the shower. I don't have any sherry, but I can get you a glass of wine or a drink."

"I'd love a glass of white wine if you have it. Chardonnay would be great. But I'll take a shower first."

"Okay, now relax. Everything will be okay. You're safe here."

Mackenzie said, "I know I am. I can't thank you enough for letting me stay here. I can't quite get my head around the idea that someone tried to kill me, but I feel better knowing you're here to protect me."

"We'll find out in time if you agitated Quenneville enough that he felt he had to take action against you. He continues to be one of my prime suspects."

She said, "I promise to be good from now on. The only thing I need is a warm shower and maybe afterward I can give you a giant hug to thank you for saving my life."

Clay wasn't sure what she meant by that. "I'll look forward to it. I'll see you in the kitchen for your chardonnay after you shower." Clay closed the bedroom door behind him and left her to unpack and shower. He visualized her naked in the shower, covered in suds, then shook his head trying to clear his thoughts.

Several minutes later the bathroom door opened a crack. "Clay, I showered, but I can't find the bathrobe now."

"It's hanging near the shower," he said.

"No, it's not here."

"I have another. I'll get it for you. Give me a minute."

He heard the shower running. "Are you decent? Can I open the door to give you the bathrobe?"

He opened the bathroom door and stood wide-eyed. She was naked and standing in a model's pose as she held the bathrobe in one hand and placed her other hand on her hip. Behind her, the shower was running and filling the room with a cloud of steam.

"I found it," she purred.

"I see." He stood mesmerized by her magnificent body.

She said, "I'm ready for that hug now."

Clay moved toward her. She was tall, but he was a huge man and easily wrapped his arms around her.

"I would like to kiss you," she said. She looked up at him like a fledgling bird accepting food from its mother.

They kissed with open mouths brushing each other's tongues, both of them moaning with sexual intent. He stroked her shoulders, then her back, and allowed his hands to work his way over her taut body.

She looked into his eyes and saw an eagerness and excitement as he struggled to remain calm. She pulled off his shirt, then slowly unbuckled his belt. He let his trousers drop to the floor and kicked them aside.

She reached down to hold his arousal. "Whoa, I thought so."

He said, "You did, huh."

"Yes, very nice."

He said, "I thought you said you were going to be good."

"I will be, you'll see."

He laughed, "That's not what I meant."

"Shut up and hold me." She pulled him gently into the shower and let the flow of warm water further stir their senses. She wrapped her arms around his neck and kissed him hard on his lips. She rubbed her naked body against his and kissed him on his neck and chest and more.

He lifted her up and bent over to kiss her breasts. She turned around slowly with her back to him, braced her hands on the shower wall and reached behind to guide him into her. She moved her hips in rhythm to his thrusts, and after a long number of seconds, they climaxed together with shouts from her of "Yes, yes, yes!" and groans of pleasure from him.

They were both exhausted. He turned her around and held her tight. They kissed again and again until they finally stepped out of the shower and took turns toweling each other. In less than a few seconds, they both became aroused again. He picked her up and carried her to his bed.

Standing over her, he said, "What just happened?"

"We made mad love, and it was wonderful. I can't wait until we can do it again."

"I'm ready when you are," he said.

"Already? I am too."

She pulled him down on top of her and allowed him to explore every part of her body. Then she gently pushed him off her and rolled on top of him. He laid on his back and allowed her to play with his arousal slowly, softly as their lips continued to explore each other's body.

She slowed down when she sensed he was ready to explode a second time but held him back for a moment longer until her passion caught up to his. They climaxed together.

CHAPTER 32

They fell asleep with her arm draped over his chest, Mackenzie with a smile on her face and Clay with thoughts that he was the luckiest man in Santa Fe.

In the middle of the night, Clay sensed Mackenzie was cold. He got up and covered her with a blanket that was folded at the bottom of the bed. Mackenzie woke, glanced at Clay, then purred and went back to sleep. He put on a pair of boxers but before he returned to bed, he heard the creak of a floorboard in the living room. He cocked his head toward the noise for a few seconds and rationalized that the sound was merely the expansion and contraction noise a house makes after a full day of the sun beating down on it. But then he heard another sound closer to the bedroom.

Clay reached for his service revolver that he normally kept on his bedside table. But he remembered he had left it in the foyer, along with his handcuffs and cell phone. He cursed himself.

He gently shook Mackenzie awake, put his hand over her mouth to keep her quiet then whispered into her ear that there was an intruder in the house. She reacted silently by nodding that she understood. Her eyes were wide with fear. He whispered, "Where is your cell phone?"

"In the other bedroom."

He told her he was going to confront the intruder and when he did, she should get to her phone if she was able.

Clay approached his open bedroom door and peeked into the living room. He saw a man in silhouette wearing a ski mask, standing motionless in the living room outside the bedroom and holding a gun. Clay looked back at Mackenzie.

He held his forefinger against his lips until she nodded that she understood. She was lying totally still and afraid to roll out of bed because she thought her movement might alert the intruder.

The guy shuffled from one foot to the other and moved toward the open bedroom door. He had not yet adjusted to the darkness of the room. Clay took two steps and threw himself at the intruder with a violent tackle that caused him to crash into the coffee table. His gun went off, the bullet thudding into the wall to the left of the bedroom door.

Mackenzie flew out of bed. Clay shouted, "Get your cellphone. Call 911."

She tried to get her cell phone, but Clay and the intruder were struggling in the doorway of Clay's bedroom and blocking her passage. She yanked a lamp from the end table and slammed it against the intruder's back. He was stunned but continued to struggle.

Clay wrestled the intruder for control of his pistol. In their struggle, another shot went off and embedded in the living room's wooden floor. Clay clutched the intruder's wrist, clamped it as tight as a setscrew, and shook the gun out of his hand. The gun clattered across the hardwood floor to the far wall.

The intruder continued to struggle until Clay picked him up and body-slammed him down to the floor.

Clay shouted to Mackenzie, "Turn on the lights and get my handcuffs, phone and gun from the foyer."

She hurried to the foyer and handed him his handcuffs first, then his phone and revolver. "Put your hands behind you," he shouted to the intruder, who continued to struggle.

Clay spoke loudly. "Calm down. You're just making it worse for yourself."

The intruder did not comply, so Clay forcibly bent his arms behind him and handcuffed his wrists.

"You're hurting me."

"Then stop fighting me." Clay said. "Who are you?"

He was out of breath from wrestling with Clay. "I'm your conscience."

Clay grabbed the intruder's ski mask with one hand and yanked it off his head.

Mackenzie shouted, "Oh, my God, it's Gardner Hicks."

CHAPTER 33

Clay continued to restrain Hicks and phoned Sergeant Rizzo. "Sarge, I have Gardner Hicks, the fugitive from Española, in custody. Send a couple of uniforms to my house to take him to headquarters and have him booked for attempted murder. I'll complete the booking of a half dozen other charges when I get into headquarters. Please inform the Española Police Department about the arrest."

Turning to Hicks, who was lying face down with his cheek against the floor, he asked, "Why did you break into my house?"

"I didn't break in; the door was unlocked."

"Try that again." Clay bent Hick's wrists more severely.

"Okay, okay. I'll tell you. I wanted to ask Mackenzie a few things."

"Like what?"

"Like why she talked Alys into leaving me."

Mackenzie had put her clothes on and was standing by, watching the scene unfold. She responded defensively to Hicks' accusation. "Gardner, I did not talk Alys into leaving you. You made that happen on your own. Alys did not want to be with you anymore because of the way you treated her."

"That's not true. You were the one who convinced her to leave me. Why did you? I didn't do anything to you. Alys and I were in love. We were destined to be together forever."

Clay heard multiple sirens approaching. The cops were arriving.

Mackenzie asked, "Gardner, that was you at the hotel yesterday, wasn't it? What were you going to do to me?"

Gardner lifted his head slightly from the floor to look up

at her but did not reply and dropped his head to the floor again.

Mackenzie asked again, angrily this time, "Answer me. That was you at the Emerson Hotel, wasn't it?"

Silence.

Clay said, "We have you on the surveillance tape abducting Mackenzie. What I want to know is, why? First you killed Alys and then you tried to kidnap Mackenzie, apparently because you wanted to kill her, right?"

"What the hell are you talking about? I wasn't at any Emerson Hotel. Where is that?"

"You told the Española police that you were staying at the Emerson, so don't tell me you don't know anything about it."

Mackenzie said, "You do know that Alys is dead, don't you?"

He laughed, "You're crazy. She is not."

Mackenzie's patience was over. She raised her voice. "Yes, she is dead and you're the one who killed her."

"Wrong."

"No, I'm not wrong, you are. And now you want to kill me, too. Remember when you threatened both Alys and me?"

"No, you're imagining things."

"I'm not. It was in our condo. You got what you wanted, didn't you? You killed Alys, now you only have me left to kill."

"You're crazy. I didn't threaten you or Alys or anyone for that matter."

Two patrol officers knocked loudly on Clay's front door. "Detective Bryce? Officers Hausen and Briggs here."

Mackenzie opened the door for them.

The cops entered cautiously and surveyed the damage to Clay's living room. "Looks like the suspect wasn't cooperating with you."

"Not at first."

They asked Mackenzie, "Are you okay, Miss?"

"Yes, I'm fine."

Clay said, "You can take the prisoner to headquarters. I spoke with Sergeant Rizzo and told him to book Hicks for attempted murder, assault, and kidnapping. I'll be along shortly."

After the two cops drove Gardner to police headquarters, Clay spoke with Mackenzie. "Hicks doesn't make any sense. He won't believe that Alys is dead. And yet, there seems to be no question he's the guy who tried to kidnap you at the Emerson."

She said, "The more I play it over in my mind, the more I realize it may have been Gardner, but I'm still not sure. If it was Gardner, at least now he's in custody and not a threat to me anymore."

Clay said, "He tracked me here. And then to make matters worse, I failed to secure the house, so he was able to just walk in through the front door."

Mackenzie said, "Clay, don't beat yourself up. No excuse, but we've been a little distracted."

"Is that what you describe it?"

CHAPTER 34

An evening of passion had turned into a chaotic morning. Mackenzie was shaken by the likelihood that Gardner had been hunting her down and came within an eyelash of succeeding. If it weren't for Clay's heroics, she realized she might be dead now.

It was nearly six-thirty a.m.

Clay told Mackenzie, "I'll be back in a couple of hours. I'm heading out to question Hicks at police headquarters, then I'm going to Quenneville's house to interview the doctor."

"It's awful early, Clay."

"Yeah, if I can't sleep Quenneville won't either."

She asked, "Are you going to say anything about me visiting him yesterday?"

"No, all I want to do is find out if there is a tie-in between his deceased wife and Gardner Hicks, and if Max Bruder was linked to his wife in any way."

Mackenzie looked away from Clay and said in a barely audible whisper, "I know I'm not supposed to be involved but we know now that Max knew Quenneville's wife, and they probably were in a sexual relationship."

"We'll see if you're right. I won't bet against you, but I'll be amazed if you're right. Okay, listen. I'm leaving but please do not answer the door for anyone. Don't answer the phone. Don't peek out the windows. Don't walk out of the house to get a breath of fresh air. If someone tries to get in the house, call 911, then call me."

She nodded and promised, "I'll be good."

❊ ❊ ❊

Clay arrived at police headquarters and phoned the police in Española. He confirmed that Hicks was now in custody and would have to stand trial in Santa Fe for the new charges of attempted murder and multiple other felonies.

Interview room number 3 was designed to provide safeguards in the event the individual being questioned decided to take out his or her ire on the interviewer. A two-way mirror allowed witnesses in the adjoining room to observe the interview.

Gardner was seated at a plain three-by-five-foot metal table. The chair was bolted to the floor, which prevented Gardner from using it as a weapon against Clay, and he was shackled to a handcuff bar attached to the table.

Clay greeted Hicks. "I know we got off to a bad start this morning, but let's start from scratch, okay?"

He answered nonchalantly. "Sure, why not."

"Is it okay if I call you Gardner?"

Hicks shrugged. "I don't give a rat's ass what you call me, just get me out of here. I've got a wedding to get ready for. I can't expect Alys to do it all."

Clay gave him the Miranda warning and pointed out the interview was being video recorded. Gardner waved off the warning.

"Gardner, I would like to start by asking you if you were Alys Chapman's boyfriend?"

"I am her *fiancé*, present tense. We are engaged to be married. I told you that this morning. Weren't you listening?"

"You don't seem to be aware that Alys is dead?"

Hicks narrowed his eyes. "She's not dead. I was with her a little while ago. We're getting married tomorrow at the Loretto Chapel."

"Congratulations."

"Thanks. In fact, I would like you to come to the wedding. I hope you're not too busy and if you can make it, I would like you to be my best man."

Tongue in cheek, Clay said, "I'll check my schedule and let you know. But for right now I want to know why you assaulted Alys' friend, Mackenzie Stanton, at the Emerson Hotel yesterday?"

"It wasn't me. I swear. It wasn't. It was probably that doctor friend of hers."

"You mean Doctor Ronald Quenneville?"

"Yeah, that's the guy."

"What did the doctor have to do with Mackenzie?"

"The two of them arranged to have Alys break up with me."

"What about last night at my house, do you blame Dr. Quenneville for that too?"

"I don't know what you're talking about."

"You don't admit you broke into my house with the intention of killing Mackenzie?"

"I did no such thing."

"You mean you deny breaking into my house?"

"You got it pal. It wasn't me. It was that two-timing doctor. I've been following him to find out what he was really like. I figured if I could find out he's a two-timer then Alys would reconsider and not marry him."

Clay asked, "What do you mean by a two-timer?"

"He's been cheating on his wife. He's been deceiving her by having secret relationships with other women."

"His wife is dead, so you can't say he's cheating on her."

Hicks cackled. "Ha, that's very funny. How do you think she died?"

"Are you saying he killed his wife?"

"I'm not telling you he did and I'm not telling you he didn't. You'll have to find out for yourself. I'm not going to do your job for you."

"Thanks for the heads-up. I'll take your word for it. But let's get back to Mackenzie Stanton. Our surveillance tape shows it was you who tried to abduct her from her room at the Emerson Hotel."

Gardner was getting very agitated. "Bullshit. It wasn't me. I don't lie. You know what I'm beginning to think? I think it was you who abducted her. And I know the reason why. It was so you could have her for yourself. The way I see it, you kidnapped her and took her to your house, forced her to have sex with you, and then you planned to kill her, like you did with Alys."

"I thought you said Alys was still alive."

"She is. What makes you think she's dead?"

Clay tried one last time to reason with him. "Gardner, what you said is not true. We know it was you who tried to abduct Mackenzie yesterday at the hotel and again last night in my house. You say you don't lie, and if you're telling me the truth tell me yes or no, did you try to abduct Mackenzie. Remember you told me you don't lie."

"Well, alright then I'll tell you the truth. I did try to save Mackenzie from you. I pretended I was going to hurt her, but I really wasn't going to do anything to her." Hicks contorted his face in anger. His cuffs clanked loudly against the metal table as he tried to free his wrists from the cuff-bar.

"Calm down, Gardner."

Hicks raised his voice. "Get these damn handcuffs off of me."

"I can't do that. We have to keep you cuffed. It's protocol."

Gardner quieted as Clay continued. "Let's go back to why you wanted to kill Mackenzie."

"Not again. I did not try to kill Mackenzie."

"But you just admitted that you did. Why would you want to harm her?"

"To get even with her."

"Because she ruined our relationship."

"What relationship?"

"Are you listening to what I've been saying? Good God, pay attention. Are you deaf and dumb? I told you before that she ruined my relationship with Alys."

"I suspect it was the opposite. From what I understand, she was trying to protect Alys from your physical abuse. Isn't that true that you were abusing her?"

"That's pure, unadulterated BS!"

Clay wasn't getting anywhere with him. "Let's change the subject for a second. Did you know a man by the name of Max Bruder?"

"No."

"What about Dr. Quenneville's wife, Maura Quenneville, did you know her?"

"No. I didn't even know he was married."

"Yes, you did. You just told me he was a two-timer and cheated on his wife."

"I did not. You're imagining things. How would I know her?"

"What are you saying? Yes, or no, did you kill Maura Quenneville? And Max Bruder?"

"I told you I don't know them, so why would I kill them? You know who probably tried to kill them was Alys' friend? What's her name?"

"You mean Mackenzie?"

"Yeah, right, that's her name? She's good at pretending she's someone that she's not, especially with her ESP crapola."

Nothing Hicks said made any sense. Clay was going to try one last time to make heads or tails what he was saying. "Tell me what happened last night in Española."

"You mean in Brazil. I've never been there."

"Not Brazil. Española, it's half an hour from Santa Fe. You had a bar fight there last night and got arrested for assault."

"I did not. I flew in from New York about half an hour ago, so I could not have been there last night."

Clay said, "That is impossible. I know for a fact that there is no direct flight into Santa Fe from New York."

"That's true except for private aircraft like my Learjet that I just landed at the airport."

"You have a Learjet? I'm impressed."

"Yes, I'm a pilot now. If you ever need to get to New York, let me know, I can fly you there."

"Good to know. I'll keep that in mind."

Hicks said, "Alys and I are going to get married later today. Didn't you hear the church bells? I told you to take these damn handcuffs off me. I don't want to get married with them on. I've got to get going. She's expecting me at the church for rehearsal. You've got to be there, too, since you're my best man. I love her, and she loves me. We are going to get back together. She told me herself that she wants to have me back. She told me just before I came here. I am not lying to you."

Clay was uncertain if Hicks was mentally ill or if he was faking a mental illness to avoid prosecution. He was not making any sense. It was time to end the interview. Clay planned to suggest to the presiding judge during arraignment that Hicks undergo a mental health exam conducted by a forensic psychologist to determine if he could comprehend the charges against him.

CHAPTER 35

Clay called Mackenzie to see how she was doing, and to reinforce to her that even though Gardner Hicks was in custody, she should continue to restrict her activities and remain housebound. "I'm heading to the Quenneville home to interview the doctor about Max Bruder. I'll call you when I'm finished. Please remember what I said about staying safe."

Clay rang the buzzer at the driveway entrance at Doctor Quenneville's home. No one answered. He buzzed again, then buzzed steadily for several seconds before Quenneville answered angrily. "Who is it?"

"Detective Bryce. I need to talk to you."

Clay heard a female voice, and a child crying in the background.

"It's too damn early. Can't it wait?" he said. "Come back this afternoon. Sunday morning is the only chance I get to relax."

"Listen, I'm not having a great morning either, so don't let me have to ask you again—buzz me in!"

"Dammit Bryce, I will exercise my First Amendment rights and tell you that you're getting to be a pain in the ass."

"That's what I get paid to be."

"Do you have a warrant?"

"No, I don't. I don't need one to talk to you. But if you don't let me in, I will be happy to rouse the judge at his home and arrange to get a warrant. In addition, I can find ways to have you spend the day with me downtown at police headquarters on obstruction charges." He paused. "Or you can buzz me in. It's your choice."

Quenneville muttered a string of curses loud enough for Clay to hear, then reluctantly buzzed the gate open. A few minutes later, he met Clay at the front door, wearing woven slippers and blue silk pajamas. When he opened the front door, a smell of Chanel No. 5 wafted in the air.

"So go ahead and tell me what is so damn important for you to bother me on a Sunday morning."

Reveca called from the second floor. "Doctor Quenneville, what is it?"

Quenneville answered. "It's Detective Bryce, Reveca. Everything is okay."

Clay asked, "Did I wake her?"

"Yes, you did." He said with impatience, "Now that you've wakened my entire household, what do you want?"

"Did you know a man by the name of Max Bruder?"

He answered without hesitation. "No, should I?"

"Are you sure? Is there any chance that your wife used him to do handyman work at your home?"

"Not that I know of. Why are you asking?"

"Unfortunately, Mr. Bruder died two days ago."

"And what does that have to do with me?"

"He indicated in a note that he was responsible for your wife's murder as well as the murder of Alys Chapman."

"No kidding. Are you saying you found the guy who killed Maura? I never heard of him. Maybe my wife used him to do odd jobs, but she never mentioned his name that I can remember. She ran our household and did what she wanted to do, and that included hiring any contractor."

Clay heard activity in the kitchen and smelled coffee brewing. He nodded toward the kitchen. "Is that Reveca?"

Reveca called out. "Doctor Quenneville, I have coffee. I will serve it to you and Detective Bryce?"

She came around the corner from the kitchen to the living room carrying a silver tray with a decanter of coffee and a platter of morning biscuits she had warmed up. She had that "just woke up" sleepy appearance with her hair frenzied yet still sexy-looking, and that ever-present smell of expensive perfume.

Clay said, "Hello Reveca, thank you for the coffee. Did you bake the biscuits?"

"Yes, it is a recipe from my grandmother in Slovakia."

"They're delicious. Reveca, I have something to ask you. Is there any chance you know a man by the name of Max Bruder, a rough-looking man, usually unshaven and with long wild hair?"

"Yes, Mr. Bruder. He works here sometimes for Mrs. Quenneville."

Quenneville asked, "Are you sure?"

"Yes, I have not seen him since the Missus died, but he was here a lot when something had to be fixed."

Clay asked, "Anything unusual you can tell me about him?"

"He never smiled. He always looked mad," she mimicked a gruff look. "But he was a nice man to Missus and to me. No matter what she asked him to do, he would say it was *no problem*. Detective Bryce, why are you asking about him?"

"Unfortunately, he has been found dead in his home."

She glanced quickly at Quenneville then back again to Clay. "Oh, no. How did he die?"

"We're not certain but we think he died from a self-inflicted gunshot."

"I'm so sorry," she said.

Clay continued. "We discovered a trove of jewelry in Max's house. We think Mr. Bruder could have been the person who stole Mrs. Quenneville's jewelry when the house was burglarized six months ago."

"Mr. Bruder was a nice man. I'm surprised if he was a criminal. I'm so sorry to hear that about him."

"Do you know if he was working in the house for Mrs. Quenneville the day the burglary occurred?"

"I don't remember for sure, but maybe yes."

"I understand that you were taking Adam for a stroll in his carriage when the burglary occurred. Is it possible that Max stole the jewelry when you were with Adam outside of the house?"

She looked at Quenneville again and shrugged. "I don't know what to say. Maybe yes, but I don't really know."

"Okay, that was a while ago and I understand you wouldn't know exactly when the burglary occurred. However, if you happen to think of anything else about Mr. Bruder, please call me. In the meantime, thanks for the coffee and for the wonderful biscuits."

Reveca took the hint, smiled, and left the platter as she retreated to the kitchen.

Quenneville asked, "Apart from asking if Reveca or I knew Max Bruder, what else do you need from me this early on a Sunday morning?"

"Is there any chance you know two individuals, one by the name of Gardner Hicks, and the other a woman by the name of Mackenzie Stanton? Mackenzie was Alys Chapman's best friend from Santa Barbara. And Hicks was Alys' ex-boyfriend. Mackenzie flew to Santa Fe from California on Friday to seek closure about Alys' death."

Clay studied Quenneville for his reaction. His face was emotionless, frozen from expression of any kind—no eyeblinks, no looking away, no breathing changes.

"The names don't sound familiar."

Quenneville had met Mackenzie at his office only yesterday, but he denied meeting her. *Why lie?*

"Gardner Hicks blames you and Mackenzie Stanton for Alys' death. Let me show you a photo of Hicks."

Clay took out the beach photo of Alys and Gardner.

"No, I don't recognize him. I never saw him before."

Clay said, "Hicks is the person who we believe tried to abduct Mackenzie at the Emerson Hotel."

"To what end? What would be the reason he tried to abduct her?"

"He blames Mackenzie for his breaking up with Alys a year ago."

"Do you have a photo of Mackenzie Stanton?"

"No, I don't, but I can get one from her very quickly."

Clay took out his cell phone and called Mackenzie. "Mackenzie, please take a selfie of yourself and send it to me right away. No, I can't explain it right now. Just send it please."

He continued explaining to Quenneville. "The attempted abductions occurred yesterday at the Emerson Hotel, then again last night when she was staying at a safe house."

"Is she okay?

"Yes, fortunately, she was not harmed."

The photo of Mackenzie came through to Clay's cell phone. "Here it is."

Quenneville studied the photo. He had no choice but to admit he knew Mackenzie. "Oh, yes, I know her. I met her yesterday when she pounded on my office door, insisting on speaking with me. I let her in, and she immediately accused me of having an affair with Alys."

"I thought she was a crazy lady. I denied her accusations and I asked her to leave. She was strange, to say the least."

"She accused you of having an affair with Alys? And Hicks accuses you as well. Are they right? Did you have an affair with Alys Chapman?"

"No. But what difference would it make if I did?"

"For one thing, it would provide motive for your wife's murder and motive also for Alys' murder."

Quenneville did not respond.

"Doctor, I understand from the case file about the burglary at your house six months ago that you had a gun, a .38 caliber pistol that was stolen along with your wife's jewelry."

"Yes, that's true."

"We found a gun in Max Bruder's home, a .38 pistol that might be yours. Unfortunately, as of now, we can't identify the owner because the serial number has been obliterated."

Quenneville said, "You are aware from that case file that I reported the loss of the pistol and jewelry to the police. They investigated the crime and combed the pawn shops in Santa Fe, but they never located any of the stolen items."

"Do you own another gun?"

"No."

"What about the pistol that was stolen from you. Did it have the serial number filed off?"

"No. I bought it brand-new, not from some thug on a

street corner," he sounded as though he was insulted by the insinuation that he would buy a gun from a straw buyer in the underworld.

"I'm sure you did buy it legitimately. However, the one we found had the number filed off."

"So why do you think it was my gun?"

"Our forensics team believes they can determine the number using a new technological process. We'll have to wait and see. It may or may not be your gun."

Clay took a sip of coffee and asked, "Tell me about your plans for Reveca. Are you planning to retain her as a nanny? She seems to be very loyal to you."

Quenneville again was exasperated by Clay. "That's a personal question, and it has no relevance to your investigation. The truth is, I don't know what I plan to do. I know she wants to stay in the States, but I don't want her to be tied down with Adam and me. However, I'm not sure what I would do with Adam if she weren't here to take care of him."

"It's none of my business, but it seems to me you'll have to find another nanny."

"Yes, that's the simplest solution. I've told Reveca to give me as much notice as possible if she decides to leave so I can find someone else. She's young and very pretty, and I think it's only a matter of time until she finds someone who sweeps her off her feet."

Clay asked Quenneville directly, "You mean someone like you."

"You always know how to get my goat, don't you? What exactly are you implying now?"

"Well, it's obvious to me that she seems to be taken by you. Was your wife aware of her attraction to you?"

"Are you trying to tie her infatuation with me to Maura's murder?"

"It wouldn't be the first time that the murder of a spouse occurred because of a husband's affair with a nanny."

"You continue to piss me off with your insinuations. Let me answer your questions before you ask them—no, I have not had an affair with Reveca. Yes, she's beautiful. Yes, Maura told me that she thought she was infatuated with me. And finally, yes, Maura insisted that we should fire her and hire someone not so young and pretty."

"In other words, your wife was jealous of your relationship with Reveca. Why didn't she go ahead and fire her?"

"Because we didn't have someone who would replace her. Confidentially, we held interviews with several other nannies, and even Maura realized we couldn't find someone as good for Adam as Reveca. As I told Maura, Reveca is years younger than me. If she's infatuated with me, it would pass quickly. I'm almost old enough to be her father."

"Maura was jealous of your relationship with Reveca, is that what you're saying?"

"Yes, admittedly it's a nice ego-boost to think a young, beautiful woman is infatuated with me, but like I told Maura, I am more of a father figure to Reveca, not her lover."

"What about your relationship with Alys Chapman?"

"There you go again. We didn't have a relationship. She was my patient. That's all. You're the second person in the last twenty-four hours to imply that I had an affair with Alys."

"Who was the other?"

"It's not important because it's not true. It's time for you to leave, Detective."

"One last question, do you know if your wife had an affair with Max Bruder?"

"First, like I told you, I don't know who the hell Max Bruder is. And secondly, Maura was not that kind of person. She was happy in our relationship."

Clay heard shuffling outside the kitchen and realized Reveca had been eavesdropping on their conversation.

CHAPTER 36

Clay drove to his house and was greeted by Mackenzie, who was dressed casually in blue jeans and a tight red sweater that showed off her extraordinary figure. The two hugged tightly, with Clay's intentions obvious to Mackenzie after only a few seconds. She playfully pushed him away. "You are so bad. Not now. Maybe after dinner, if you're a good boy."

Clay pretended to pout. "Okay, so what are we having for dinner?"

"Broiled chicken breasts with olive oil and garlic seasoning, and side dishes of mashed potatoes and green beans. I hope you will enjoy."

"Where did you get all the ingredients? I didn't have a lot in the house."

"I tried to be creative."

He took a bite of the chicken and savored the taste. "Wow, excellent. Not only are you beautiful, you're a great cook. I couldn't ask for anything more. If you were better in bed, I might have to ask you to marry me."

"Ha, very funny." She took a bite. "The dish is pretty good, isn't it?"

Clay tilted his head toward her. "Was the chicken in the freezer. I don't remember having any in the fridge."

She purposely avoided answering him and asked, "How did your interview go with Gardner?"

"I think I'm making some headway with him. We'll find out if he is capable of standing trial when the forensic psychologist determines his mental health. I discussed Gardner's status with Captain Ellsworth and the DA, and everyone agrees that he needs to be evaluated to determine if he should stand trial. He's been placed in a psychiatric unit at the Behavioral Health Institute to determine his competency."

"Good. I feel safe now."

Clay asked, "Was the chicken in the freezer?"

Mackenzie answered irrelevantly, "How about your interview with Quenneville?"

Clay continued to enjoy his meal. "Yeah, it was good."

"Well, tell me about it."

"I'll fill you in later. Tell me, did something happen today when I was gone? You're acting strange. I've asked you twice now where you got the ingredients for our meal, and you haven't answered me yet."

Mackenzie dropped her head and avoided looking at him.

"Can't you simply enjoy the meal?"

"Okay, you're holding out on me. What did you do today? Did you order this meal from a restaurant?"

"Kind of."

"What do you mean by 'kind of'?"

"Okay, yes I ordered it from an Italian restaurant called Roberto's."

"I can't believe you went against my very specific instructions not to show yourself to anyone. My house is no longer safe for you."

"Oh, you're getting carried away. We're fine. The delivery guy was a teenager, hardly a threat to me."

"Who else did you have contact with today?"

"No one."

"Mackenzie, I know you well enough to know when you're lying. Who else did you have contact with?"

"It was no big deal. I called the security office at the Emerson and talked to the guard there."

"John Paul? Why? My God, you are incorrigible."

"Clay, you're being unfair to me. I still haven't gotten over the trauma of being assaulted at the hotel. We don't know for sure if it was or wasn't Gardner who tried to kidnap me. If it wasn't Gardner then someone is still out there hell-bent on killing me. All I wanted John Paul to do was email me the tapes so I could study them myself."

"Did he?"

"Yes, but first I had to convince him you would approve of him sending the tapes. I told him I was staying at your house and to promise me he wouldn't tell anyone that I was here."

"So now John Paul knows."

"Yes, but he promised to keep it to himself."

"Apart from the security guard and the food delivery guy, who else did you have any contact with?"

"No one else, I swear."

"After you viewed the surveillance tapes who did you think was your assailant at Emerson?"

"I couldn't tell. It might have been Gardner but I'm not sure about that. As I told you at the hotel, Gardner and Quenneville have the same kind of build. And speaking of similar builds, so does Jeremy Voit. I was hoping you could watch the tape with me and maybe together we could determine who my assailant was."

"You promised me that you would not intrude in my investigation, but you did anyway. Now you want me to watch the tapes to see if we could come up with the guy's identity. Why shouldn't I be unhappy with you?"

"Will you forgive me for what I did? I knew I was wrong, but I really thought I could help you."

"No matter what you promise, you'll just do it again. I think the solution is to get you to another safe house under the watch of cops who won't take any guff from you."

"Oh, come on, I promise to be good. I don't want to leave you, for a lot of reasons. Please. This is reason number one." Mackenzie got up from her chair and sat on his lap. She ran her hands through his hair and smothered him with kisses, unbuttoned his shirt, stroked his chest and kissed his neck. "If you let me stay, I can show you reason number two." She felt him getting aroused.

"My God, I thought I was bad, but you are unconscionable."

She kissed him.

"You're killing me. Now stop."

"I can't and I won't."

"Dammit, you win, you are a devil."

He lifted her from his lap and with one powerful motion carried her into the bedroom, lowered her onto his bed, and watched as she removed her clothes. He slowly kissed every inch of her bare skin.

She watched him as he tore off his clothes, then she pulled him down on top of her, skin on skin. They stroked each other until their excitement erupted in incredible orgasms.

They stayed in bed, bodies entwined for several minutes, softly caressing each other. "We should finish dinner, shouldn't we, or no?" she asked.

"Not quite yet."

"You're ready already, aren't you?"

"Yes, how about you?"

"I can't wait."

They had intense sex again and collapsed after they climaxed.

She said, "You are wearing me out. Can we please check out the surveillance videos?"

"Okay, but you should know that I'm not happy with you regardless of how good you are in bed. I told you not to leave my house, not to talk to anyone, and what did you do? The total opposite. How can I ever trust you?"

"I'll grow on you."

The two sat down in front of her laptop to view the surveillance tapes, but after more than an hour, they could not determine who the individual was who had tried to kidnap her.

She said, "This is the second time I've gone through the tapes, and I still don't recognize who it is."

"Neither do I," Clay said. "But one thing is curious. The maid was right in the middle of the attempted kidnapping, but the surveillance tape of the fourth floor shows she never said a thing or tried to intervene in any way."

Mackenzie said, "Yes, that was odd. I remember thinking she was going to shout or do something, but she never did."

"I'm going to bring her in to question her about that. And while I'm at it, there's something suspicious about her relationship with Steve Aldrich, too. I'm going to bring them both in. I want to review the details of their encounter with Maura Quenneville at Albertsons and what if any contact they had with Alys."

CHAPTER 37

Clay instructed Emily and Steve to be at police headquarters at two o'clock that afternoon to be interviewed.

Upon their arrival, Emily spoke for both of them. "Why us?"

"First off, I want to talk with you about the kidnapping attempt of Mackenzie Stanton that occurred at the hotel yesterday. I want to know if you can shed any light on who the assailant was. And then I want to ask you about Maura Quenneville and Alys Chapman's murders."

Steve said, "Emily and I have spoken with you before, and we gave you all the information we knew about the two women. I, for one, do not know anything about the second woman, Alys Chapman."

Clay explained, "Frankly, my investigation into both murders is at a dead end. I want to start from scratch with you and learn about your argument with Maura Quenneville. I will interview each of you separately so I can have each person's individual recollection of the events with her. Then I want to question you about Alys Chapman and what contact you might have had with her. Because you may have had encounters with either or both women, relevant facts may emerge from our interview that will assist me in solving both homicides. I believe one or both of you saw or might know who killed the two women, but in the words of a friend of mine, your subconscious has not released the information that would help identify the killer. Perhaps our interviews can help you release details about that person."

Emily, I'll start with you first."

Clay escorted Emily to an interview room.

She was worried. "Am I a suspect or something?"

"No, as I said earlier, I've asked you to be here for a fact-finding interview. Yesterday, a man tried to kidnap a woman by the name of Mackenzie Stanton. She was a guest at the Emerson Hotel.

"We were able to track the kidnapping attempt on the hotel's surveillance cameras. And what we saw was the attempted abduction occurred when you were cleaning the room only three rooms away. You did not seem to be concerned about what was occurring. You didn't do anything to help her. You didn't cry out. You didn't confront the attacker. Why didn't you try to help?"

"I don't know what you're talking about. I work with earbuds in and listen to music all day because what I do is boring, and that helps me get through the day. Most likely I couldn't hear what was going on. I do remember you tapped me on the shoulder and asked if I knew where someone was, but that's all I remember."

Clay believed she was telling the truth and couldn't be blamed for not being aware of the attempted abduction.

"Let's switch gears. Let's talk about Maura Quenneville. Did your argument become so overheated that your acrimony developed into a homicide?"

"What is acrimony?"

"Anger. Were you and Steve so angry toward Mrs. Quenneville that you plotted to kill her?"

"No, I did not. Can I go now?"

"The answer is no. Not until I say you can go. Were you a party to her murder?"

"What party? I didn't go to any party with her. What are you talking about?"

Clay couldn't help but chuckle. "I don't mean were you at a party with that woman. I mean, did you assist Steve in murdering Maura Quenneville? Or did Steve assist you?"

"No, I did not. And Steve didn't either."

"Where were you the morning that Mrs. Quenneville was murdered?"

"Hell, I don't know, probably at work or driving to work. I don't know when she was killed. You can check with the Emerson to see what time I was there that morning."

"Do you take the Breeze Canyon Road to get to work?"

She hesitated before she answered. "Yes."

"Were you on the road when Mrs. Quenneville was killed? She was killed sometime Sunday morning."

"I was probably at work already."

"You've explained about the issue you had with Maura Quenneville in our previous discussions. Let me ask you again, did the extent of the problem you had with her escalate to threats against her?"

"If you mean did I threaten to kill her, the answer is no. I did not threaten her. And if you mean did I kill her, the answer is no again. She was a pain in the ass, but that's life. I mean, I run into bad guys almost every day, especially in the kind of jobs I have."

"What do you mean the kind of jobs?"

"You know what I do. I'm a maid half the time and a grocery store cashier the other half. Nothing sexy about what I do."

"I understand you do excellent work at both jobs."

"The problem with those jobs is that sometimes I get my share of malcontents and difficult people."

"Like Maura Quenneville."

"Yes, she was one of the biggest jerks I ever had to deal with. Maybe the worst! She was rude, rich, and a bitch. She thought she was the center of the universe. She's someone who probably got whatever she wanted whenever she wanted it, no matter if she hurt other people in the process. When she barged into Steve at Albertsons, she made such a scene and purposely embarrassed him in front of me and a lot of other customers."

Clay said, "Yes, he told me he was embarrassed. In your view, was Steve embarrassed enough, let's say mad enough, that he would have harmed her if the opportunity presented itself? Do you think he took revenge against her?"

"I don't know the answer to that."

"Let's talk about how Steve reacted to the news that Mrs. Quenneville was killed."

"I don't think he was sorry. He felt she was a mean-spirited woman. You know how people ask, 'Why do bad things happen to good people?' Well, she wasn't good people. There was nothing good about her. She was bad people, and bad things happen to bad people, too. I mean, Steve wasn't doing summersaults, but he thought she probably got what she deserved. That's how much he had been embarrassed by her."

"How about you? Did you feel the same way when you learned Mrs. Quenneville was killed? Did you believe she got what she deserved?"

Emily looked away from Clay for a few seconds and when she looked back to him her eyes were narrowed. "I wasn't happy she died, but I wasn't unhappy either. It's like when a judge sentences a person to be executed for killing someone, it don't make no never mind if death is by electric chair or by hanging. It's an eye for an eye, a tooth for a tooth that matters."

"That's a pretty heavy analogy for an argument that began in a grocery store," Clay said. "I mean, you're comparing a rude customer with a criminal who dies in the electric chair. That's over the top, don't you think?"

"You think I'm being politically insensitive, don't you? Well, I don't care. It's my opinion, right or wrong. I bet you've investigated Mrs. Quenneville's reputation and found she was a bitch to a lot of people. Probably a few folks would have gladly thrown the switch on her day of reckoning."

"Do you think Steve killed Mrs. Quenneville?"

"I don't know. He's a sweet and kindhearted guy. I like him a lot. But did he kill that woman? I don't have a clue."

"What about Alys Chapman, the woman who was killed in the Emerson parking lot? Where were you the night she was killed?"

"Probably asleep. I put in long hours every day at two jobs, so I go to bed early most nights. And besides, what reason would I have had to kill her? I didn't even know her."

Clay asked, "Do you think Steve had a reason to kill her?"

"You'll have to ask him. I can't imagine why he would have had any contact with her."

"What we know about the two homicides is that the same person killed both women."

"If you think that was me, you're barking up the wrong tree. I didn't kill nobody."

Clay said, "Steve admittedly is a sensitive guy. From what you've told me, might he have let his anger get the best of him, and that led him to kill Mrs. Quenneville as a way to impress you?"

"Well, he likes me I know, but would he kill for me? I don't think so."

"Why is it that both you and Steve denied you were in a relationship?"

Emily looked away from Clay. "I don't know what you're talking about."

"I believe you've been honest with me, so please don't lie to me now. Both of you deny having a relationship with each other, and yet I've spotted you and Steve together acting pretty chummy the last several days. Why deny that?"

She shook her head and chewed on her upper lip for a few seconds before she answered. "You're right. We've been reluctant to show that we liked each other because we thought you would try to tie our relationship to Mrs. Quenneville's murder. That's exactly what you're trying to do, ain't it?"

"I'll ask you again, did you kill her?"

"Absolutely not."

"Did Steve kill her?"

"You'll have to ask him."

CHAPTER 38

Emily and Steve bumped knuckles as they passed in the hallway that led to the interview room.

Clay pointed to the video camera mounted in the corner of the room. "Your interview will be recorded."

Steve said with obvious irritation, "What you told Emily and me was a lie, wasn't it? You believe we had something to do with that woman's murder, and that's the real reason you brought us in here, isn't it?"

"As I said, I'm at a standstill in my investigation. So yes, I'm looking at everyone who might have had a reason to harm Maura Quenneville and Alys Chapman."

Steve said, "I haven't missed a day of work since the day I was hired, and I don't want to end that record now. I told my postmaster you wanted to interview me but to hold my mail until I got back. There was no need to get a sub for me. I told him I'll get my route done."

"That's impressive of you to want to do your job. What did your boss say?"

"He said he would put my deliveries on hold as long as I got back at a reasonable hour, so let's get this over with."

"Steve, you told me about the argument you had with Maura Quenneville at the grocery store, but I want you to tell me again exactly what happened."

Steve recited the details of his encounter with Maura and did not vary from his earlier account when Clay first visited him at the post office.

Clay said, "I've seen you and Emily together several times now. You and she seem to be close. Why did you lie to me about the two of you saying you didn't know each other?"

"Truthfully, we thought you were going to try to connect us to that Quenneville lady's murder if you saw us together because of what happened at Albertsons."

"Why would I do that?"

"Because there had been such a ruckus at Albertsons and then a week and a half later that lady was murdered."

"Are you so much in love with Emily that you would want to harm someone who was mean to Emily, like Maura Quenneville was?"

Steve shook his head. "You think I would murder someone like that bitch? Hell, no. I can't believe you're asking me if I murdered someone because Emily and I were in a fight with her."

"Not accusing you, just looking to see how far you would go to protect your girlfriend."

"I'd go a long way to protect her, but I'm not a killer. I draw a line."

"You'll be able to get to work in a short while if you cooperate with me. Start off by telling me a little about yourself. You said you've never missed one day of work?"

"That's right, never, not one day in twenty-five years. I always wanted to be a mailman. It's been my dream job—it really has been. Honestly. I get paid well, I have a great pension, and I like the people I service on my route. The postmaster general himself announced my name in the post office monthly newsletter as someone who has never missed a day of work in twenty-five years. I was the only carrier in the entire U-S-of-A who could boast about that. He called me the Cal Ripken of mail carriers."

Clay nodded that he was impressed. "Twenty-five years. That's amazing."

"Yep. I'm proud of that, but you know I almost had my streak broken a couple of weeks ago. I had an auto accident on my route. My first-ever accident, and it wasn't even my fault. A car cut me off when I was driving my postal truck, and I ended up in a drainage ditch on the side of a road. I got banged up, but I was not about to miss work. And I didn't. I was lucky."

"You have a very impressive work ethic. Was the guy who cut you off texting or what?"

"No, I think he cut me off intentionally, and I'm pretty sure it was my next-door neighbor."

"Seriously? Why would your neighbor run you off the road?"

"Because we've had a running feud about his damn dog. It barks day and night. Keeps me awake."

"Was your neighbor Max Bruder?"

"Yeah, that's him. How did you know that? And what do you mean, 'was' my neighbor?"

"Are you aware your neighbor is deceased?"

"No kidding, he's dead? How? What happened to him?"

Clay lied. "Actually, he died of a self-inflicted gunshot."

"Is that why you're interviewing me? Do you think I killed him or something?"

"I discovered him dead because he failed to show up for his job at the Emerson Hotel, and I was asked to do a well-visit to see if he was okay."

"That explains why I saw cop cars over there. I thought it was about that damn dog and his constant barking."

"Why didn't you file a complaint about the dog if he barked as much as you said he did?"

"I did. That made matters worse, and that's probably why Bruder ran me off the road. The township fined him three hundred dollars for violating the noise ordinance. When he found out it was me that filed the complaint, he waved his gun at me and threaten to shoot me. It wasn't a coincidence that someone ran me off the road afterward—it was him, no question about it. Frankly, I'm not sorry about him dying. By the way, what happened to his dog? I don't hear him barking anymore."

"I had animal control take him away."

"Thanks. I'm finally getting some sleep."

"So you live in that rancher next to Max's house? You keep a nice property."

"The problem is the market value of my home has plummeted because Max didn't take care of his property. There was always stuff in his yard. Once he put his lawn tractor up on blocks in his front yard, just to piss me off. You've been there so obviously you could see for yourself what a slob he was. I know he served in Iraq and Afghanistan and came back with PTSD. And I'm sorry about that. I really do appreciate that he was in the service, but his yard was always a mess, junk all over the place, rusting machinery, his lawn was always overgrown with weeds."

"Tell me what else you know about him? Were you ever in his house?"

"No, and I had no interest in hanging out with him."

"Do you remember over the past couple of days if you saw anyone visiting him?"

"He had a visitor recently at night that set the damn dog barking again. And of course, there were a few cop cars there the last couple of days."

"Do you remember the make of any car that was at his place during the last few nights?"

"No, not one that I could identify in the dark."

"The bartender at the Emerson said he was there one time and recognized that Max maybe was a hoarder."

"He sure was."

"I thought you said you were never in his house."

Steve realized he misspoke and tried to cover for his gaffe. "I wasn't ever in his house, but occasionally he would leave his garage door open, and I could see what a junk bin his house really was." Steve attempted a bit of humor. "There was so much junk in that garage he probably died in there because he couldn't find his way out."

Clay stared at him. "Actually, I found him dead in his garage."

"No way, I was only joking about finding him dead in the garage."

"Is that so? Were you just joking?"

CHAPTER 39

Captain Ellsworth called Clay into his office to learn about the status of the Quenneville and Chapman homicide investigations. The captain was just back from a two-week vacation with his wife.

"I hope you and Debbie had a nice time."

"We did, thanks. Now fill me in. I understand we had another murder in my absence."

"Yes, a guy by the name of Max Bruder was the victim. He was a maintenance employee at the Emerson Hotel and we're not sure, but somehow, he ties into the murders of Maura Quenneville and Alys Chapman." Clay described in detail that he discovered Max dead in his garage and that the forensics team concluded he had been murdered, and the murder was rigged to appear to be a suicide. Forensics discovered a .38 caliber pistol and a cache of jewelry when they searched his house and garage. They ran ballistics tests on the pistol and learned it was the same weapon that was used to kill Quenneville, Chapman, and Bruder. But we don't know yet what the motive is that links the three victims."

"What about the jewelry?"

"Most likely stolen from the Quenneville home six months earlier in a burglary. We're working with the insurance company to determine if that's the case."

"You said the murder was rigged to appear to be a suicide."

"Yes. Forensics said Max's prints were on the pistol, but the prints seemed to have been forced on the gun by the killer after Bruder was dead. The murderer left a suicide note in the form of a prayer card, but Dan Carton's team believes the note was bogus and is convinced he was murdered. I agree with Dan."

"What did the note say?"

Clay pulled his notepad from his jacket and read, "*I killed m.q. and a.c. They do not deserve my grief. I am not sorry. Forgive me my sins and through the mercy of God may their souls rest in peace!!!* The initials obviously stand for Maura Quenneville and Alys Chapman."

Ellsworth surmised, "Is the killer a fake religious nut trying to mislead you by covering up his heinous crimes, or is he really into religion?"

"I don't know, but we've learned he left prayer cards at Bruder's and Alys Chapman's murder scene too."

"Who owned the pistol that was used to kill Bruder?"

"We don't know yet. The serial number had been filed off, but forensics is trying to identify the number. I should find out shortly."

Ellsworth said, "In addition to the murder of Bruder, I understand there was an attempted kidnapping of a woman by the name of Mackenzie Stanton. Who is she?"

"She was Alys Chapman's best friend. She flew to Santa Fe from Santa Barbara to visit with me because she said she knew who killed Chapman and wanted to help me capture the killer."

"Who does she think the murderer is?"

"Quenneville, but she doesn't have any evidence. And to further complicate matters a guy by the name of Gardner Hicks is the person who has tried to abduct Mackenzie."

"Hicks is Alys' ex-boyfriend, and Hicks thinks Mackenzie convinced Alys to break up with him."

Ellsworth leaned back in his chair and exhaled deeply. "This is beginning to sound like a soap opera."

Clay smiled at the analogy. "You're right, but there's more. I need to explain about Mackenzie. I first met her in Santa Barbara when I was there to look for evidence in Chapman's homicide. Hicks first attempted to abduct Mackenzie at the Emerson Hotel, where she had been staying. When she escaped from Hicks, I realized we needed to get her out of harm's way. Since it was too late in the day to try to work out the details of her staying at a police-authorized safe house, I had her stay in my house where I could safeguard her."

Ellsworth tilted his head at Clay. The captain was a by-the-book cop, but he let Clay's safe-house arrangement fly without argument. "I'll let that fly for now, but go on," he said. "Just be careful."

Clay nodded. "I will be."

"Where do we stand now?"

"Captain, this saga continues to grow exponentially. Sometime after midnight last night, Hicks broke into my house, armed with a pistol trying again to abduct Mackenzie. Fortunately, I was able to subdue him. I had him booked for attempted murder, assault and kidnapping this morning."

"Does Stanton still think Quenneville killed Alys, even though it's Hicks who has been after her?"

"Yes, she does. Here's another twist. When I questioned Hicks, I couldn't make heads or tails what he was saying. He made no sense whatsoever. Either he was pretending he was mentally ill, or he's schizophrenic. With your permission I will talk with the D. A. about petitioning the judge to have Hicks examined by a forensic psychologist to determine if he's fit to stand trial."

Clay's cell phone rang. He removed it from his jacket

pocket. "Sir, it's Dan Carton. He promised to call me right away if forensics learned who the owner of the pistol was. I should take it."

"Go ahead."

Clay asked, "Dan, what did you come up with?" After a few seconds of silence Clay nodded, smiled, and told Ellsworth. "The pistol belongs to Doctor Ronald Quenneville. Maybe Mackenzie Stanton is right after all."

CHAPTER 40

The captain summarized the status of the case. "This all started when the ME found a slug that killed Maura Quenneville. Since then, we've had two additional homicides and two attempted abductions. Since Hicks is in custody and being examined for his mental competency, your focus seems to be on Quenneville as the owner of the murder weapon. What do you think his motive would have been to kill both his wife and his lover?"

"I've learned that the New Mexico State Medical Board has the right to suspend a doctor or revoke a physician's license to practice medicine if it is determined that the doctor had sexual relations with his or her patient. And that applies even if the affair is deemed consensual.

"A few days ago, I contacted the medical board and inquired if Quenneville had ever been cited for sexual abuse with a patient. I was told that an anonymous complaint had been filed against him several months ago. The complaint stated that he was having an illicit affair with his patient, Alys Chapman. The board questioned Quenneville and Alys, but since the complaint provided no corroborative evidence, the complaint was dismissed without prejudice.

"Here's my theory: Maura devoted so many years of her life to have her husband become a surgeon—she was selfless on his behalf. When she believed he had forsaken her and taken up with a younger woman, it probably was more than she could stomach. I think it may very well have been Maura Quenneville who filed the complaint with the medical board. I also think it was more than a coincidence that she and Alys Chapman were killed a few weeks later. I think those events were connected. Both women were shot with the same gun. It would seem we have the motive behind the murders of the women, and that was to keep them quiet about his affairs."

"Do you know for a fact that the doctor was actually having an affair with Chapman, or are you hypothesizing so you can create a motive?"

"I don't have anything concrete."

Ellsworth was skeptical. "So let me get this straight: you and Stanton think Quenneville killed Alys Chapman, but you have no proof. No physical evidence at the crime scene, no DNA, no fingerprints, nothing, only your intuition. And you can't tie this guy, Bruder, into the killings. You have three homicides, and no link except the same gun was used to kill all three individuals. You see where I'm going with this? At the very least, you would need to get Quenneville to admit he had an affair with Chapman. Short of that, you'd be hard-pressed to charge Quenneville and then convince the D. A. to take the case to trial."

Despite her unwise interference in the murder investigation, Mackenzie believed that Quenneville was the killer. If she could get Quenneville to admit he had an affair with Alys, it would provide Clay with the motive to charge the doctor with murder.

She thought of a way to have Quenneville admit his affair, but she would need Clay's help to pull off the sting. "I have an idea how to get Quenneville to admit he had an affair with Alys, but I need your help."

Clay was not forgiving. "I don't want to hear it."

"I know you're upset with me about meeting with Quenneville, and I apologize for doing that without your permission, but if you help me, I know we can get him to admit his affair."

"Mackenzie, what you did was give him a reason to believe that we're investigating him. He will be super cautious now."

"I understand, but please hear me out."

"You are incorrigible. I said no."

She pouted. "If you listen to me and think it's a bad idea then I'll back off, I promise. But at least hear me out."

"Alright, go ahead, what is it?"

"I can tell him that I decided to let him see the diary and tell him we should do it over a drink so I could get to know him better. I'm sure he'll agree to a rendezvous."

"That's your idea? No, it's too dangerous."

"It won't be dangerous if I use the diary as my security chip. He's not going to hurt me. He wants that diary, and he won't rest until he has it. But here's where I need your help."

"To do what?"

"To back me up. If you can arrange to have me wired, you can monitor our encounter and if things go bad, you can intervene."

Clay shook his head. "No, I'm not doing that."

She continued to badger Clay. "What do you have to lose?"

"No, I said."

"Come on. Do this, and if we can get him to admit to an affair, then we have his motive why he killed his wife, and Alys, too."

"No. Now drop it."

"I'm not going to drop it. I know this will work. All you have to do is get approval to wire me so we can record his confession. I'll do the rest. Please, let's try it."

"Is this all about your *gift* again?"

"Yes, I'm sure this will work, and if it doesn't work, there's no harm. It can't make things any worse."

Clay shook his head. "I don't know what to do with you. Okay, dammit. But you'll listen to me and do exactly what I say, or I'll blow up the encounter immediately. Got it?"

She hugged him and looked him in his eyes." Thanks, Clay. You'll see this will work."

"Okay, listen. I still need to get the okay from my captain to wire you and a warrant from the D. A. so don't count your chickens yet."

Mackenzie said, "I'm not worried. You'll get what you need, I'm sure of it. Afterward when we've got all the necessary authorizations, I'll call Quenneville and arrange to meet him in his office after it closes."

CHAPTER 41

Clay hid a miniature radio transmitter in Mackenzie's purse and had her test it out. He would be listening from his car in the parking lot outside of Quenneville's office.

The scene was set. At a few minutes before five o'clock, Mackenzie began to play her part. She entered Quenneville's office dressed in sculpted black slacks, five-inch-high heels, and a white silk blouse. Clay was in the parking lot in his car, listening.

Quenneville's receptionist asked Mackenzie if she could assist her. "Yes, please tell Doctor Quenneville that I'm here. My name is Mackenzie Stanton."

"He's busy right now and we're closing in a few minutes. Is there anything I can help you with?"

"I'm a friend of Dr. Quenneville. Please tell him I'm here. He promised to take me out to dinner tonight."

The receptionist examined Mackenzie suspiciously but buzzed Quenneville.

He responded, "Tell her to wait for me in the lobby. I will be a few minutes yet. I'll be out as soon as I can work my way through some paperwork. You can call it a day. Lock up for the night. I'll get the lights and AC when I leave. See you in the morning."

Ten minutes later, Quenneville appeared in the lobby. "Hello, Mackenzie. I'm surprised, but actually I'm pleased to see you."

"Doctor Quenneville, I wanted to take you up on your offer of a drink before I left to go back to Santa Barbara. I have the diary. I thought you might want to have it." She smiled softly. "I'll show you over a drink, and dinner."

Clay was able to listen in on their conversation.

"Okay, give me a few seconds to wash up and we can leave."

Mackenzie cooed, "You know, the truth is, I have been jealous of you and Alys for quite a while. I don't want to sound heartless, but now that she is out of the picture, I felt it was okay for you and me to get to know each other, if you know what I mean?"

"As long as you're not a patient, I think we'll be okay. You know I've got to be super-careful. A complaint has already been sent to the state board about me."

"I understand, but we're just going out for a drink, and ..." she paused for several seconds.

"And what?"

"I was hoping if you would advise me if I can have my breasts enhanced, like you did for Alys."

He stared at her chest for several seconds. "I'm not sure why you would want larger breasts. Alys' breasts were very small, while you certainly do not have a problem with yours. In any event, you'll need to contact my office to set up an appointment if you want to consider surgery."

"Oh, for God's sake, can't you examine me now, so I don't have to come back for an examination? Then we could get that drink you promised me."

"You are persistent, aren't you?"

"Yes," she smiled.

"Okay, let's go to my office. I'll get you a hospital gown."

"You don't have to do that. It looks like everyone's gone for the day. But if you're uncomfortable giving me an exam here, we can always go back to my hotel room." She suggested her proposal in a sensual whisper. "I'm all in for an exciting rendezvous. As you can tell, I'm not shy. I'm not like Alys, she was always understated. And I know how to keep a secret. I don't do diaries like Alys did."

"Let's stop bringing up Alys' name. I know you and she were friends and I have good memories of her, but unfortunately, she's deceased now. I'm starting to get cold feet about meeting like this."

"You're making me feel anxious. Are you bailing out on me?"

"No, not at all. I'm just being cautious."

Quenneville flicked the lobby lights off and escorted Mackenzie back to his office. He began his foreplay with a compliment. "I love women. Always have and always will. But you, my dear, stand alone in the pantheon of beauty."

"Wow, that's poetic and a heck of an ego boost, but I bet you say that to all your girlfriends, don't you?"

"Not exactly everyone, and I don't have girlfriends, plural. I don't play the field. I feel I can be honest with you. At one point, I was going to divorce my wife so Alys and I could get married. Neither one of us wanted it to be only a one-night stand. It was one thing to enjoy the excitement of an affair. And our affair was always exciting, but I thought it could be more than that. Alys wanted to get married, and although I wasn't ready for that kind of a move, I told her when my wife was out of the picture, I would definitely consider marriage."

"What do you mean, 'out of the picture'?"

"I mean Maura and I were working toward a divorce. We both wanted to move on past our bad marriage."

"Was Alys aware of what you and your wife were planning?"

"Yes. I told her everything. You know the sad thing about her death is, she had it all. I really did love her. It was a shame that she was killed."

Without asking, Quenneville got close to Mackenzie and began to unbutton her blouse. She was wearing a bra. "You understand since you're not a patient of mine that what we're doing is perfectly okay."

"I know."

He placed her blouse neatly on the chair next to his desk and reached around her to unclip her bra.

His breathing quickened. "You are very pretty."

She pushed him away teasingly and hid a grimace. "Did I tell you how jealous I was of Alys? You two had it all. All she ever talked about was the two of you. You shouldn't be upset about what was in her diary. You hung the moon and told it to shine. She wrote about how you couldn't get enough sex. To tell you the truth, I'm pretty good in bed too. You won't be disappointed." She rubbed her tongue across her upper lip in a slow, sensual way.

Quenneville let out a long breath. "Whew."

Mackenzie giggled.

Quenneville was beside himself. "We were good in bed, that's for sure. I can't wait to read about us."

Suddenly, Mackenzie changed her demeanor completely and backed away from the doctor. "Every time I think we can talk about you and me, you bring up that damn diary. This is ridiculous." She snatched her blouse from the chair and quickly put it on. "I've had it with this charade. I'm leaving."

He was perplexed. "What's the matter? What did I say? So, I had an affair with Alys. I didn't think you cared."

"Did your wife know about you and Alys?"

"My wife's dead."

"You didn't kill her, did you?"

"Don't be ridiculous. No, I didn't kill her. Why are you leaving?"

"Because this doesn't feel right. The only thing you want is that damn diary. I can't go through with this. I can't do it. I feel like you're using me. It's not about me, it's about the diary, isn't it?"

"I thought you said when you came here that you were going to give me Alys' diary. Listen to me, I need to have that diary. I don't want the police to find out about it. They will think I had something to do with her murder."

"I don't know why they would think that. So, you had an affair. You said you didn't kill her."

Quenneville became defensive. "My wife and I were in a sexless marriage, so I strayed with Alys. And then Maura was killed. But I didn't kill her."

Mackenzie got what she schemed for—acknowledgement from Quenneville that he had an affair with Alys. It was going to give Clay a motive to work with.

She walked toward the door of his office in a huff.

Quenneville shouted after her, "Wait a second."

"No. I don't want to talk to you."

"I don't know what the hell happened. All I said was that I wanted to have the diary."

"No thanks. I'll hold onto it for now. I see you really aren't interested in me, are you? It was always about Alys and the diary, wasn't it? I know, I don't measure up to Alys, do I? What a mistake I made. I'm leaving." She turned away from him, closed his office door, and hurried into the lobby.

Quenneville followed and grabbed her arm.

"Let go of me. And open this door. I realize now I made a terrible mistake thinking I might want to have sex with you."

Clay recorded the entire conversation. It was time for him to intervene. He pulled up to the front of the office building, flashed his headlights, and reached across the passenger seat to open the door for Mackenzie.

"How did I do?" she asked.

"Good. Very good." Then he sarcastically said, "The part about you being good in bed was a little bit of an exaggeration, but you almost had me convinced."

She responded in turn, "You are sooo bad. Well, the truth is I had to exaggerate since I couldn't tell the truth about how bad you are."

"Touché."

* * *

Quenneville stood at the front door and watched as Mackenzie got into Clay's car.

"Well, I'll be a sonofabitch. That's Bryce's car."

CHAPTER 42

An hour after Mackenzie's sting, Clay called Quenneville. It was after six o'clock.

"This is Detective Bryce."

"Was that you outside my office a little while ago? What do you want now, Bryce?"

"I need to talk to you about Alys Chapman's death."

"Again?"

"So talk."

"Face to face."

"I'm on my way home. Call me tomorrow."

"I am advising you to change course and come to police headquarters. I'll be waiting for you. When you get here, ask for me. And if you're not here in half an hour, I will put out an APB on you and notify the media that you are a suspect in the death of your wife."

Clay heard Quenneville mutter and curse under his breath.

"That's blackmail, you bastard!"

* * *

Clay reviewed information from the burglary at the Quenneville home prior to the doctor's arrival. He learned the jewelry found in Max's garage was the jewelry stolen from the Quenneville residence, but the case was unsolved, not unusual since most burglaries do not end in arrest or conviction.

Detective Donald Arnoldson, since retired, was the investigator in the Quenneville burglary case. He had interviewed Doctor Quenneville, Maura Quenneville and Reveca Gabova, the Quenneville's nanny. There was no obvious suspect. It appeared the burglar or burglars probably entered through an unlocked rear sliding glass door. Entry was not forced. Clay was surprised to learn from Detective Arnoldson's report that Max Bruder was not interviewed, nor was his name mentioned in any context dealing with the burglary.

Max most likely was not the burglar. And although the pistol was discovered in his garage, it was unlikely that Max killed the two women with that pistol. His purported suicide had proven to be fallacious. Max was murdered, and the .38 most likely had been planted in Max's hand by his killer."

Twenty minutes later, Clay was informed that Quenneville had arrived.

"Have him escorted to interview room number one. I'll be there shortly."

Clay went to the room adjacent to the interview room to observe the doctor's reaction to being brought in for questioning. It was quickly obvious that Quenneville was not happy. He stomped around the room while he waited for Clay.

When Clay arrived, he motioned for Quenneville to sit down.

Quenneville was irate. "What the hell do you want from me now?"

"First off, I want to inform you that your interview will be recorded."

"Yeah, okay. Let's get this over with. I'll ask you again, what do you want from me?"

Clay glared at Quenneville. "Let's understand our roles—I do the asking, you do the answering, not the other way around."

"Yeah, I get it, so ask." Quenneville was agitated. His eyes darted from Clay to the video recorder, to the two-way mirror on the wall facing him, then back again to Clay.

"I am going to read you the Miranda warning." When he finished, he asked, "Do you understand your rights?"

"You consider me a suspect, is that right?"

"Do you want to call your lawyer?"

"You tell me. Do I need a lawyer?"

"You have to be the judge of that."

"Let's get started. If I feel I need a lawyer, you'll be the first to know."

Clay glowered at the doctor. "Let me start by asking you about the burglary at your house. It was about six months ago, right? Tell me what happened."

"Short and sweet. We were burglarized. I called the cops. They came in. They looked through the house to make sure the burglars were not still there. Afterward, a detective came in. He asked me a bunch of questions so he could file a report. Then he asked me to put together a list of everything that had been stolen. He said he would inform the pawn shops in the city about the stolen items, and he would notify me if any of my stolen property showed up. That was all of it."

"Did any of your property ever show up?"

"No. I kind of figured nothing would. I notified my insurance company and got reimbursed for our loss. I didn't think much more about it except I decided to enhance our security system with interior motion detectors and a driveway alarm."

"What was stolen?"

"Virtually all of Maura's jewelry except what she was wearing, and my pistol was stolen too."

"Why did you have a pistol?"

"Why else? Self-defense."

Clay said, "Several weeks ago, there had been an incident at the Albertsons grocery store involving your wife, a checkout cashier, and a customer named Steve Aldrich. I interviewed Mr. Aldrich, who identified your wife as having instigated the disagreement. He described her as wearing a lot of expensive jewelry. But you said all her jewelry had been stolen."

"Yes, and I also told you that the insurance company made good on the stolen jewelry. But instead of giving Maura money to replace what was stolen, they offered her comparable jewelry. She probably was wearing some of the replacement jewelry at Albertsons that day."

"How did she react to the fact that someone had stolen her jewels?"

"She said she felt violated, and no matter how often I told her we were safe with the improved security system in place, she still worried about our safety. After the burglary, she never felt comfortable being alone in the house."

"But she wasn't alone, was she? I presume Reveca was there, right?"

"Having Reveca in the house did not calm her fear. If anything, it made her more anxious. She didn't like Reveca very much."

"I can't say for sure, maybe because she was envious of her. You've met Reveca, she's young and very pretty."

"And your wife, wasn't she pretty?"

"She was attractive, but frankly not striking like Reveca is. She insisted on having some minor plastic surgeries to smooth out her skin, trying to replicate Reveca's beauty."

"Were you the surgeon who performed surgery on her?"

"No. That's never a good idea. I had a colleague perform the surgery."

"Did Reveca feel the same way about your wife? Did she not like her very much either?"

"No, she didn't. She confided in me that Maura was always finding fault with her, snapping at her about one thing or another."

"I understand when the burglary occurred, Reveca was not in the house."

"We don't know when the burglary actually occurred, but we think it happened when Reveca and Adam were out for a walk. Reveca explained it was a nice day, so she took Adam for a walk in his stroller. She said they were out for only an hour."

"What about Maura, where was she?"

"She said she was at the Santa Fe Country Club playing golf with some other women. It was not until later that night that we learned we had been burglarized. Maura realized it first. She found all her jewelry was missing and immediately accused Reveca."

"Where was the jewelry—in plain view, or was it in a safe?"

"Hidden, but not very well. She put her jewelry on a shelf in our bedroom closet, underneath a stack of her clothes. We have a wall safe, but Maura could never get the combination right, so she always hid her jewelry under her clothes in the closet. I know it wasn't smart, but I could never get her to change her ways. The burglar obviously must have spotted her flaunting her jewelry when she went out and targeted her."

Clay nodded that he understood. "My ex-wife used to leave her rings and things in a dish on her vanity or in the kitchen or wherever she happened to be."

"I understand from the file on the case that the investigating detective questioned Reveca. Was she ever considered a suspect in the burglary?"

"No, he didn't find any basis for accusing her of the theft. Nor did I. She blamed herself that she was not in the house when the burglary took place. From that point on, she never let Adam out of her sight, thinking that the burglar might want to kidnap Adam and hold him for ransom. Her imagination ran wild for quite a while. She finally calmed down somewhat, but still is concerned about Adam's safety every day and locks every door in the house when she's alone."

"Your wife was killed sometime after the burglary? Do you think the burglary was tied to her murder in any way?"

Quenneville paused for a moment, bit his lips, and shook his head at the suggestion. Finally, he responded, "I can't see how."

"Was your pistol in the bedroom closet with your wife's jewelry?"

"No, I kept it in the drawer of my bedside table."

"When did you learn the gun was missing?"

"The night after we realized Maura's jewelry was stolen. I do crossword puzzles to relax. I had been working on a crossword puzzle and opened the drawer where I kept it and realized the pistol was missing. I notified the police the next day and gave them the serial number."

"Where was the serial number recorded?"

"On the bill of sale, and that was in my wall safe."

"You might want to know that we found your gun yesterday. And the serial number was filed off. Would you have had a reason to file it off?"

"I didn't file it off. Why would I? And if it was filed off, how do you know it was mine?"

Clay said, "Our forensics lab was able to reconstruct the number using an advanced search technique. Interestingly, forensics informed me that they also conducted ballistics tests and learned that the pistol stolen from you was used to kill your wife and Alys Chapman, too."

Quenneville stared into space, shaking his head for several seconds.

Clay broke the ice. "Let me ask you, did you use your pistol to kill your wife?"

"What?"

"Did you kill your wife? Did you shoot her when she was driving on Breeze Canyon Road?"

The doctor spit out the words. "You've got to be kidding me. What kind of question is that? No, of course not. Why would I? Is that why I'm here? Because you think I killed my wife?"

"Where did you get your pistol?"

"From a licensed gun dealer in Philadelphia when I was in residency at Jefferson Hospital. I've owned it for over twenty years, and I've never fired it, not even at a gun range."

"We've learned that the pistol was used a few days ago

in another homicide, this time to kill Max Bruder. Do you remember me asking you if Max did any handyman work for you or your wife?"

"Yes, I remember. And I told you no. However, I also said maybe Maura employed him and didn't mention it to me. She ran the household and arranged for whatever had to be done whenever it had to be done. She wasn't under any budget constraints."

"We believe Max may have stolen your gun and used the gun to kill your wife. Did you arrange for Max to kill Mrs. Quenneville?"

"What? No, I did not hire him to kill Maura. I don't know how many times I have to tell you that. No, I did not arrange to have my wife killed, and no, I did not arrange to have Alys Chapman killed."

"We know now that you were having an affair with Alys Chapman and we believe your wife may have found out about it. And if she did find out, we have reason to believe she sent an anonymous complaint to the New Mexico State Medical Board."

"You're nuts. She did not file a complaint with the medical board. Go ahead, check with them. You'll see. Maura would not have done that. Not after all the work she put into seeing me become a surgeon."

"We have checked, and we know a complaint was filed."

"Why would you jump to conclusions that it was Maura who filed the complaint?"

"Here's my theory. After all the sacrifices Maura made for you, it probably ate her up that you were having an affair with Alys Chapman. Alys was a beautiful young thing, too beautiful for you to pass up. Wasn't she? Were you thinking that you would divorce your wife and marry Alys? But then things got complicated for you, didn't they? You found out about the complaint and thought it had to be Maura who ratted on you. And if she did it once, she would do it again, and the next time not anonymously. That's when you decided you had to kill her. If she filed another complaint, your career would be over. Goodbye to your license, your income, your celebrity. It was only a matter of time, wasn't it?"

Quenneville responded angrily. "None of that is true."

"I believe it is. What did you do when she confronted you about your infidelity? Was Alys the only affair, or did Maura discover others? Your apology was not enough, was it? What did she want from you? A divorce? Did she attack you physically? Try to poke your eyes out, scratch your face? Exactly what happened? I know for a fact that she had a hell of a temper. She probably let it all out with you."

"She didn't do anything like that because I never cheated on her. I'm not a fool. I have everything I ever wanted and everything I worked for. I'm perfectly happy with my life as it is, but I miss Maura very much. Someday I'll find another soulmate."

"You know Doctor, you come across as an inveterate liar. You don't ever tell the truth about the women in your life, do you? What about Mackenzie Stanton, is she your new romantic interest? We know about your rendezvous with her."

"Rendezvous? You're kidding me. I did not have sex with her. I don't know what she told you, but I did not have sex ... with that girl. And even if I did have sex with her, she's not a patient of mine, so it would not be an issue with the medical board."

"She arranged to meet with you this evening to have you

admit you had an affair with Alys. Yes, Mackenzie recorded you, and I have the tape from your meeting."

"You're kidding me. That's why you were there at my office. Okay that's it. I'm leaving." Quenneville stood, looked directly at the video recorder, and said, "If you think I killed my wife and Alys Chapman, then charge me. Let's get this over with. Otherwise, I'm through talking to you."

"Sit down. I'm not through with you." Clay stood and hovered over the smaller man. "Sit down, I said!"

"I will not."

Clay called his bluff. He went to the door and beckoned the cop who was stationed in the corridor to come into the interview room. "I want you to cuff Dr. Quenneville and book him for suspicion of murder. Allow him to call his lawyer."

Quenneville panicked. "Okay, okay." He returned to his chair. "I'll tell you the truth about everything. What do you want to know?"

CHAPTER 43

Quenneville sat across from Clay and took three or four deep breaths to compose himself. He had promised to tell Clay the truth about his relationship with Alys. "I probably should have my attorney here to counsel me, but I'm totally innocent, and I think you'll agree with me."

"Tell me about you and Alys. How long had you and she been together?"

As Quenneville began to answer, there was a knock on the interview room door. Clay was irritated by the distraction and shouted out, "What is it?"

Captain Ellsworth opened the door and beckoned Clay into the corridor.

Clay said "Sorry, Captain, I didn't know it was you. What do you have for me? I'm on the verge of getting a confession from Quenneville."

Ellsworth announced, "I thought you needed to know that I just got word that Gardner Hicks escaped from the maximum-security unit of the Behavioral Health Institute and he's still on the loose."

"Damnatiions! Okay, let me finish this interview. I'll check in with you as soon as I'm through with Quenneville."

Clay returned to question Quenneville. "Sorry about that. I had asked you about Alys Chapman before we were interrupted."

"Yes, Alys and I had an affair, but it was a relationship that began well before she became a patient. When the American Society of Plastic Surgeons held a convention in Santa Barbara I got to know her through my role as the chairman of the Society."

"Go on."

"She was the one who sold me on having our convention at the Hilton Beachfront. We worked together to coordinate all the details, and over the course of the event I fell hard for her. She was a lovely person. After a relatively short while, I was contemplating getting a divorce from Maura so we could marry. It's something we both wanted, but then Maura was killed. It didn't change how we felt toward each other, but we decided to hold off on getting married so people wouldn't talk about how I rushed to another woman. Furthermore, we worried that the police would look at me suspiciously, thinking I was responsible for her murder. Alys and I loved each other. I was willing to give up medicine to be with her, if necessary. Someone ended my dreams by killing her. It wasn't me. Why would I? I loved the woman, and she loved me."

Clay asked, "I need to have you clear up something. Did you rendezvous with Alys in room 412 at the Emerson when she flew in from California?"

"Yes."

"Why that room, and 410 too?"

"No reason. Habit on her part, I guess."

"Your relationship with your wife was a rocky one, but you told me you were beholden to her for getting you through your medical degrees. Frankly, there didn't seem to be a whole lot of love between the two of you."

"The truth is, Maura and I had an incompatible relationship."

"Did she know about your affair with Alys?"

"I don't know. I didn't flaunt our involvement, but as it turns out, Maura was unfaithful to me, too. I reasoned if she could be unfaithful, why couldn't I? It was what's good for the goose is good for the gander."

Clay said, "That's an interesting take on infidelity. Who was your wife unfaithful with?"

"That woolly-haired maintenance guy from the Emerson. It seemed to me that she could have chosen someone a little more upscale. Nevertheless, that's who it was."

"Then you knew Max Bruder after all?"

"Yes, I did. I lied that I didn't know him, but I did."

"Why did your relationship with your wife fall apart? You told me you owed your career to her."

"I did. I owed her for getting me through my education, but once I started my practice and began to do well financially, she and I didn't have a lot in common. She was a world-class nagger. It didn't make any difference what the subject was, she had an opinion about it, and in her mind, she was never wrong. It got to the point where I couldn't tolerate being alone with her. After a while, I would work late into the evening, so I didn't have to put up with her nagging. She was a pain in the ass about everything, not only to me but to just about everyone. The two of us didn't socialize very much because she was so unpopular with people. Every discussion with her always turned to how she worked her butt off to get me through medical school, and how much money we had, or didn't have, and on and on. It was always about money. I don't know who killed her, but my guess is she created a lot of enemies with her negativity. *Enemies* might be too strong a word, but for sure she rubbed people the wrong way."

Clay asked, "Did you kill your wife?"

"Emphatically, no, I did not."

"Do you believe it was your wife who sent the anonymous complaint to the medical board informing them that you were having an affair with one of your patients?"

"I think it was, but luckily it never went anywhere."

Clay said, "Have you thought of anyone she might have pissed off to the point where she became a target of their rage?"

"No, I can't say that I know anyone like that. A lot of people were annoyed with her for one reason or another, but I can't think of anyone with strong enough feelings about her to want to murder her."

Clay said, "Interesting that you should mention she annoyed people. As you know, she had a problem with that guy in the Albertsons supermarket when she cut in line and caused a ruckus. I guess it was possible that argument led to the guy killing her. But killing someone in a grocery store over cutting in line sounds a bit far-fetched, doesn't it?"

Quenneville said, "She told me that she had words with a guy there, but she never explained what had happened and insisted it wasn't her fault. However, I know very well, it was always the world against Maura, so I have no idea who was at fault?"

"What did she say happened?"

"Hell, I don't know if anything happened. I can't imagine it caused the guy to kill her, but I guess anything is possible."

"Did she describe him?"

"The only thing she said about him was that he wore a mailman's uniform."

CHAPTER 44

After Clay interviewed Quenneville, he drove to the Behavioral Health Institute, a state-owned and operated psychiatric hospital in the southeast corner of Santa Fe to learn from Dr. John Cole, the Institute's administrator how Gardner Hicks had managed to escape from the maximum-security wing of the hospital.

"Apparently, he hid in a stall in the lobby bathroom most of the night, then walked right out the front door early the next morning. The lobby guard said he left his post about four o'clock in the morning to go to the bathroom. That's when Hicks came out of a stall, dressed in hospital pajamas, slippers, and bathrobe, said good morning to the guard, then walked right past him and out of the hospital."

"How the hell did he get from the third floor to the lobby without someone spotting him? And he was dressed in pajamas? What was the guard thinking, that Hicks was going to a slumber party?"

Dr. Cole said, "I don't have the answers to any of that, but I will do my best to get to the bottom of this debacle."

"When did someone on his floor notice Hicks was missing?"

"At breakfast this morning, the nursing staff took a count and realized he was gone."

"Did you do a search of the building? Sometimes in these situations, the escapee will hide out in the hospital itself."

"Yes, we searched the building, inside and out, as well as the surrounding hospital grounds. The police are searching for him too. I realize he was only here for a short period of time, but we learned quickly that he was trouble. He picked a fight with the staff and intimidated other patients. He punched one patient for not moving out of his way quick enough when he wanted to get by him."

"What conclusion did your staff arrive at regarding his mental state?"

"Our diagnosis is not complete, but the psychologist assigned to his case says he showed signs of paranoid schizophrenia."

"Is he considered dangerous?"

"Yes, absolutely. But he wasn't here long enough to provide a complete character risk assessment to determine if he was competent to stand trial for the criminal charges against him."

"What was he wearing when he escaped."

"The best we can tell, he left here dressed in the pajamas and bathrobe."

Clay called Sergeant Rizzo. "Broadcast an all-points bulletin for a fugitive, Gardner Hicks, who has escaped from the maximum-security ward of the Behavioral Health Institute. He was last seen wearing hospital pajamas, slippers, and a bathrobe. He should be considered dangerous.

Within minutes after the APB was transmitted, Clay was informed that a man who appeared to be Hicks attacked a man of similar size at a bus stop at 5th and Ingersoll Avenue and tried to force the man to give him his clothes. Gardner bloodied the man, but the guy fought him off and called the cops. He then tried to board the bus, but the driver refused to let him on.

Clay raced to get there but by the time he arrived at 5th and Ingersoll Hicks was gone. Clay called his dispatcher and asked him to determine the next scheduled stop for the bus.

The next stop was at the corner of Fencil and Gailor

Roads. But the bus had already left by the time Clay could get there.

He raced to the next stop and pulled alongside the bus. He turned on his flashers and motioned for the driver to pull over.

Clay parked diagonally in front of the bus, jumped out of his car, gestured for the driver to open the front door, and then climbed the two steps onto the bus. He looked up and down the rows of passengers, but Hicks was not there.

He asked the driver, "Did you have a passenger who was dressed in pajamas and a bathrobe?"

"There was a wacko dressed like that who tried to get on a couple of stops ago. He didn't have any money, so I told him he couldn't get on."

"Where did he go?"

"I have no clue."

A passenger shouted, "He crossed the street. He was in the middle of the road, trying to hitch a ride."

"Did anyone pick him up?"

"No. He pounded on the hoods of cars driving past him when they didn't stop."

"Did anyone see where he went from there?"

One lady raised her hand and said, "He got into a cab."

"Going which way?"

"That way," she said, gesturing in the opposite direction.

Gardner was able to get the cab to stop. The Pakistani cabbie asked Hicks, "Where to?"

He gave the cabbie Clay's address.

The driver asked, "Do you have money to pay me?"

"Not on me, but my wife has money. She'll pay you when you drop me off."

"None of my business, but why are you dressed in your pajamas?"

"My wife threw me out of the house after an argument."

The driver looked in the rearview mirror at the tired-looking Hicks and did not believe his story, but it had been a slow day and night with very few fares, so he didn't argue.

Clay contacted the cab company to seek their help in finding Hicks. He explained who Hicks was and where he was seen hitching a ride with a cab.

In turn, the cab dispatcher announced on the cab radio, "Be on the lookout for a fugitive from the Behavioral Health Institute. He is dressed in pajamas, slippers, and a bathrobe. Notify the Santa Fe police immediately if seen. He is considered extremely dangerous."

The cabbie jammed on his brakes and reached under his seat to pull out a pistol he carried for self-defense. He got out of the car and aimed the pistol at Hicks. His tremulous voice belied his false bravado. "Get out of the car. Do what I say. I don't want to use this gun."

Hicks put up his hands in surrender. "I'm not the guy he was talking about. That guy stole my clothes and left me with these pajamas."

The cabbie said, "Why did you lie to me then? Why didn't you tell me the truth from the beginning?"

"I didn't think you would believe me, but that's the truth. The guy came up from behind me and knocked me to the ground, then he told me to take my clothes off. I didn't have any choice but to do what he said."

The cabbie was scared. "I'm calling the police."

"I wish you would. I didn't have a chance to call them myself. That guy took my cell phone from me. Look at the bump on the back of my head. It's when he hit me. You'll see I'm telling the truth."

The cabbie was skeptical, but he circled around him to examine the fictitious bump on Hick's head.

Hicks was quick. He threw a punch at the cabbie and caught him across the side of his face. As the cabbie staggered back, Hicks was on him in an instant and yanked the gun away. He said angrily, "You should have believed me. Now because you didn't, I'm going to have to kill you." Hicks aimed the gun at him.

The driver flung his arms up and covered his face cowering in fear. "No! No!"

Hicks ordered, "Take off your shirt and pants."

"I said take your shirt and pants off. Now!"

The cabbie complied and quickly undressed down to his underwear.

Hicks said, "Get on the ground. You make one move and I'll blow you away. Understand?"

Hicks put on the Pakistani's clothes and said, "Sorry pal, but I can't wait for you to tell the cops what happened."

Click. Click. Click. He pulled the trigger three times, but the pistol jammed each time.

The cabbie sprang up and ran from the scene, zigging and zagging down the country road as Hicks unjammed the gun and fired twice at him.

Hicks shouted, "Son of a bitch," then jumped into the cab and drove off in the opposite direction.

CHAPTER 45

The cabbie pounded on the door of the first house he came to in the rural neighborhood, a dozen miles from the heart of Santa Fe. "Help me! Someone's trying to kill me. Help me!"

The homeowner came to the door and pointed a twelve-gauge shotgun at the half-naked Pakistani. "What do you want? Don't try to come in or I'll blow you away."

The cabbie could barely get the words out. He kept looking over his shoulder. "I ... I'm a cab driver ... I picked up a fare about fifteen minutes ago ... then I learned he was ... he was a fugitive who escaped from the psychiatric hospital ... he ... he knocked me down and took my gun away."

"Where are your clothes?"

"He took my clothes and put them on himself. When I picked him up, all he was wearing were pajamas and a bathrobe."

The homeowner questioned his story. "Why did you have a gun in the first place?"

"For protection in my taxi, but I've never had to use it. The guy wrestled it from me and fired at me a couple of times when I was running from him."

The homeowner was uncertain about the driver's story. "Stay right here. I'll call the police." He locked the door behind him. The driver cowered behind a juniper near the entrance to the house and waited for the police to arrive.

A few minutes later the owner opened the front door again. He continued to aim his shotgun at the cabbie. "I called the police. They're on their way."

A car arrived with flashing lights and its siren blaring. The cop asked the driver to explain what had happened.

The cabbie tried to compose himself and explained, "My dispatcher made an announcement to be on the lookout for a fugitive wearing pajamas who escaped from the psychiatric hospital. He was considered dangerous. I figured my passenger was the guy the police were looking for. I took out my gun from under my seat and told him to get out of the cab. But he knocked me down and took my gun away from me. He aimed it at me when I was on the ground and pulled the trigger three times. Three times! Thank God the gun didn't fire. I got up and ran until I got here. I banged on this man's front door, and I told him what happened. That's when he called the police."

"Do you know where the fugitive is now?"

"No, but he stole my cab. When I looked back, he was driving it away in the other direction." He pointed in the direction the cab was headed. "He went that way."

Clay received news of the incident within minutes. "Get me the name of the cab company."

He called the Rancho Santa Fe cab company and spoke with the cab dispatcher. "We've located the cab the hospital fugitive used in his escape. I need the GPS tracking data for the vehicle's location. Where is he now?"

After a few questions verifying Clay's identity, the dispatcher answered. "He's across town at 136th Street and Alma, heading northwest."

"I'll head in that direction. Keep me informed about his route."

A minute later, the dispatcher advised, "Now he's at 136th and Hacienda. But he's not moving. It could be he's stuck in traffic. No, wait. There's a 7-Eleven there. He's probably at the gas station to fill up with gas. My guess is he'll abandon the cab and try to hijack another vehicle."

Clay called the dispatcher. "Notify Sergeant Rizzo that fugitive Hicks is at 136th and Hacienda. Advise if any cars are available to proceed to that location."

Clay turned on his siren and LED flashers and raced to the scene. By the time he arrived, three cops were already there, encircling the empty cab, questioning customers and employees alike. The fugitive was not in the vicinity.

A woman in her thirties with her two children in the back seat of her Toyota sedan approached one of the cops. "I saw a man walk up to a middle-aged woman who was pumping gas and, I can't be sure, but it looked like he got into her car from the passenger side. At first, he approached me, but when he looked into my car and saw I had two children in the back seat, he left and walked over to the car where that lady was pumping gas. I can't be sure, but I thought he had a gun."

The cop said, "Stay right here. I want you to tell the detective what you saw." He shouted to Clay. "We might have an eyewitness. This lady saw someone get into a car driven by a middle-aged woman."

Clay identified himself, "My name is Detective Bryce. Tell me what you saw?"

"Like I told the officer, it looked to me that a man forced himself into a lady's car. At first, he came up to my car and looked in. When he saw I had two kids in the back he walked away and went over to that other lady's car. I can't be sure, but I thought he had a gun."

"It sounds as though it could have been our fugitive. What kind of a car was the lady driving?"

"Oh, my, I don't know for sure, but I think I remember that it was a white SUV type of a car. I think it was a

Mercedes-Benz. I didn't think to get the license plate number. Sorry, but I can't even be sure that he was the guy you're searching for."

Clay thanked the lady, asked the cop to take a statement from her, then went into the 7-Eleven to talk to the manager. "You have surveillance cameras, right? I need to see the video from the last fifteen minutes."

The manager led Clay to his small office in the back of the store and quickly replayed the video Clay asked to see. They saw a man walk past several cars and look into each one. He stopped at a car where a woman driving a white Mercedes SUV was replacing the gasoline pump nozzle into the gas pump. She took the receipt from the pump and got into her car. The man who had been looking into other cars walked around the Mercedes to the passenger side. He entered the car, but the video did not show what transpired in the car. The Mercedes did not move for a few seconds, then slowly entered traffic on 136th Street. Clay tried to read the license plate number, but it was not clearly visible on the grainy footage.

Clay contacted Sergeant Rizzo and asked him to issue another all-points bulletin for a white Mercedes SUV with two occupants, a middle-aged woman being held against her will, and an armed and dangerous white male about thirty years of age.

Half an hour later, Clay was informed that the woman who owned the SUV had been released by Hicks and had sought help from a man who was walking his dog. The man called 911.

The officer who first arrived on scene was instructed to drive the Mercedes owner to police headquarters where Clay was to interview her.

The woman was not physically harmed but obviously nervous from her ordeal. Clay introduced himself and said, "I'm thankful you are okay."

The woman was shaken. "I am thankful, too," she said with a nervous laugh.

"Are you okay to answer some questions?"

"Yes, I think so."

"What is your name?"

"Mrs. Marybeth Aguila."

"Mrs. Aguila, I understand you were carjacked from the 7-Eleven at 136th Street. Did he ask for a ride, or did he force his way into your car?"

"He didn't force his way in. He got into the car without asking and showed me that he had a gun. I asked if he was going to shoot me. He said no unless I did something stupid. He said I was to do what he asked."

"Then what?"

"He pointed the gun at me the entire time he was in the car and told me to drive. I drove for about five or ten minutes then he asked me where my purse was. I told him it was under my seat. He asked me to retrieve it and hand it to him. He proceeded to tear through it. He said he was sorry, but he had to take my money because he didn't have any. He took my credit cards and put them in his pocket. Then he took my cell phone and told me to pull over and get out of the car. I did as he told me. He got out of the car and came around to sit in the driver's seat. Then he thanked me for the ride and drove off. He actually was a very polite young man."

"Did he talk about what he was going to do, or where he was going to go?"

Marybeth said, "The only thing he said was he had to clean up some loose ends."

Clay thanked Mrs. Aguila and had the dispatcher announce the Mercedes SUV license plate number to all patrol officers and to emphasize that the fugitive was armed and dangerous.

CHAPTER 46

Hicks drove slowly through the city, observing all traffic rules so he would not be pulled over by the police for a traffic violation and in the process be identified as the fugitive on the run. He planned to wind his way to Dr. Ronald Quenneville's home at the foothills of the Jemez Mountains to meet face-to-face with the man who stole his girlfriend from him. He wanted to learn what Quenneville offered Alys that he did not.

He had not slept all night and decided to catch a few winks on the side of the road. When it was dark, he would drive the rest of the way to Quenneville's house.

He pulled into a feeder road off Route 25, drove to the end of the road, and then drove a short way farther into what appeared to be a hiking path in the desert. He parked under the shade of a cottonwood tree. Hidden from traffic, he set the Mercedes driver's seat as far back as it would go and slept fitfully for a short time. He was suddenly awakened by someone rapping on his window.

A wizened farmer barked at Gardner. "Hey mister this is private property. What are you doing out here?"

Hicks snapped awake. He rolled down his window, and pleaded, "I'm sorry. I was heading to Albuquerque and was falling asleep while driving so I decided to pull off 25 and take a quick snooze. Sorry, I'll leave right away. I have to get going anyway. I'm getting married tomorrow."

The farmer didn't care what his plans were. "Yeah, good for you, now make it quick." When he walked back to his beat-up old pickup, he turned around to ensure the trespasser was preparing to leave his property.

Hicks waited a few seconds, got out of his car, yawned

massively to impress the farmer that he indeed had been taking a snooze from a long drive. He walked to the pickup and raised his forefinger to the farmer to indicate he wanted to tell him something.

The farmer rolled down his window. "Yeah, what is it?"

Hicks asked, "I was wondering if you know a man by the name of Doctor Ronald Quenneville? He supposedly lives around here someplace."

"I don't know any such person."

Hicks looked over the top of the farmer's pickup, did a double take, then feigned that there was something of interest for the farmer to see in the field. Hicks shouted out. "Hey what's that?"

"What?" the farmer asked suspiciously.

"Take a look, you can see for yourself."

When the farmer exited his pickup, Hicks pointed over the farmer's shoulder to the horizon and said, "There it is over there, about eleven o'clock."

As the farmer turned, Hicks pulled out his handgun from his back pocket and hit the old man viciously on his right temple with the butt of the cabbie's handgun. The farmer dropped to the ground, unconscious.

Hicks opened the trunk of the hijacked Mercedes to see what was in it and noticed a tool kit provided by Mercedes. With the farmer lying unconscious on the ground outside of the pickup, Hicks opened the kit. He pulled a Phillips screwdriver from the kit and removed the license plate from the pickup, replaced it with the Mercedes plate, then switched the farmer's plate from the pickup to the Mercedes.

When he was through switching plates, he got into the car, merged onto Route 25, and continued to Quenneville's house.

CHAPTER 47

Using the Mercedes GPS, Hicks found Quenneville's house, parked up the street a distance away from the driveway entrance and waited for the doctor to show up.

It was dark when Quenneville arrived. He used his remote to open the gate. As the gate swung open slowly, Hicks got out of his car, sneaked to the foot of the driveway and, unseen by Quenneville rushed into the property before the gate closed. He crouched low and rushed to the back of the house and onto the patio that surrounded a large swimming pool and spa. He peeked through the window alongside the sliding glass door to see Quenneville enter the kitchen from the living room and flick on the lights.

Reveca entered the kitchen a few seconds later. The doctor and the nanny greeted each other with an embrace and a long passionate kiss on the lips. The doctor rubbed her back and slid his hands down to her butt.

That son of a two-timing bastard.

When Reveca left the kitchen, Hicks snuck along the house and peeked through a living room window to see her making Quenneville a gin martini straight up and serving him his drink with another kiss on the lips, then returned to the bar and made a rum and Coke for herself. They toasted each other with clinks of their glasses and another short kiss.

The two lovers sat alongside each other on a large leather couch and chatted. Hicks could not hear what they were saying.

Hicks moved back to the sliding glass door and checked to see if it was unlocked.

It was.

Hicks slid the door open just enough to quietly squeeze through and into the kitchen. The doctor and his nanny were so fixated on each other that they did not hear him tiptoeing across the Mexican tile kitchen floor.

"Boo!" he shouted from behind them.

The doctor spilled part of his drink as he and Reveca turned to see who it was that startled them.

Hicks cackled, "Ha! That was fun to do. Scared you, huh? Let me do it again. Boo!"

Quenneville stood up. "Who the hell are you?"

"Gardner Hicks is my name." He waved the Pakistani's gun at them. "They say revenge is not justice, but I disagree. Revenge is my game."

Quenneville and Reveca set their drinks on the coffee table. "What do you want?" Quenneville demanded to know.

"Sit down before I use my gun to make your body a sieve."

The doctor sat.

"What do you want? Are you the same guy who burglarized us before?"

"Nah, I'm not into burglary. My hero is Spiderman. Just like him, my creed is to transform wrong into right. And you, my friend, are my project *du jour*. That's French, if you don't know."

"Is this a joke? Who put you up to this?"

Hicks waved his gun at them, then fired a shot into the ceiling. "You tell me if you still think this is a joke?"

Quenneville hunched his shoulders. Reveca cowered and grasped Quenneville's arm with both her hands. She said, "What do you want from us?"

"I want justice, that's all. You see, I'm like one hundred and ten percent sure that the doctor killed my girlfriend."

Quenneville asked, "Who was your girlfriend?"

"Alys Chapman. Beautiful Alys. My one and only love. And you killed her. Why?"

Quenneville said, "Good grief, you're the second person to accuse me of killing Alys."

"Who was the other person?"

"Her friend from California."

Hicks said, "Ah, yes, Mackenzie."

Quenneville said, "Yes, she's the one. Let me tell you that I did not kill Alys, and I don't know who did."

Hicks disagreed. "I don't believe you. First you tried to make Alys look like a fake Barbie doll, then you couldn't be satisfied until you had sex with her."

"I really don't know what you're talking about. What do you mean, 'fake' Barbie doll?"

Hicks shook his head and continued to wave his pistol at Quenneville. "I guess you're not as bright as some people think you are, so let me explain. You made Alys' boobs bigger, didn't you? And then, as if that wasn't enough, you talked her into having an affair with you. Why? Wasn't your wife good enough? Couldn't she satisfy your sexual appetite?"

"I didn't talk Alys into anything. She came to me wanting to have her breasts enhanced, so I did the surgery. I don't talk people into having a surgery. She talked herself into having that done."

"And your wife? Don't lie to me and tell me you didn't kill her."

"I did not kill my wife. Did you?"

Hicks unexpectedly fired another shot into the ceiling.

Both Quenneville and Reveca ducked.

"I told you not to lie to me and there you did it again. The next shot is going to be at your lying lips. That's it. Sounds like a country song, doesn't it?" He hummed something unintelligible.

Reveca shook her head. "I do not understand." She continued to show fright.

Hicks responded, "Oh, what would you know? You're like from Russia or someplace. What would you know about country music?"

Reveca looked away. She didn't want to anger him.

Quenneville asked, "What do you want from me? I've told you the truth about Alys. I did not talk her into having surgery. She said, she wanted to please you, and that's the only reason she wanted her breasts enhanced."

"You had sex with her, didn't you? I know you did. Admit it."

Quenneville did not respond.

Hicks turned to Reveca, "And you, do you know that your lover is two-timing you? He'll use you, then dump you when he finds someone younger or prettier, although you're very pretty. Trust me, he'll throw you away like a piece of trash."

Hicks stood in front of Reveca. "Stand up!"

Quenneville said, "What are you going to do to her? Can't you see that she doesn't know what you're talking about?"

"Just shut up." Hicks grabbed Reveca's arm and shoved her into the powder room. He warned her, "If I hear a peep from you, your lover will be shot dead. Understand?"

Reveca answered, "I understand, but please don't shoot him. He's a nice man."

"You're wrong about him being a nice man." Turning to Quenneville he said, "You have her hoodwinked, don't you?"

Hicks jammed a chair under the doorknob to the powder room to ensure Reveca could not get out.

Hicks said to Quenneville, "Let's you and I have a seat and chat for a while, okay with you?"

CHAPTER 48

A state trooper stopped an old pickup truck on Cardonia Road off Route 25 outside of Santa Fe. The trooper called his state police dispatcher. "I have stopped a vehicle with the tags of the Mercedes SUV that you broadcast was involved in a carjack. But it's not a Mercedes. The plate is on a 1990 Ford pickup. I'm going to check it out further."

The trooper cautiously walked to the driver's side door and confronted the farmer who had chased Hicks off his property. "Do you know why I stopped you?"

The farmer said, "I have no idea."

The trooper noticed blood on the side of his head. "That's a good size bump you have on your head."

"Yeah, tell me about it."

The trooper asked, "How did you get it?"

"Some yahoo was parked on my property off a feeder road alongside 25. He was sleeping and I woke him up to tell him to leave, and I guess he wasn't too happy about that. The next thing I knew, I was waking up on the ground. When I was able to get up, I had a brutal headache, and the guy was gone, and I had no idea what the hell had happened."

"Do you know that you have a license plate on your vehicle that belongs to a stolen Mercedes-Benz?"

"No kidding. Well, as you can see, my pickup ain't no Mercedes-Benz."

"Then how did you end up with that plate?"

"I'll be darned if I know. Maybe that guy who hit me switched plates."

"What's your pickup's actual license plate number?"

The farmer recited it to the trooper, who called in the

plate number as a probable stolen plate on a probable stolen car. The trooper was told to stay with the farmer and advised that Detective Bryce would be there shortly.

❊ ❊ ❊

Clay rushed to the scene and asked the farmer to tell him what happened.

The farmer related to Clay how he had asked Hicks to get off his property, and the next thing he remembered was waking up and looking at the sky from flat on his back. "He must have clocked me when I wasn't looking. When I came to, my head hurt like the fires of hell, and the guy was gone. I woke up next to my pickup."

"Did he say anything to you like where he was heading?"

Rubbing his head gingerly, and checking his fingers for blood, the farmer explained. "Yeah, he said he was driving to Albuquerque and got off 25 to rest a while before he was going to continue on his way. He said he was getting married tomorrow. That was it. All told, I talked to him about twenty seconds."

"Anything else? Did he have a gun?"

"I can't be sure, but I think he hit me with the butt end of a gun. He faked me out by pointing to something behind me. He said, 'What's that?' and when I turned to look, he must have knocked me out cold."

"Do you need an ambulance?"

"No, I'm okay, I've been kicked harder milking cows. Oh, and one more thing I almost forgot. That yahoo asked me if I knew a doctor named Ronald something or another."

"By any chance was Quenneville the last name of the guy he was asking about?"

The farmer answered. "Yes, that's it, by golly that's the name."

"What did you tell him?"

"That I didn't know him."

❋ ❋ ❋

Clay realized Hicks was hunting for Quenneville, and probably Mackenzie too. He put Quenneville's house address on Mountainview Place into his GPS. The navigation system informed him that the house was twenty minutes away from Clay's current location. He decided to head there first. On the way to Quenneville's house, he called Mackenzie.

She answered cheerily. "Hi handsome, when will you be home?"

"Mackenzie, listen carefully. Hicks escaped from the psychiatric unit at the behavioral center and I'm pretty sure he's headed to Quenneville's house and then to my house to meet up with you. Although he might decide to go to you first, then Quenneville. No question, one way or another you are still a target. I'm going to have my Sergeant dispatch a couple of cops to protect you. Gardner knows you've been staying at my house so it's no longer safe for you. We don't have a lot of time to find a suitable safe house."

"Your house is only ten or fifteen minutes away from the Emerson. Why not use the hotel as a safe house? I can be safeguarded there as well as anywhere else."

Clay paused for a moment. "Good idea. The cops and John Paul can protect you there."

"I will pack my stuff and be ready in five minutes."

"The cops will be there in a few minutes. I will call John Paul and alert him what's happening and tell him to take every necessary measure to keep you safe at the hotel. Stay put until the officers arrive."

"Clay, I'm scared."

"If you are scared, that's good. Do exactly what I'm asking you to do, and you'll be okay. No freelancing, got me?"

"But Clay ..."

"Mackenzie, I don't have time to argue. I'll get in touch with the security guard as soon as we hang up."

Clay called John Paul. "I need your help. We've identified the guy who tried to abduct Mackenzie Stanton at the Emerson. He's Gardner Hicks, Alys Chapman's ex-boyfriend. Long story short, Hicks escaped from the behavioral facility where he had been in custody. We're searching for him now. We believe Hicks is targeting Mackenzie. I've decided to safeguard her at the Emerson until I'm able to get there. Right now, she is being escorted to the hotel by patrol officers. When Mackenzie gets there, I want you to put her in one of your conference rooms and make sure no one gets in the room. I'll be there as soon as I get freed up here. You and the officers will have to be on guard."

"I understand. No problem."

"I've already informed Mackenzie that you will be guarding her. Be extra vigilant. John Paul, the thing to remember is that she is very headstrong. She has a mind of her own. You will have to be firm with her. I realize this is outside the scope of your job, but I do not have time to get her situated in a police safe house. Hicks is moving fast, and I know he wants to take revenge for reasons I don't have time to explain right now."

"Got it. I will be ready for him. You can count on me."

CHAPTER 49

Clay sped to Quenneville's house, turned off his headlights, and parked his car on the street. He walked several yards in both directions, looking for another entryway other than through the locked driveway gate.

He spotted a white Mercedes parked about seventy-five yards farther up the street and sprinted to the vehicle to confirm it was the car that Hicks had hijacked. He checked the license plate against the plate belonging to the farmer and found it matched.

The Mercedes was Mrs. Marybeth Aguila's car.

Clay called Sergeant Rizzo to arrange for officers to escort Mackenzie to the Emerson Hotel and to remain on guard until Clay got there. He asked to have other officers back him up at 10429 Mountainview Place. "Fugitive Gardner Hicks is holed up in that residence. There must not be any sirens or lights. Order backup to remain well outside the premises' perimeter until I can address the situation. Also, I will need you personally to assist me after I get Hicks in custody."

Clay reasoned that Hicks had somehow made his way over the eight-foot wall that encircled the entire property and was already in the house. Urgency was called for. He decided to park against the wall, climb on top of his car, and hoist himself over the top of the wall.

It worked. He dropped to the other side and raced to the patio at the back of the house. His long strides allowed him to reach his destination quickly. He peeked into the kitchen through the sliding glass door and saw Hicks holding a pistol against Quenneville's temple and then shove Reveca into the powder room just inside the foyer.

Clay waited until Hicks' back was to him, then he slowly opened the slider and stepped inside. He crouched behind the wide granite kitchen counter and stayed out of sight, listening as Hicks rebuked Quenneville, "You've ruined everything. Did you know Alys and I were supposed to get married tomorrow, and now we'll have to wait until another minister is available? Tell me, who is that woman you were kissing a minute ago?"

"She's the nanny for my son."

"Your nanny? One woman isn't enough for you I guess, huh?"

Quenneville answered, "I don't know what you're talking about."

Hicks asked, "Where is your son?"

"He's upstairs asleep, unless you woke him up by shooting into the ceiling."

"Don't change the subject."

Quenneville showed some boldness and responded angrily, "I'm not. You're the one who asked about my son."

"Tell me about your fling with Alys. What a crying shame that you ruined it for us. We were in love. We had our whole lives ahead of us. But no, you had to prove that you were a big shot. Other people don't matter to you, do they? How selfish could you be? Now what are we going to do with all the food we bought for the wedding reception? And the flowers? Alys worked so hard to make our wedding something special and you botched it up for us."

Quenneville tried to reason with Hicks. "I didn't know you were going to get married. She never told me anything about the two of you getting hitched."

"You continue to lie, don't you? I hate liars. That means I have only one recourse since you've screwed up my life."

"What's your recourse?"

"I'm going to have to kill you and your lover. Do you hear me in there?" Hicks shouted as he pounded on the powder room door. "Your lover can't stop lying to me, and that means I'm going to have to kill him."

Reveca cried, "No, don't."

Clay heard the threat. He peeked over the counter and saw Hicks with his left arm around Quenneville's neck and a gun pointed at Quenneville's temple. Gardner bellowed, "I'm going to count to ten and if I don't hear an honest apology, you will be a dead man. Got it?"

It appeared to Clay that he had to act quickly. He burst into the living room and pointed his service revolver at Hicks. "Gardner, drop the gun!"

Startled by Clay's sudden appearance Hicks fired a shot at him which missed Clay and thudded behind him into the kitchen wall.

Clay held his revolver with his right hand tucked into the palm of his left hand and aimed it at Hicks. "Do not shoot again. Do you hear me? I will blow you away if you try to shoot again. Now you either drop the gun, or I drop you."

"Ha, not doing that. You shoot me and my finger will twitch on this hair-trigger pistol and your doctor friend will be dead. If you're okay with that, go ahead and shoot me. I don't have a lot to live for anyway."

Clay tried to change Hicks' focus away from Quenneville. "I know you're pissed at him but let me handle it. And why do you have his nanny locked up in the bathroom? She hasn't done anything to you." He decided to stretch the truth. "She even asked me if she could be a bridesmaid in your wedding."

"She did? I'll have to check with Alys about that. Did you know the doctor and that woman in the bathroom are lovers? I swear they are. Doesn't that beat all? He can't have a relationship with one woman alone."

"Listen to me, Gardner. I don't want to have to shoot you."

"Do what you've got to do. I don't care."

"Yes, you do. You're getting married to Alys, remember? What will she think?"

Hicks had a forlorn look. "Do you think she'll be mad at me?"

"Yes, if you don't show up. She's gone to a lot of trouble to make the wedding just right. You know how women are with weddings. Everything's got to be perfect."

"Yeah, but I think I'm going to call the wedding off now."

"Why?"

"Because."

"You don't really want to do that, do you?"

Gardner insisted, "You do know he killed Alys, don't you? I'm going to avenge her murder by shooting him between his eyes, and then I'm going to shoot his lover."

Hicks' thoughts were irrational. "And you know what else, Detective Bryce, this guy killed his own wife."

"Hold off on killing him. If you do, I'll tell you who actually killed his wife."

"Who was it?"

"I'll tell you when you let him go. And you've got to let his nanny go also. I promise to tell you. But in the meantime, forget about the doctor. Alys is waiting for you. You're delaying the wedding plans. Obviously, the wedding can't go on without you. And remember, I'm supposed to be your best man. If you kill the doctor, I will not be able to take part in your wedding. I will be busy testifying in court."

Gardner curled his lips. "Is that true?"

"How's this for an idea? How about we take you to the church for the rehearsal. I can arrange for a police escort to zip you there in no time."

Suddenly submissive, Hicks had a blank look in his eyes and said, "Okay, I'll let them go if you promise to tell me who killed Alys."

"That's a deal."

Hicks released his hold on Quenneville and removed the chair that wedged the powder room door tight. "Hey lady, you can come out," Hicks announced.

Reveca stepped out. Her eyes were swollen from crying. She saw that Hicks still pointed a gun at Quenneville and hurriedly stood behind the doctor, hugging him with both arms around his chest. "Why does he want to shoot us?"

"Stop crying," Hicks shouted. "I hate it when women cry to get their way. Stop crying!" he ordered.

Quenneville tried to comfort her. "Hush, everything will be alright. Detective Bryce will take care of it."

Hicks said to Clay, "Didn't I tell you they were lovers?"

Clay said to him, "Yes, you did. You proved your point, so please put your gun down on the floor. You don't need it anymore."

Hicks put his gun on the floor and said, "Okay, now you promised to tell me about Alys, right?"

"I promise I will, but I'll tell you after we get you married. Come on now. Let's hurry before the minister has to leave. Remember, you're going to get a full-blown police escort."

Hicks nodded, and responded to Clay in a childlike manner, "I can't wait. And I'm excited that you're still going to be my best man."

"Yes, absolutely, if you still want me."

Hicks allowed Clay to handcuff him.

❋ ❋ ❋

The street outside the Quenneville mansion was jammed with police cars, the cops waiting for instructions from Clay.

Clay had Quenneville open the entrance gate to allow the cops to flood into the property.

Clay asked Sergeant Rizzo to arrange for Hicks to be transported to headquarters, where he was to be placed in custody until Clay and the district attorney decided on a course of action for him. "Tell your officers to treat him with kid gloves. He's got a mental illness. It's not his fault."

❋ ❋ ❋

Quenneville extended his hand to Clay. "Thank you, Detective. I thought we were goners. I've never laid eyes on the guy before. Why was he accusing me of killing Maura and Alys?"

"He has never gotten over the fact that Alys had plastic surgery. He has the convoluted belief that you were responsible for their breakup because you performed surgery on her."

"He was off-the-wall. I had no idea what he was talking

about. He kept talking about Alys as though she was still alive, and they were getting married."

Clay said, "I'm not a psychologist, but I believe he is mentally ill. And yes, he blamed you for Alys' death. He also blamed Mackenzie Stanton, Alys' best friend. He believes she talked Alys into having the plastic surgery."

Quenneville said, "Now please tell me who killed my wife and Alys?"

"I'll tell you later."

Quenneville said, "You don't know, do you? Were you lying when you told Hicks you knew who the killer was?"

"I did exaggerate a bit when I said I knew who killed them. However, I will put an end to all this and disclose who it is after I have a meeting shortly with all the individuals who are possible suspects."

Quenneville showed concern. "You think it was me, don't you?"

Clay did not respond.

Reveca came forward and extended her hand to Clay. "I thought that man was going to kill us. Thank you for saving us."

"You're welcome, Reveca."

Clay noticed Reveca was limping. "What happened to your leg?"

"Clumsy me. I cut it when I ran into the edge of the dishwasher door in the kitchen."

"Looks like you're really hurting."

"It's really not too bad."

"Doctor, these officers will escort you and Reveca to the Emerson Hotel, for reasons you'll understand shortly. I need to talk to everyone there. You both will refrain from speaking to one another in the meantime."

Quenneville was concerned about Adam. "What about my son? We'll need to have a babysitter take care of him while we're at the hotel."

"Do you have a babysitter in mind?"

"Yes, we have a young lady who cares for Adam when Reveca needs a break."

Speaking aside, Clay said quietly, "Sergeant Rizzo, help him out getting that babysitter please. We need to get the sitter here as soon as possible. Then arrange to have Doctor Quenneville and Reveca escorted to the Emerson. I will be there shortly. Keep them apart and make sure they do not speak to each other when they arrive at the hotel."

Addressing the doctor and Reveca, Clay said, "When you get to the Emerson, the security guard there will make sure you're comfortable. Please cooperate with him. His name is John Paul."

Quenneville was anxious to know what Clay was planning. "You can't do this. I really want to know what is going on and what you're planning to do with us."

"I promise to inform you as soon as I arrange for several other people to join you at the Emerson. When everyone is situated there, I'll let you know who murdered Maura and Alys through the process of elimination."

CHAPTER 50

Clay instructed Rizzo to round up Emily Embers, Steve Aldrich, and Jeremy Voit to join Quenneville and Reveca for a meeting he was convening at the Emerson. He explained to Rizzo that in addition to those five individuals, Mackenzie Stanton would be in attendance, and he would require two patrol officers to stand guard and maintain order.

"I will need you and the Emerson security guard to be present to assist me as needed."

The conference room's tables were positioned in a u-shaped arrangement that allowed Clay to walk down the middle and speak face to face with each participant. When Clay entered the room there was complete silence at first then buzzing and outright objections from everyone in attendance. Everyone asked, "Why are we here?"

John Paul quieted everyone. "Everyone pipe down. Detective Bryce wants no interaction among the participants. He will explain why you are all here."

Clay said, "Thanks, John Paul. As you all know, I am investigating the murders of Maura Quenneville and Alys Chapman. To get you all up to date, recently there was a third murder: a man by the name of Max Bruder who, as some of you may know, was the Emerson maintenance employee. Max was killed in his home by an unknown assailant. He was discovered in his house, dead from a gunshot wound. We believe that the same person who killed the two women also killed Max. At first we believed he committed suicide but now we are virtually certain that he was murdered.

There was buzzing among the participants.

"Keep it down," John Paul barked.

Clay explained. "I have interviewed all of you about the murders of Maura Quenneville and Alys Chapman. My intent now is to review the circumstances surrounding the deaths of the three individuals. I believe this intervention will ultimately point to one of you as the killer."

More buzzing.

"Most of you do not know Mackenzie Stanton." He pointed to her.

"I invited Mackenzie to be present because she, too, has been a target of an assailant and, frankly, is lucky to be alive. I'm hoping that today she might be able to help us identify her assailant. And if so, there's a likelihood that person might also be the killer of the three victims."

Mackenzie nodded to the people who turned to see who she was.

Clay asked, "Does anyone have any questions about my intent?"

Emily Bruder raised her hand. "Yes, I have a question. Why am I here? I have a job to go to. I am totally innocent of any murders. Other than Max, who I worked with, I did not know the other two people who were murdered."

"What about Mrs. Quenneville?"

"I didn't really know her. The only time I had anything to do with her was when we had an argument at Albertsons grocery store, where I work."

Steve Aldrich who was in his recognizable post office uniform said, "I agree with Emily. We've told you before that we're totally innocent. You don't have any right to keep us here." He stood up and said to Emily, "Let's go. He can't stop us. I'll be damned if I'm going to lose my job over this foolishness."

Clay knew the legality of this gathering of suspects was questionable, but he stayed the course and warned, "I strongly advise you to sit down. If you or anyone chooses to leave before he or she is dismissed, that person will immediately be escorted by one of these fine officers to police headquarters, and he or she will be charged with obstruction. If you don't know what that means, I will define it for you. It's engaging in an act that interferes with the investigation or prosecution of a crime."

Steve looked at Emily and reluctantly sat down.

Clay said, "For those of you who are not aware, Emily was referring to an argument that she and Steve Aldrich had at the Albertsons grocery store with Mrs. Quenneville, the wife of Dr. Ronald Quenneville."

"Let me ask you Emily, when Maura Quenneville broke into your grocery line and banged her cart into Steve, why didn't you just have her escorted out of the store? Because you did not settle the dispute quickly, the disagreement grew into a full-scale argument and a total embarrassment for everyone involved. We can only be thankful that no one pulled a gun to settle the argument. Was it your intention to find a reason to justify murdering Mrs. Quenneville?"

Emily defended herself. "What do you mean by that? It is not my role to evict anyone who shows unpleasant behavior. I'm not a cop."

"But the least you could have done was to summon your supervisor?"

"Yes, I could have, but I didn't. Someone else in this room killed her, but I did not kill the bitch."

Quenneville stood up and said with a raised voice, "I object to her portrayal of my late wife as a bitch."

"I'm sure Ms. Embers will apologize to you later." He gestured to Quenneville to be seated.

Clay addressed Emily again. "Is it possible that you and Steve orchestrated Mrs. Quenneville's murder after that episode?"

"You're crazy. Why would we do that?"

"Steve admitted he followed Mrs. Quenneville after she left the grocery store. And then, several days later, Mrs. Quenneville was murdered. Was it Steve who killed her, or did you shoot her?"

"Neither one of us shot her."

Steve intervened, "Yes, I followed Mrs. Quenneville out of the grocery store, but I did not kill her."

Clay exaggerated the truth. "I told you before that we have a witness who swears he saw an old Honda Civic tailgating a Mercedes on Breeze Canyon Road, the Honda was following so close to the car that the witness thought it was being towed. That same witness said he heard a shot before the car veered over the cliff and into Breeze Canyon."

Steve insisted. "As I told you before, it was not me. First off, I don't own a gun, and secondly there are a lot of old Civics on the road. I was not on Breeze Canyon Road the day Mrs. Quenneville was killed. I am totally innocent, and so is Emily."

Clay said, "That's very noble of you to defend your girlfriend, but let me ask you this: since you followed Mrs. Quenneville and learned where she lived, did that set the stage for the both of you to kill her several days later?"

Steve raised his voice. "Absolutely not true. We're not sorry she's dead, but we didn't have anything to do with her murder."

Clay stood in front of Jeremy Voit and stared at him for a few seconds. Jeremy squirmed in his chair.

"I have checked on you and your history. You didn't tell me that you were arrested for sexual assault eight years ago."

"I didn't think you needed to know. I was totally innocent. It was a bogus charge made by a girl I dated a few times. We had an argument one night over watching a show on TV and I reached for her arm to calm her down. She yanked her arm away. I didn't harm her but I left a bruise on her arm. She called the cops and said I had sexually assaulted her. She was a screwball. I had to spend the night in jail. But the next day she withdrew her complaint. She said she called the police on me because I wasn't paying any attention to her. And that's the truth. She had me arrested but the charge was dropped. I didn't have to register as a sex offender or anything like that."

"What about Alys Chapman? You said that you were really infatuated by her. Did you try to hook up with her?"

"I told you before that I flirted with her, but I never got anywhere."

"You were upset with her because she turned down your overtures, weren't you?"

"No. I was disappointed but not upset. I've been turned down before by women."

"And what about Max Bruder? You said you were not his buddy, but you were at his house and understood he had mental health issues, PTSD you said. And you guys drank a few beers."

"It was one beer, that's all."

"When you were there did he talk about a pistol that he had?"

"Yes, he showed his gun to me. I'm not sure why he wanted me to know he had it, but that was Max. You never knew what to expect. He told me he had it because he was thinking about using it against his next-door neighbor in some dispute about Max's dog. I told him I didn't think that was a good idea and would he please change the subject and put the damn gun away, what with us drinking beer and everything."

"Interesting. As it turns out, the gun Max showed you was the same gun that was used to kill the two women whose murders we are investigating. Having a gun in your possession if you are emotionally unstable is not a good combination. Why didn't you tell me about the gun?"

"At the time, I didn't think it was important enough to bring up. I didn't think he was going to use the gun. I thought he was just showing off, being macho, you know."

Clay said, "So you have a man who had a gun, who at one time threatened to shoot his next-door neighbor, and yet you found it not to be important enough to bring it up to me? Why? Was it you who killed Max?"

"No, it was not me. If I had to do it all over again, of course I would have told you that Max had a gun. I'm sorry now that I didn't."

"To get back to Alys, did she act uppity to you, like she

believed she was too good for you? You know, a beautiful girl like that …"

"No. I liked her. I wouldn't have killed her even if she was stuck on herself. Besides, she was going with someone else at the time."

"You mean Doctor Quenneville, don't you?"

"Yes."

"How did you learn his name?"

"Alys let it slip one evening. It was about five o'clock. I had just opened the bar. I asked her if she would like to go out with me to see the town after I closed at midnight. She said no thanks, she was meeting up with someone later. I said she didn't have to lie to me if she didn't want to go out. She said honestly, she was meeting Doctor Quenneville and that was the only chance she had to see him that day. Then she shook her head and said, 'Please forget that I mentioned his name.'"

CHAPTER 51

Clay stood in front of Quenneville and did not say a word for the longest time.

Quenneville reacted badly. He squirmed in his chair, looked at the other participants and finally told Clay. "You're crazy if you think it was me. I did not kill anyone."

Clay nodded but said nothing.

Clay finally broke the ice. "Of everyone here, you had the most likely motive. You were in an admittedly loveless relationship and wanted to end your marriage. How long had you been having an affair with Alys?"

Quenneville glanced nervously at Reveca, then Mackenzie. He shook his head and said it barely loud enough for everyone to hear. "I had been seeing Alys for nearly a year."

"You told me in an earlier interview that you and Alys would rendezvous in room 412 at the Emerson, the connecting room to 410 where Alys stayed. Isn't that correct?"

Quenneville put his forefinger underneath his collar. He looked at Reveca again and wiped non-existing perspiration from his upper lip. "Yes, that's where Alys and I met on weekends when she was in town."

He mouthed to Reveca, "I'm sorry."

Reveca started to cry softly and buried her face in her hands.

"Doctor Quenneville, did you meet with Alys the night she was killed?"

"No, I met with her earlier that day. I couldn't meet with her that night. I had another... ah, engagement."

"And that other engagement was with Reveca, wasn't it?"

The room lit up with people murmuring about Quenneville's admission of his affair. Emily said, "I knew it was him." Other people nodded in agreement.

Quenneville said, "Yes. It's true I was having an affair with Reveca at the same time as I was having an affair with Alys. I'm not a playboy. I really did love both women."

"You promised to marry them both, did you not?"

"Yes, I was sincere. I wasn't faking it. Of course, I couldn't marry both at the same time. I knew I would have to decide who I wanted to be with for the rest of my life. It was a tough decision, but I decided it was Reveca I would marry."

"It was hard for you to manage two affairs, wasn't it?"

"Yes, because I loved both women, and I wasn't sure what I should do." He turned to Reveca. "That's true. You know I love you, don't you, and I still want to marry you?"

Reveca dabbed at her swollen eyes and said sincerely, "I know you're telling the truth. I love you."

Clay said, "Doctor, let's talk about the burglary that occurred at your house. The fact is, there never was a burglary, was there? You planned it all. You planted the gun and jewelry in Max Bruder's house."

"That's not true. I don't know where you're coming up with that tale. I don't know who the burglar was, but no, it was not me."

"Max was a convenient foil, wouldn't you say? You used him to try to throw me off track. You told me that you didn't know Max Bruder, but you did, didn't you?"

Quenneville did not answer.

"You can answer yes, because I know you did know him,

and yes, you were in his house. Why did you go there? To kill him? And was Reveca your accomplice?"

"I wasn't in Max's house. Why would you think that?"

"Doctor, this is going badly for you. You must tell me the truth. I cannot accept your lies any longer. Do you understand?"

He glanced at the other participants. "Yes, okay. I know everyone's looking at me as the killer, but I am not."

Clay said, "Let me review some facts. Reveca told me she cut her ankle on the dishwasher door, and that's why she was limping. Isn't that so, Reveca?"

He explained it to the group. "I noticed in Doctor Quenneville's house before we all convened here that Reveca was limping. She told me she had cut her ankle when she scraped her leg on the dishwasher door in the doctor's kitchen. But the truth is she suffered a dog bite, and it required several stitches. Isn't that true, Reveca?"

Reveca hesitated to answer.

"I'll ask again, is that true, Reveca?"

She cast her eyes to the floor. "Yes."

"You were most likely bitten by Max Bruder's dog, a dog who attacked anyone who dared to show up at Max's house. We know at the very least that Reveca was there with you, Doctor Quenneville."

"Why do you assume that?"

Clay explained, "When I went into Bruder's house to perform a welfare check, I noticed there was a very faint smell of Chanel No. 5. Reveca always seemed to wear that perfume, and oftentimes I smelled it on you also because the two of you were having an affair, and no doubt you and she embraced more than once."

The group tittered.

"I put two and two together. Either the smell was from Reveca or from both of you when you were there to kill Bruder."

Quenneville objected loudly. "That's not true. Bruder was already dead when we went to his house."

Reveca spoke up. "The reason why we were at his house was because Doctor Quenneville found out that Mrs. Quenneville was having an affair with Mr. Bruder, so the doctor wanted me to accompany him when he drove to Mr. Bruder's house. The truth is, he wasn't going to hurt Mr. Bruder. He told me all he wanted to do was tell Mr. Bruder he knew about the affair with his wife and to tell him to treat her with respect. He never said anything about killing Max. I wouldn't have gone with him if I thought that's what he was going to do."

"Doctor, even though you admitted you were having two affairs, including one with Reveca, you wanted your wife to stop having an affair, isn't that true? It was okay for you to have an affair, but it was not okay for Maura? That sounds like a double standard to me."

"Yes, I guess it was. I simply wanted him to treat her well. I know that's crazy logic, but that was my rationale. And frankly by showing up at his house I was hoping he would stop seeing Maura altogether."

"I really find it difficult to understand that logic, but let's go on. Reveca, you went to Mr. Bruder's house with the doctor."

"Yes, I stayed in the car when he went in to talk to Max. After a while I got out of the car to see what was happening and that's when Max's dog attacked me. When I screamed,

Doctor Quenneville rushed out of the house to see what the matter was. He wrapped a handkerchief around my wound to stop my bleeding and later on he took me to his office to stitch up my wound. When I asked him what happened in Max's house, he said he found Max dead. And he was scared that he would be blamed for his death. He swore Max was dead already and asked me to come into the house to see for myself. He didn't want me to think he killed him, so I agreed to go and I hobbled into the house. I needed to see if he was telling me the truth."

"Was Max dead?"

"Yes."

Clay tested Reveca. "Where was the body?"

"In the garage. It looked like he had been dead for a while, and there was a terrible smell."

He asked Reveca, "Let's go back to the burglary at the doctor's house. Was Max alone in the house when the jewelry and gun were stolen?"

"I don't remember. I think Max was working inside when I took Adam for a walk, but I'm not sure of that. I usually did not pay much attention to him when he was at the house. He had a job to do and my job was to take care of Adam."

"Was Mrs. Quenneville there that day?"

"No, only Mr. Bruder and me."

"I asked you several days ago if you knew the name Alys Chapman. Do you remember me asking you that?"

"You answered that you did not know the name, but actually you did, didn't you, and Mrs. Quenneville did too, isn't that right?"

"Yes. Mrs. Quenneville knew who she was. One night I heard her arguing with the doctor. She was shouting that she had followed him to the Saddleback Saloon and saw Alys there with him in his car and they were kissing."

"What happened afterward?"

"I asked the doctor what the argument was about, and he told me he planned to divorce Mrs. Quenneville when she left him."

"Where was she going?"

"I do not know. He told me not to worry about her. He would take care of her."

"What did you think he meant when he said he would 'take care of her'? Did you think he wanted to kill her?"

"No, he meant she would be gone when they divorced. I don't believe he killed Mrs. Quenneville. He's not a murderer."

"Reveca, did Mrs. Quenneville know you and the doctor were having sex?"

"I think so, yes. But the doctor told me not to worry, because she was having an affair too."

"With Max Bruder, right?"

"Yes."

"Final question, Alys Chapman was killed around midnight. Do you know where the doctor was that night?"

"Yes, with me."

CHAPTER 52

Clay addressed the group. "Each of you had a motive that could point to you as the suspect responsible for the deaths of the three individuals."

Clay stood in front of each person and gave his summary of their possible motives.

Clay nodded to Reveca. "You admitted you knew that Alys and the doctor were having an affair. Logically, If Alys was out of the picture, that would open the field for you to marry Doctor Quenneville."

"Yes, I love Doctor Quenneville. But I am not a killer. And why would I want to kill Mr. Bruder?"

"You make a good point. Bruder was the odd piece of this puzzle. But let me go on."

* * *

He turned to Emily and Steve. "You two had motive also. It's possible you both planned to confront Mrs. Quenneville and teach her a lesson because of her bad behavior toward you. Did Mrs. Quenneville's behavior at Albertsons create the probable cause to kill her? I don't believe so. I believe her barging into Steve was purely coincidental."

* * *

"Jeremy, you did not have motive other than she turned you down for a date. I read your police file, and I agree you were innocent of the sexual abuse charge. Your record is clean. I believe that as a bartender your job may put you in a position to date a lot of women, and you probably have. There's something about tending bar that attracts people to the male or female bartender, isn't there."

"I agree. That's part of why I like what I do."

"Now Doctor Quenneville. You had the motive to kill Maura and Alys. You had to put up with a nagging wife. You fell in love with not only one woman but two. If you could find a way to end your marriage, you would be able to marry either one of the two women you say you loved. It was a burden of riches, wasn't it? You realized that it most likely was your wife who filed a complaint with the medical board to get even for your infidelity. And yes, as hypocritical as it seems, you were not happy that your wife was having an affair with Max Bruder. But I'm convinced you did not kill anyone."

Quenneville breathed a sigh of relief.

Clay asked rhetorically, "So who killed Alys?"

As if on cue, the conference room door opened and Dan Carton, Santa Fe's Forensics Chief Examiner, walked in and motioned to Clay that he needed to talk to him. The two men spoke in confidence. After a few minutes Clay thanked Carton then returned and walked to the center of the u-shaped table arrangement. He stopped abruptly in front of John Paul and stared at the security guard for several seconds.

"John Paul Koslowski, I am arresting you for the murders of Maura Quenneville, Alys Chapman, Max Bruder, and Cinnamon Stixx."

CHAPTER 53

John Paul appeared to be shocked at the accusation. He stood up and raised his voice at Clay. "What? Are you crazy? Is that a joke?" His voice cracked. "I know you're kidding me. Why would I kill all those people? I'm the security guard, not a killer."

"No, it's not a joke.

"Let me explain. You have told me that you've been at the Emerson for fourteen or fifteen years as a security officer. You told me you've seen a lot of things during that time: people having sexual rendezvous in conference rooms, in connecting hotel rooms, in the kitchen, and pretty much throughout the hotel."

"That's true. I have spoken the truth about my observations."

"How did you feel about that behavior? Were you in turn excited about what you were observing? I think I know the answer. You are a voyeur, aren't you? You enjoy watching people have sex, don't you? You told me watching surveillance tapes all day long was a pleasure for you. Did you mean that the sex you eavesdropped on got you excited sexually? Like the arsonist who sets a fire because it turns him on. Are you a fire starter?"

"No, you're way off base. The truth is, I abhor people who have illicit sex. I have felt that way from the moment I first witnessed such acts. I find them offensive, indecent, and immoral."

He was losing control and spoke loudly. He looked at each of the participants in the room. The Emerson is home to a den of sinners." He paused. "I told you, there was a murder here the very first month I was on the job and I've been witness to adulterous behavior nonstop ever since with countless number of people, including all of you."

"You told me you were the one who found the hooker dead in the parking lot where Alys was also killed, right? The hooker went by her street name of Cinnamon Stixx, right?"

John Paul's eyes continued to flit nervously from person to person. "Yes, I found Cinnamon dead in her car in the parking lot fifteen years ago. The police called her a high-class escort, but she was nothing more than a prostitute, a whore, a common streetwalker."

"And the police never found the killer or killers of that hooker back then, correct?"

"It was a killer, yes, one person."

"How do you know that?"

He shrugged. "I just assumed it was."

"You killed her, didn't you? You had to. You loved her but you hated her too. Your parents would have insisted that you kill her. She was no good. She was an ordinary streetwalker, right? Was Cinnamon the first prostitute you killed?"

He didn't answer.

"John Paul, when is your birthday?"

"October sixteenth. Why do you need to know?"

"I happen to know your birthday but play along with me, please. What year were you born?"

"1978."

Clay looked around at the others seated at the tables and asked, "Does anyone here know what event occurred on October 16, 1978?"

No one knew.

"How about you John Paul, what occurred on that date in history? Of course, you know, don't you?"

He answered, "Karol Wojtyla was elected Pope on that day—Pope John Paul II."

"You were born on the same day that Wojtyla was made pope? Is that why your parents named you John Paul?"

"Yes, I am honored to be named John Paul."

"Obviously, your parents were very religious?"

"Yes."

"By the way, I notice you wear a gold cross around your neck. You're very religious too, aren't you? I understand you go to church every day."

"Yes, I haven't ever missed a day. I am able to endure the lewd and lascivious acts and thoughts in this world when I go to church."

"How are you able to do that, by murdering those people who you believe to be sinners? Do you pray for sinners? And do you ask for forgiveness too? For the people you've killed in the name of God?"

"I go willingly to pray for people because my parents taught me to do that."

"So did you pray for Alys Chapman, and Maura Quenneville?"

"Yes."

"And Max Bruder, and even for Doctor Quenneville."

"Yes."

Clay asked, "What about me?"

"Yes, I pray for you, and your girlfriend too. You both are living a life of sin."

"Did your parents warn you to be wary of all women?"

"Yes. I never married. Because my parents and I never found a woman who believes as we do, in living a pure life."

"Cinnamon Stixx was your first love, wasn't she? Did you kill her?"

"I loved her, but I couldn't stand the thought of her making love with other men. She knew not what she was doing."

"So you did kill her. Otherwise, why would your DNA have been on the prayer card that you left behind in Cinnamon's car?"

"What are you talking about?"

"When I reviewed Cinnamon's case file, I had forensics check if there was any DNA on the prayer card. And remarkably, I have just been informed by Santa Fe's Forensics Chief Examiner that your DNA was still viable from fifteen years ago. At the time, no one bothered to check if you were the match for the DNA. DNA was not as useful a tool as it is today. Besides, she was a prostitute, and you were the security guard. No one was going to accuse you. So now, after all these years, we learned your DNA was a match. Further, we discovered your DNA on the prayer card that was left in Alys' car also, and in Max Bruder's home too. We know without a shadow of doubt that you are the murderer."

Looking at Quenneville, John Paul said, "Doctor, you can think whatever you want about Alys and your wife, but they were nothing but common whores who lived a life of sin." He pointed to Reveca. "And Doctor, I am convinced your Slovakian girlfriend is the same—she's not any better than a prostitute."

Quenneville stood and shouted at him, "If you say that one more time ..." He didn't finish.

Clay interceded. "Calm down, Doctor."

Quenneville sat back, breathing hard.

"You can agree or disagree with me, but the simple fact is that Doctor Quenneville will face the wrath of God because he has lived a life of moral turpitude. He will have to walk in the embers of hell for all eternity because he's been in a constant state of sin. And you can't arrest me for killing someone who lives a life of sin."

"You are not God. You cannot determine who lives or dies. You are guilty of murder. The physical evidence proves your guilt."

"Detective Bryce, I can disprove every point you might make in a court of law, not here in these sham intervention proceedings. But instead of trying to frame me as the killer, what you should be doing is turning your attention to Quenneville. He and that Slovakian prostitute girlfriend of his who both live a life of sin are the ones you should be arresting."

Quenneville responded with rage. He jumped to his feet and threw himself at John Paul, knocking him off his chair.

The two rolled around on the floor for a few seconds before Rizzo and the two cops who had been safeguarding the proceedings finally separated them and stood them up. As John Paul pretended to dust himself off, he pulled out a pistol from his jacket pocket and fired at Quenneville, but the bullet missed.

Clay drew his revolver and shouted to John Paul, "Put the gun down!"

John Paul aimed his gun at Clay, "You too are a sinner. It is time for you to meet your maker."

Clay did not hesitate and fired his revolver, striking John

Paul in his side and dropping him to the floor writhing in pain.

Quenneville kneeled alongside John Paul trying to stop the flow of blood from his wound. Clay and Mackenzie stood over both of them.

John Paul looked up at Clay and said, "Detective Bryce, you can judge me as a killer if you wish, but it has always been my God-given right to punish sinners who live a life of sin." His voice became more bombastic, sounding more like a TV preacher's pleading.

"As Matthew sayeth in chapter 5, verse 28: '*I say to you that everyone who looks at a woman with lust has already committed adultery with her in his heart.*'"

Clay turned to Mackenzie and whispered in her ear. "I guess I'm going to hell."

EPILOGUE

John Paul was convicted of first-degree murder of Maura Quenneville, Alys Chapman, Max Bruder, and Cinnamon Stixx. He was sentenced to four consecutive life sentences without the possibility of parole.

After his conviction, Clay met with him in prison from time to time to learn the names of other victims of John Paul's self-anointed religious crusade.

There were many.

❋ ❋ ❋

Mackenzie returned to her airline attendant position and arranged for regular layovers in Santa Fe to be with Clay. She spoke often of her intention to team up with him to solve crimes. "You and I should partner together to solve crimes using my ESP *gift* as our forensic tool."

Clay said, "You mean, partner like Batman and Robin."

"Yes, but only if I could be Batman."

"Why did I know you would want to take the lead?"

"Maybe you really do have ESP."

❋ ❋ ❋

True to his word, Quenneville proposed marriage to Reveca, but she turned him down unable to forgive or forget his deceit regarding Alys.

She gave Quenneville notice and helped him select and train another woman to care for his son. Not surprisingly, the new nanny was beautiful and young.

Reveca remained in the U.S. and in time became a citizen.

Using knowledge gained from her work as a nanny, Reveca founded a company that hired women from Slovakia and other Eastern European countries to work as nannies and au pairs for wealthy patrons in the U.S.

Gardner Hicks was diagnosed with paranoid schizophrenia and due to his mental impairment, was found to be unfit to stand trial for the crimes of attempted murder, kidnapping, and assault. He was committed to the maximum-security ward of the Behavioral Health Institute, the same psychiatric unit for violent prisoners from which he had escaped earlier.

❋ ❋ ❋

Steve Aldrich and Emily Embers married. They bought Max Bruder's house, flipped it for a nice profit, then decided to team up to buy and sell other houses on their way to owning and leasing a number of houses in and around Santa Fe.

THE END

Made in the USA
Middletown, DE
10 November 2024